ERIN
GOSSAMER HALL

> "Fans who enjoy their horror seasoned with generous amounts of religious symbolism and zealotry — Bram Stoker's DRACULA, Stephen King's CARRIE, etc. — should give Samiloglu's DISCONNECTION a try."
>
> —*bn.com/Explorations*

Medallion Press, Inc.
Printed in USA

ERIN SAMILOGLU

GOSSAMER HALL

DEDICATION:

For Daddy

Published 2007 by Medallion Press, Inc.

The MEDALLION PRESS LOGO
is a registered tradmark of Medallion Press, Inc.

Typeset in Times New Roman
Printed in the United States of America
10-digit ISBN: 1-9328158-9-9
13-digit ISBN: 978-1932815-89-4

10 9 8 7 6 5 4 3 2 1
First Edition

ACKNOWLEDGEMENTS:

A big thank you to family and friends. Keena Grissom, editor extraordinaire, a simple thanks just doesn't cut it. You're fantastic.

London, as always, nothing would be anything without you. Thank you for the joy and laughter. You are my Reason. I love you.

PROLOGUE

The bones had memory.

Their silence spoke of a vicious past, and like anything that could recall history, they sought vengeance.

In the hills above the lake, buried deep in the earth, they rested in an evil that did not sleep, in soil that did not nurture, in a state of unforgotten hate.

In this place of damnation, the bones waited and listened.

Years passed before they heard him coming.

Their champion, the one who would bring them alive again.

Their *maker*.

CHAPTER ONE

MACK "MAD" MARON WAS HIS NAME. MURDER WAS his specialty, mass murder. Dr. Killian Hastings wrote a best seller about the madman a decade ago, and since then scholars and nonscholars alike knew he was the go-to man for everything Mad Maron.

It was Wednesday night, and Hastings sat at his desk, relaxing before his class began. He took a silver flask out of his briefcase and ran his fingers along the engraved initials while he poured its content into a glass. The dry whiskey smell made everything about Hastings's plan feel more real to him, and he swallowed the liquor whole to block out the enormity of the next few hours.

Very soon. Hastings's palms crushed together in anticipation. *Very soon now.*

The professor set the flask back into his briefcase. He pulled open his desk drawer and reached in, taking out the hardback copy of the Mad Maron biography a *Los Angeles Times* critic had once hailed as, "The most wildly engaging nonfiction book of the year."

Hastings set the book on his desk and studied it thoughtfully. *Devil of the West* was written in bold red just above an enhanced, yellowed, black-and-white portrait of the handsome thirty-two-year-old gunman. Maron was positioned with one hand casually folded over his stomach, the other hand tense on his holster, as if to announce that even in leisure he was still pre- pared for battle. His customary cowboy hat was tilted to the side, hiding his dark hair and shadowing his left eye, and a scarf was tied crookedly around his neck.

"A picture says a thousand words." Hastings re- peated the cliché to himself while he studied the photo. It was hard to tell from the drab black-and-white pic- ture, but Hastings knew the killer was dressed in his customary black garb. The professor had often joked during interviews that Maron could have been the Johnny Cash of the nineteenth century, the way he never wore anything but the shade of night.

This evening, it was Mad Maron's face, not his

clothes, that held Hastings captivated. The gunslinger appeared to be boiling off the page, building cell by cell into reality. His eyes burned with a menacing evil, intense with its desire, enraged by certainty, as if the gunslinger knew exactly what the professor had planned for the night.

Dr. Hastings, the picture threatened. *Don't do it. I'll be coming for you.*

Hastings blinked hard, hoping his eyes were playing tricks on him, but when he looked again, it remained—the feeling that Mad Maron was coming to life.

I'll be coming for you, Dr. Hastings, the killer warned. *Get ready, partner. Saddle up.*

Hastings abruptly grabbed the book and threw it back into the desk, slamming the drawer closed with a violent push. *Just the alcohol,* Hastings thought, and lightly kicked the briefcase beside his desk.

That's all it is—a little whiskey-induced hologram.

Hastings took off his glasses and rubbed his eyes. He concluded that along with the alcohol, it was also the excitement that was wearing on him. No one could deny his plan was ambitious. He wasn't even sure it would work.

Can it really be done?

Of course it can be done, he answered himself while he unfolded his glasses and put them back on.

He stood up from his desk, walked to the window, and looked out onto the darkening October evening. The purple twilight had deepened like a funnel into the day; all that was left were the sun's dying rays of orange and pink scattered across the sky. Half an hour remained before Hastings's class began, and unlike any other time before, he was eagerly anticipating its arrival.

The little-known Presbyterian school, Brookhaven College, had forced him into teaching the night class, Texas History, after Dr. Matthew Simon had dropped dead of a heart attack last summer on a trip through Yosemite. The recently deceased professor had always taught the shitty classes. Hastings had made sure of it. It was part of the beauty of heading the history department—handpicking his own classes and making sure the other poor sucker got the leftovers.

Hastings considered himself a superstar among college history professors, and Brookhaven, in his esteemed opinion, was lucky to have him. It didn't matter that murderers and derelicts were his specialty. A published book counted for something, by God, and if he couldn't teach at Brown, his alma mater, or another ivy-league school, he could at least teach the good classes at pissant holy-rolling Brookhaven College.

The college dean, Dr. Gretchen Kurcan, had called Hastings a week before the fall semester started. "Got news," she said. "You're teaching the night class." The lady was never one for beating around the bush.

Neither was Hastings. "Want to bet on it?"

"Had any other teaching offers, Kil?" It was her way of reminding him that his specialty wasn't a well-received topic for college curriculums.

Hastings inhaled sharply. "Haven't you hired any-one new?"

"Part-timers. No one wants to teach at night." She sounded tired and irritable, as if calling him was the last chore on a long list at the end of a very long day.

Hastings felt doubly insulted. "Find someone," he hissed into the receiver.

"It's too late. You're it." He could hear her fingers drumming impatiently on her desk at the other end of the line.

Hastings hung up and flung the phone against the wall. The crash resounded in the room and echoed throughout his empty south Austin home. Hastings waited for Kurcan to call back, but she didn't. Look-ing back, it was stupid hanging up on her like that. He could have lost his job at Brookhaven College, and he would never have taught Texas History. He would never have met Juan. He would never have discovered what Juan could do.

Hastings smiled to himself, shaking his head at the series of fortunate events that would, in just mere hours, make him a rich man.

The professor pulled back the curtain wider, and Juan Fuentes appeared on cue, as if he were in a play in which he was unconsciously starring.

Hastings watched the boy cross the width of the yard. To a casual observer, the student looked like any other. Slumped posture, slight build, a backpack slung over his shoulder, a bored expression shadowing the contours of his dark face.

Just another college kid.

But Hastings knew better.

CHAPTER
TWO

SOMEONE'S WATCHING ME.

It was just a feeling Juan had. Nothing could really explain it. Apprehension crawled down the length of his spine while he stood at the building's expansive, cracked stone staircase and looked up at the dark, caged windows. His gaze roamed the place, looking for another pair of eyes watching him. He saw nothing.

Stupid, he chided himself. *Who would be watching me?*

It was the building, Juan decided. Students called it the Prison, but its real name was Gossamer Hall, and it was the old man on campus, a sprawling fortress built in the late 1800s and named after the first Brookhaven College president, William Gossamer. Its garish red brick reminded Juan of dried blood, and the caged windows were like those of old timey insane asylums he'd seen in horror films.

It has a bad aura, Juan mused. What his Mexican grandmother would call *el sentido de la mal*.

While he climbed the steps, he felt a twitch at his side, and he looked down to see his left hand was shaking. *No, please. Not now,* he thought while he reached down and grabbed his left hand with his right.

Something about Gossamer Hall always made his hand shake.

"Be still," Juan whispered. "Please be still. Don't betray me now." He stopped on the last step and squeezed his eyes shut. If his hand kept shaking, Juan knew what would happen.

Making.

He called it *making* because there was no other verb for what he could do, no definition. He and his mother had looked in Webster's once, when he was a child, when his *making* began. *Telekinesis, clairvoyant*, nothing seemed to pinpoint it.

His mother had looked at him. "There's no word for it because you're the only one," she said while her eyes widened with growing trepidation. Her expression reminded Juan of the time she had seen a tarantula crawling across the floor in her bedroom——that kind of frightened, unbelieving shock.

Juan knew what she was thinking. *What monster have I created?*

"Your great-great-grandfather was a Monhu medicine man," his mother told him after a short period of silence. "Perhaps . . ." she began, but no words followed.

Perhaps that's why I'm a freak, Mom? Perhaps that's why you're looking at me like I have eight arms?

He couldn't blame her. How could he? She had feigned acceptance for a long time——longer than most God-fearing folk. It was a miracle she had gone this far with him. Really. Every parent, at some point, must recognize their baby has become an individual, good or bad. Time was a weapon.

The final bullet to his mother's love came on Juan's tenth birthday, when he had *made* fireworks pop over his cake. A spark went the wrong way and almost blinded a kid sitting nearby. The boy was visibly shaken, and his mother was shaken because her son was shaken and she threatened to sue. "Wetbacks!" she had screamed before she and her Aryan baby boy left the premises.

"It's not safe to be around him," he heard his mother whisper in the phone to an unknown caller the next morning.

Juan had been sitting under the dining-room table,

hiding from his older siblings, when he heard her conversation. Years later, the moment was still engraved in his mind like a blowtorched brand to his skull. The horror of learning his mother was afraid of him was a blow from which he had never recovered.

If his hand had shaken at that moment, he'd have cut it off. He had thought fireworks would be the grand finale to a super-cool birthday.

I didn't mean to hurt anyone.

"Don't send me to live with Nana," Juan begged his mother on the morning he was due to leave for Austin. "I promise I won't *make* anymore."

"Juan, that's not why I'm sending you there. Nana is in bad shape. She needs you."

"Send Lucinda," Juan pleaded.

"Lucinda's too young, *mi amor.*" Before Juan boarded the bus, his mother leaned in and whispered in his ear, "If anyone finds out about your gift, they'll treat you like a *ejemplar anormal.* You must, under all circumstances, keep your gift a secret."

That was ten years ago. Juan had lived with Nana ever since.

Opening the door of Gossamer Hall, Juan's mind drifted back to what had happened that morning. Juan was in the living room working on his homework when Nana walked through the door from the kitchen.

"Juan, honey . . ."

Juan looked up and waited for the request for a chore that was bound to follow. *Juan, honey,* were always the opening words of an inevitable demand.

"What is it, Nana?" he asked.

She is getting old, Juan noted. The energetic woman he had known when he was a child had shriveled with age and the weight of her life. Nana, who was nearly deaf and almost blind, walked with a curved spine and arthritis-ridden feet. There were some mornings when she didn't bother getting out of bed, and some nights when she never went to sleep.

Nana tousled her grandson's dark hair with gentle, decrepit fingers. "Honey, there's no sugar, and I wanted to make some tea."

"There's sugar substitute in the cabinet above the stove, Nana." Juan flipped a page in his textbook and continued reading, trying to ignore the shadow of the old woman standing above him.

Nana pursed her thin lips and stared down at Juan with the concentration of a poker player with a bad hand. "I've never used substitute sugar in my life!" she exclaimed. "Juan, honey . . ."

Juan sighed and laid the book to his side. "Okay, Nana." *Forget the work I have to do.*

Juan was halfway to his car when it occurred to him that this was a perfect opportunity to use his *make.*

He lowered himself to the pavement while the wind shuddered through the nearby trees. He sat Indian-style and looked up at the wide, blue Texas sky, and willed himself to remember the image of sugar.

Making involved extreme imagery, not in the way people remembered objects or places they had once visited. Juan had to really get into the *mind* of the object, inside its corners and ceilings, its surfaces and elements. He had to imagine that the item encompassed everything like a vacuum, and there would be no release until the item was formed . . . until the item was *made*.

His concentration deepened, and he felt his ring finger tremble, and then it extended to the palm, which also moved. In a matter of seconds, Juan's entire left hand was vibrating like it was spinning in an electrical current.

Work your magic, Juan told his hand while it shook uncontrollably. The following moments were filled with a mixture of nervousness and expectation as he waited and forced himself to remain focused.

The problem with the *make*, something Juan could never predict, was where the *make* would appear. Sometimes it developed right in front of him, or in his hand or by his foot. Sometimes it showed up in unseen places. In the past, Juan had looked for hours for a toothbrush; the *make* had hidden itself well.

Maybe it took seconds. Maybe it took minutes. The smallest item like sugar could take forever, while a leather coat he had once *made* for a begging homeless man was *made* in mere moments.

There were rules to what he could *make*. He could never *make* anything heavier than himself. He could not *make* complicated machinery like a car or an airplane.

Juan could not *make* the weather or change time. He could not *make* items made of metal or precious stone. He could *make* paper money, but it was not authentic. A quick glimpse from any poorly trained cashier could tell it was counterfeit.

Juan could only *make* one thing in an estimated hour, no more than five items in a day.

"Here's your sugar, Nana," Juan said when he entered the house.

Nana was in the kitchen at the table, staring outside at trees her poor vision saw as colliding swirls of green and brown. "What was that you said?" she asked, turning toward the sound of her grandson's voice.

Juan held up the sugar in his hands. "I have it," he replied. "Hold out your hand." He reached out and poured it into Nana's cupped palm.

Her blind eyes stared at Juan with wide-eyed suspicion. "How did you come across this?" she asked.

Juan swallowed hard. "The neighbors," he answered.

"The Phillips?" she asked.

"Yes."

"The Phillips are out of town, Juan."

Juan did not know what to say to this.

Nana fixed her unseeing eyes at her grandson for a long time while she whispered words too soft for him to hear. Finally, she lowered her head and opened her hands, letting the sugar fall through her fingers and onto the ceramic tile.

"It is the devil who gives you this gift. Don't be tempted, Juan," she warned before turning back to look at the swirls of brown and green. "Don't be like your . . ."

Her voice trailed off.

"Don't be like who, Nana?" Juan asked.

But his grandmother did not answer.

Juan went back to his work, but the recent events bothered him enough that it was hard to finish his chemistry assignment.

She knows, Juan thought. He had always suspected, but he had never had proof until now.

I am not a devil, Juan told himself while he pressed the elevator button of Gossamer Hall. The sound of the old elevator shaft rattled as the car made its way down.

I am not the devil.

I have a gift.

Juan entered the classroom from the door located at the rear. He exhaled with a sigh of relief when his eyes searched the room and found that Dr. Hastings was not there. *Speaking of devils*, Juan thought, walking into the classroom.

Juan had been warned about Dr. Hastings long before signing up for the professor's class. The students, the teachers, even the middle-aged counselor with the red-lipstick smile, had tried to warn him on registration day ("He's a real pain in the ass, sweetie pie"), but Juan had just shrugged his shoulders. It was the only history class offered at night. All of his biology classes interfered with the day history classes, and he wanted to finish his history requirements while he was still a freshman.

Juan looked down at his shaking hand. "Stop," he ordered, but his hand refused to listen.

"Hey, Fuentes, over here!" a voice called out.

Juan looked up. Mark Green was waving at him from the other side of the classroom. Juan waved back halfheartedly. Mark was a friend from his biology classes, one of the few Brookhaven students who had befriended Juan right off the bat. He was a smart, but slightly annoying character, the type of guy who would tell a joke without knowing the punch line. *He always knows the answer to everything,* Juan thought, and while this sometimes helped Juan, say on a quiz or homework assignment, it could also be irritating as hell in everyday life.

On his way to the front row, Juan passed two massive football jocks snickering over a *Playboy* spread out over their desks. "Shaved," one of them whispered, and the other one laughed.

Juan shook his head and wondered what became of athletes after their glory days were over. What would happen to the sloppy, smiling chunk of three-hundred-pound muscle staring over a spread of the Pamela Anderson-wannabe in her birthday suit? Or his bigger friend, a guy named Josh, who snored in class and picked his nose, flicking his boogers at Juan and Mark during the water break and calling them faggots?

Juan decided he really didn't care. He slowly moved away from the jocks' laughing voices, only to stall at the desk in front of them. He wanted to say something to its occupant but knew he couldn't. He lacked the courage to talk to beautiful girls.

He knew her name because everyone knew her name. She didn't belong at Brookhaven College, where most of the girls wore long dresses and crosses around their necks and believed their lifelong mission was to serve God.

This girl belonged at the University of Texas, hanging off a sorority balcony or laughing on a park bench next to someone who was equally beautiful. She belonged in a magazine spread or in a café in Paris dressed in designer garb, or on a cruise sitting by the pool sip-ping martinis. She belonged in a Hollywood movie as the love interest to a guy who saved the universe.

No, Juan corrected himself. It was she who could save the universe.

Lily.

Her name tasted like icing on his lips; Juan liked to say it over and over in the privacy of his mind. *If only I could* make *girls like her notice me,* he thought.

Juan watched her from the corner of his eye while he continued past. She sat very still. Eyes the color of violet ice stared at the front of the room. Her dark hair hung in waves along her back; her perfect hands overlapped across the desk. She had the aura of being passionate and observant, cold and indifferent, all at once.

Juan wondered what her voice sounded like. She never said anything, not even when the football players tried to talk to her. The advantage of being a beautiful girl, Juan surmised, was that you could be a boring imbecile and people still would want to know you.

Juan passed another student, an attractive, older, nameless woman. Her hair was dark red and pinned back, revealing a soft, pale face. She smiled faintly at Juan when he walked by, but her amber eyes revealed an echoing sadness. The poignant look in her eyes lingered in Juan's thoughts when he passed the next student, a rough-looking thug with one eye, who could, if he chose to, punch out the football players with one blow.

"Did you do your homework assignment for to-night?" Mark asked while Juan sunk into the desk next to him.

Juan nodded. "You mean that chapter on Mad Maron?"

"Blew your mind, didn't it?" Mark pushed his black-rimmed glasses up the bridge of his nose and ran his hands over his notebook. *Star Wars* heroes were drawn in the margin, Luke Skywalker battling Darth Vader, Han Solo and Chewbacca in their spaceship. Juan thought if someone looked up "nerd" in the dictionary, there'd be a picture of Mark.

"What did you say?" Juan asked, shaking off the ridiculous image of Mark fighting the forces of galactic evil in his chemistry goggles and "Drugs Kill, Jesus Heals" T-shirt.

"I said, that history assignment was nuts. You read it, didn't you?"

Juan's hand jerked forward and froze just below his pen.

"Juan?" Mark said. "You okay there?"

"Yeah. Just, you know, thinking about what you said," Juan replied while he hid his shaking hand under the desk. "That homework was some crazy stuff."

Juan did not tell his friend that the "crazy stuff" had kept him awake last night. It was all about murder and torture—the kind of thing Juan hadn't expected to find at Brookhaven College.

Why was Dr. Hastings so gung ho on us reading it? he wondered.

Juan remembered last week, when the professor had leaned over his desk with palms flat and said, "Read your chapter or else."

His eyes bored a hole into Juan. It was like the words had been intended for him and him alone.

To remember made Juan's hand shake even worse.

"Thirty-three people," Mark said.

His words forced Juan back into the present. "What?" he asked.

"Darn, Juan, what's wrong with you today?" Mark shook his head. "I said Maron and his cousins killed thirty-three people. Is that more than Jeffrey Dahmer?" Mark reached into his pocket and pulled out his BlackBerry. "I'm looking it up now." A pause followed while the bright screen reflected in Mark's lenses. Finally Mark said, "Fifteen. Dahmer killed fifteen. Nuts, huh? Mad Maron has Dahmer beat."

"And Dahmer only killed men. Maron killed women and children, too," a voice piped up from the back of the classroom.

Juan didn't have to turn around to know who was speaking. He had never heard her voice before, but somehow he knew it was she.

Lily.

He and Mark turned to look at the quiet, beautiful girl. She stared back at them, her gaze unwavering. Inside Juan's chest, he felt his heart skip a beat.

"You're right," Mark said, nodding his head slowly. "Maron killed three women and a child." He coughed nervously in his hand and looked at Juan as if to say, *Look at this, will ya? Lily is talking to us.*

Juan's hand started shaking faster. He reached down with his other hand and squeezed it with a death grip.

Please don't. Please, not now.

Lily placed her pencil to her lips and looked up to the ceiling pensively. "I wonder what was wrong with Maron. Was he loony or just evil? I kept reading the chapter over and over, but it didn't explain why he killed all those people. I mean, I know it was bank robbery, but then he just went nuts, you know? Body after body." Lily shook her head.

"Is there ever an explanation for murder?" Juan asked. His cheeks reddened when Lily glanced over at him.

She's absolutely beautiful.

"They could dig up his body," Mark suggested. "A bunch of scientists dug up Beethoven's body and found lead in his hair, which explained why he was deaf and nuts."

"They can't dig up Maron's body," another voice

in the classroom informed them. "They don't know the location. He was never found after the lynch mob got a hold of him."

Juan, Mark, and Lily turned in the direction of the voice. The guy with one eye stared back at them.

CHAPTER THREE

LARS CASE WASN'T HIS NAME. THE NAME BELONGED to some poor kid whose passport he'd stolen to cross the Mexican-American border.

It wasn't that he wasn't American. He was American, all right, American as apple pie, baseball, Jerry Springer, and lawsuits. His nationality wasn't the issue. The problem was his real name had an arrest warrant attached. If anyone knew his identity, he'd be in prison rather than Gossamer Hall, though sometimes Lars didn't think there was a difference.

Lars did not know why he was such a screw up. He guessed some people were just born to be trouble.

Sitting in his night class, part of a conversation about an outlaw dead and gone, his thoughts turned back to Heather and Mexico. It was always that way. One minute in the present, the next minute in the past, anything triggering a relapse.

He thought about the mess that went down south of the border. He hadn't planned for any of it. He blamed heroine—heroine and Mickey. If Mickey hadn't left Lars and Heather stranded in Tijuana with no money and no dope and no way to get money or dope, well . . . it would've been a different story.

Lars closed his eyes and tried not to remember, but it was like trying to part the sea. The images came back again, tides and tides of them.

He saw Heather leaving the restaurant with a suspicious bag, Heather walking across the street with her yellow summer dress blowing up around her like Marilyn Monroe in the *Seven Year Itch* poster. Heather speeding the beat-up ancient Volvo back to the apartment in mid-summer heat with no air conditioner.

Heather consoling him:

"Don't cry, baby, don't cry. Fuck Mickey. Fuck that guy. It's just you and me, baby. Don't cry."

Lars had been sick. Really fucking sick. Arriving at the cockroach hotel they called an apartment, he went on a withdrawal rampage. Curling up and barfing, shaking and swinging his arms back and forth, fighting to stand and falling instead.

He had gone a full twenty-four hours without junk. He thought he could handle it. He thought he could kick the habit. He didn't have a choice, did he? It was hard to score with no dough.

But Heather found the dope. She told Lars she had called in a favor. Lars knew if there were any favors involved, it usually meant Lars and Heather owing them, but what else could he do? Desperate times called for believing the unbelievable.

Lars was dying next to a flea-ridden couch he and Heather had saved from a sidewalk. His heart was beating slowly. His breath was ragged. He felt like his insides were melting and pouring out of his skin.

"Heeeeeaaaaaattttthhhheeeerrrr . . ."

I suck.

I am a wastoid rotting-away, fleshless vampire out to destroy everything around me.

"Don't cry, baby, don't cry." Heather was in the kitchen fixing the junk, banging around the cabinets looking for a clean spoon. "Don't cry."

Heather, please . . .

"Baby, it's almost ready."

Thoroughness was Heather's specialty. The general outline of a character still remained even when the rest of it went to pot. Heather might have been a hard-core fucking junkie but she still had that rigorous standard of perfection, a characteristic left over from high-school honor roll. It was she, in fact, who laid the blueprint for their addiction. They were dark plans, but they were plans nonetheless, and Lars could admit to never planning anything.

"It's almost ready, baby, one more sec," Heather said.

A heavy knock on the door altered the moment, followed by someone kicking through the wood. The door slammed open and crashed against the wall. Lars watched through slit eyes while two Mexican thugs with guns entered the apartment.

Lars tried and tried to catch his breath, tried to warn Heather, but his lungs were broken, tormented bagpipes, and the room had lost all air.

"Where is it?" asked the taller man. He motioned around the room with the barrel of his gun. His mustache reminded Lars of the Columbian guy on coffee canisters.

Lars wobbled to a weak standing position, his knees bent. "You're just a hallucination," he said, his fingers pointing wildly in the air.

You are a hallucination, and I am a loser dickhead.

Heather thought he was talking to her. "I'm real, baby, I'm real, and so is the junk, baby," she called from inside the kitchen. She hadn't heard the bang. She was too busy obsessing over the beauty of a perfect hit.

The Mexicans eyed the door suspiciously. "That her?" the taller one asked Lars.

Lars bellied over and vomited on the floor.

"Hey, fuck-fuck, you girlfriend?" He pointed the gun at the door.

I am shit at the bottom of the toilet.

"Leave her alone," Lars muttered, lifting his head from the floor.

"Baby, what is it?" Heather materialized, rushing into the room carrying a spoon and a telephone wire and wearing a weary smile. Sweat pasted her blond hair to her forehead. The scent of her desperation filled the air.

Her smile faded when she saw the Mexicans. Her eyes doubled in size with disbelief. Her mouth opened to form a scream, but she didn't have a chance. The taller Mexican raised his gun and blew her face open with one devastating bullet. She fell backward and hit the floor with a resounding thud, her legs tangling together under her pretty yellow dress. Blood sprayed against the wall and dripped around her limp frame.

Lars's breath fell out of him. Time paused while his mind took a photo of what he saw—his high-school sweetheart dead on the floor, the filthy Mexican gangsters standing at the door, their guns pointing at him.

"We not ask again," the taller one said. "Where it is?"

"I don't know what you're—" Lars began before ducking to the floor, dodging a bullet. The shot hit a cheap unframed Monet print Lars had bought for Heather at a yard sale a million years ago, and it wavered to the ground like a flag of surrender.

The gun smoke lingered in the air, causing Lars to keel over and vomit again.

I am not a man.

I am a turd. I am a filthy, little weasel—

"You fuck. You fucking A-mer-i-can liar," said the shorter of the men, lowering his smoking gun. "Drugs we need, *amigo*."

I am dead.

"The bag, *amigo*. Your bitch stole from us."

I am dying.

"Please!" Lars screamed. "I need—"

Lars eyes widened, his brain rocked back and forth in his head while the taller Mexican raised his gun and pointed it at him.

"Say *adios, amigo*."

Everything went black.

"Are you okay?"

Lars looked up. A dark-haired angel stared at him with large amethyst eyes. She wore the concerned expression of a nurse checking on her patient.

And I'm the patient, he realized.

"What?" Lars asked.

"You went white all of a sudden," she said.

Two boys sitting in the front of the class were also staring at Lars. "You were talking about Mad Maron, and then you stopped," said one of the boys, whose name, if Lars remembered correctly, was Mark.

"I was just thinking," Lars said. Silence followed. Lars had the feeling they were waiting for him to continue.

Likely chance of that happening, he thought.

The black-haired beauty cleared her throat. "So, no one knows what happened to Mad Maron after he killed all those people?"

Lars shook his head. "No. Several men, who were part of the lynch mob, came forward and claimed they killed Mad Maron, but there was no proof, and the body was never found."

"Did they say how he was killed?" asked Mark.

"Gunshot," Lars answered. "And then it's also said he just went somewhere to die."

"How do you know so much about Mad Maron?" the girl asked.

Lars shrugged. "I read a lot."

Sudden silence filled the room, and Lars looked up and realized why. Dr. Hastings had appeared at the doorway, his face etched with its usual irritated scowl. He entered the room, and the door slammed behind him with a loud bang.

He walked with long strides to the front of the class, talking all the while, "Students, class has begun. Please open your textbooks to page ninety-eight. Your little conversations end as of now."

A groan blanketed the classroom. Lars smiled, slightly amused.

Here they were, people from all walks of life, some who had never said a word in the classroom or to each other, and yet there seemed to be a quiet conformity among all of them.

Dr. Hastings was a hated man.

Lars thought the professor was the personification of Gossamer Hall—older than time and unloved by everyone. Students often joked that Dr. Hastings had been at Brookhaven College longer than the building, though in reality, Lars knew he had only been around a decade or so. Lars estimated the professor's age to be around seventy, seventy-five.

Dr. Hastings was tall—a good six-foot-something. He used his height to intimidate his class. He walked through the aisles, peering over the shoulders of his students during tests and pop quizzes. His two dark, beady eyes, fronted with thick lenses, studied his students with a bullying quietness. He often raised his hand to his beard and groaned distractingly when he saw an incorrect answer on a test or quiz. "Imbecile," he would mutter before walking away.

He was legendary for catching students off guard. Any pupil who dared be tardy or absent or asleep during his class (which was often the case with the jocks in the back row), was rewarded with a tedious lecture or an unfair grade, an embarrassing call-out or a stomp of the foot while Dr. Hastings paced the room, screaming about "slackers" and "vagrants."

And yet Dr. Hastings, for all his villainy, did not scare Lars. Very little scared Lars these days.

He thought about Heather. It was true that toward the end she had scared him—scared him with her love, her disease, her addiction. Had scared him when she jumped in the car with a bag not her own.

Had scared him when she walked in from the kitchen, that spoon in her hand, that telephone wire, that terrified look when she saw the Mexican gangsters standing at the door.

Lars had read once, perhaps in a poem, that when you love someone, you love them forever. He could feel that love still, the same jolt of fire he had felt the first time he had seen Heather in the Madison High School parking lot, watching him from across three lanes of cars with her blond hair blowing back in the wind, the smoke of her cigarette rising up in the late afternoon. The clouds had gathered behind her, their blossoming white saturating the day in translucent haze. School had just let out, students were everywhere, but for Lars, it was just he and Heather while she exhaled the smoke and breathed him in.

The drugs had not come until later, in a cruel twist of events Lars still cringed to remember. The party at his friend's house. That blazing fire in the backyard. Everyone getting out of hand. His friend had hired a reggae group from out of town. A guy named Mickey was hanging around. He wasn't even in the band—just some kid following them to gigs. Later Lars learned he was the band's supplier.

It was Mickey's dare that opened Pandora's box. His hand full of crystal meth.

Bet you can't go through this in an hour.

Heather took the bait because she was brave and stupid; Lars followed after because he had a sneaking suspicion he was in love with her. Trailing behind was all he could do, after all, to keep up.

The realization of their addiction arrived, out of the blue, on a hot summer night at the end of their senior year in high school. They sat in Lars's car in the parking lot downtown and together came undone.

Heather's hands were glued to Lars's. They were like two deformed pretzels sitting in the back seat, stomach to stomach, chest to chest, legs crossing legs. Sweat mingled with the scent of the cloves they had stubbed out in the ashtray. The radio hummed with Tori Amos' disturbingly soprano voice. Lars could hear trains from the nearby railroad roaring past while he pushed Heather's hair away from her face, revealing hazel eyes glowing with addiction.

"This is it, isn't it?" she asked, though it wasn't really a question. She had a bottle of pills in her hand she had stolen from her a job at a retirement home where she had spent her summer arriving late.

Lars did not answer. He took the pills from her hands and fired away—the red ones, the blues, the tiny jagged white ones that kept slipping through his fingers. Heather took the leftovers. When the pills kicked in, they jumped out of the car and ran up to the railroad tracks, dancing in the face of the oncoming trains, laughing at the stars, spinning to the hum of the night.

"To be young is to be immortal," Lars had recited to Heather from a poem he no longer remembered.

Lars was kicked out of his house after his second arrest. It was a bad situation; he was happy to leave. The old man was just as screwed up as his son, and his mother didn't seem to care that her son was a junkie and her husband was an alcoholic. She stood by the stove every night cooking the meat, cooking the vegetables, rolling the dough and stirring his drinks, watching Regis and the would-be millionaires and answering the questions under her breath. Lars often thought of himself as the last word in a marriage that was hardly a sentence.

Lars was getting ready to start work in an automotive shop; Heather was ready for college when she suddenly got a wild hair up her ass to go to Mexico.

Lars was against the idea from the get-go. They didn't know a soul there, how were they supposed to get the junk? But Heather clued him in on a few things.

"Mickey's there."

Lars was pouring beer down his throat, but it suddenly tasted like vinegar. He spit it out.

"Mickey? Reggae Mickey?"

"He's not so much into reggae anymore."

"I don't fucking care. We're not going anywhere near that jerk."

But Mickey, as Lars was soon to find out, was pulling out the stops in Mexico, stealing all kinds of shit in department stores in El Paso, designer duds and purses, shiny suitcases and Pottery Barn vases. He was making some fat money selling it to the Mexicans, advertising it as the souvenirs of the rich all Americans had and Mexicans only dreamed of having, and he had convinced Heather that she and Lars could get into the action.

"Lars Case?"

His fake name brought Lars back to reality. Dr. Hastings was standing over him, his condescending eyes burning a hole into Lars.

"Yes, sir?" Lars answered.

Dr. Hastings leaned back on his desk, his palms lying flat on the surface. "Mr. Case, are you paying attention?" he asked.

"Yes, sir."

"Then, you can tell me about Mad Maron's mistress?" he asked.

"Sir?"

"Mad Maron," Dr. Hastings answered. "You were listening, weren't you? Do you know Mad Maron?"

"Yes, sir." *I probably know more than you do, asshole.*

"Then you won't mind repeating to me the details about Mad Maron's mistress, would you?" Dr. Hastings leaned against his desk, his eyes glowering at Lars. Lars thought the old fart was just waiting for him to screw up.

Lars cleared his throat. "Brianna Devonport. Mad Maron killed her after the Fredericksburg Massacre. It was his last murder. She was the mayor of Austin's daughter."

The classroom went quiet. Lars could hear the rustling of paper from one of the jocks' desks. Probably that *Playboy* they had been looking at earlier. Dr. Hastings's eyes grew cold. Victory's warm embrace closed over Lars and he laughed quietly to himself.

"Very good," Dr. Hastings replied. "I wasn't sure

you were paying attention."

He hadn't been paying attention, but Dr. Hastings need not know that. The first time Lars had ever heard the name Mad Maron was at his Boy Scout campfires. There was no other surefire way to scare the shit out of adolescent boys than bring up stories of Mad Maron. He remembered many a night being dared to walk into the woods alone.

What are you afraid of? Mad Maron?

"Who is Mad Maron?" an eight-year-old Lars had asked his Uncle Frank on a warm day in mid-July while the two of them sat in a boat on Lake Travis pretending to fish.

Uncle Frank was known throughout the family for knowing a little something about everything. Lars's mother called him a busybody, but his dad swore his brother was harmless.

When Lars asked the question, Uncle Frank's first reaction was to choke on his Shiner Bach. "Where the hell did you hear that name, son?" he asked, pulling on the reel while he threw his beer bottle out into the lake. He was the reason why the Green party had put signs up along the shore reading *Littering is unlawful*.

Lars shrugged. "Just around. Who is he, Uncle Frank?"

Uncle Frank snorted. "If I told you about Mad Maron, your momma and pappy wouldn't let me take you fishin' ever again."

"I won't tell them, I promise." It wasn't like Lars was fishing anyway.

"Promises, schomises," Uncle Frank quipped. His eyes cut away from the water and peered down with muted intensity at his nephew. He had the kind of sun-burnt handsome face that looked good in beer commercials. "You ever heard of the Fredericksburg Massacre?" he asked.

"Yes, sir," Lars replied, even though he hadn't.

"Well, that was the work of Mad Maron." Uncle Frank took another beer out of the cooler and twisted the lid. Lars watched while his uncle took a long swig that emptied half the bottle of its contents.

"Is that it?" Lars asked.

Uncle Frank turned and looked Lars straight in the eye. Lars could not decipher his uncle's expression. "What has your father told you?" he asked slowly.

"Daddy? Nothing. Why, was he supposed to?"

Uncle Frank's chest rose and fell with an exaggerated breath. Lars sensed his uncle was relieved in some way.

A moment later, his uncle threw the reel out. "If you know the Fredericksburg Massacre, son, then that's all you need to know," he said.

"Tell me again," said Lars. "My memory ain't so good."

Uncle Frank cocked his head, frowning at his nephew before saying, "Thirty-three people in one night. Can you believe that? Thirty-three people. Mad Maron and three of his cousins were headin' for Mexico. They were all heavin' and hivin' about gettin' some treasures on the way outta town, and I reckon that's when they stopped in Fredericksburg. They went into a bank and killed everyone in sight, then went out on the street and killed those people, too."

Uncle Frank watched the lake for long minutes before asking, "Why are you so interested in Mad Maron anyway?"

Lars said nothing.

"To think," Uncle Frank began, "that somewhere in this land, millions of dollars in gold rests."

Lars looked up from tying a hook to his line. "Gold?"

"Hell, yes." Uncle Frank motioned at the land above the lake. "Mad Maron buried some gold out here right before the militia caught up with his condemned ass, and I'd be a monkey's uncle if I knew where the hell it is—but I'll tell you this much, it sure is out here somewhere, that's for damn sure. Sure the hell wish I could find it, you know how much money your aunt spends at the damn market every weekend?"

Lars stared out into the water, where the late afternoon sun had cast its vanishing rays on the surface, threading the brown water with gold.

"The loot's never been found?" Lars asked.

"Nope." Uncle Frank released more curses while he reeled in his lure, revealing the absence of fish. "Not even a frog turd is bitin' today," he muttered.

"And no one knows where he hid it?" Lars looked down at the water and imagined truckloads of treasure underneath.

"What?" Uncle Frank threw a confused glance his nephew's way.

"The gold. No one knew where he hid it?"

"Oh." Uncle Frank scratched his head. "All anyone knows is that he made a map right before he died, but that map was buried with his body, and Lord knows where the hell his body is."

Nowadays Uncle Frank was retired and living in New Orleans, having divorced the woman who threw all his money away at the market. Lars wanted to visit him badly, but he knew it was risky. One of two shitty things might happen—Uncle Frank would turn him in or the old man would get charged with aiding a murder suspect.

So Lars stayed in Austin, which was not too far from Lars's hometown, but not too close, either. Austin was just big enough to hide him, small enough not to choke him, like big cities often did.

Lars had chosen Brookhaven College over UT

because UT was too damn close to the politicians for his liking, and ever since one of the ugly Bush twins had started school there, the cops swarmed the campus like flies on horseshit.

And no one, Lars thought, would suspect that a guy with his past would end up at Brookhaven College, the most holier-than-thou college in Texas.

Attending Brookhaven College was part of Lars's Five Year Plan of changing his life and leaving his mistakes in the past. The plan began with college because it had always sort of saddened him, perhaps more than any of his other mistakes (and there were plenty to choose from), that he'd been too messed up at age eighteen to enter an establishment of higher learning.

But today he was twenty-five and a new person. *I have a chance to start over*, Lars thought while he leaned back in his desk and watched Dr. Hastings without really paying attention. When his pencil dropped, he reached down to retrieve it, only to match hands with fingers more delicate and beautiful than he had ever felt before, and he rose up from the floor and stared into the saddest eyes he had ever seen.

CHAPTER FOUR

CELESTE.

Celeste as in celestial, as in belonging to the sky or heavenly bodies. Celeste as in blissful, divinely good, sublime.

Celeste of porcelain skin. Wrapped in beauty. Wrapped in light.

Reagan should have known something that incredibly wonderful would never last. Even the almighty sun, in its radiant glow, would one day fizzle out into a black hole.

Oh, God, but I miss her.

Celeste. Two years had passed. The days of

concerned faces were over. No more flowers on the console table, no more condolence cards in the mail.

Life rolled forward, but Reagan remained toxic.

Her thoughts were conspiracies that overshadowed her showers, her meals, the phone calls she avoided daily. She was a postcard with no picture or words, a form with no shape.

They did not know her pain. Women looked at Reagan, but they did not speak. They avoided her as if death were contagious, as if it were dust easily blown onto their sleeves. They whispered in the market aisles between the dryer sheets and baking soda, they stared at her in the post office running past with envelopes and stamps and flower-printed packages. They walked together in the parking lot, clutching their purses, glancing behind them, looking at the woman who'd lost her child.

Lakeway was a small town northwest of Austin, a place where everyone knew everyone, and everyone knew Reagan and what had happened.

Reagan tried to blink away the pain, but it was impossible. Two years and she should have recovered something of her former self, but the endlessness of grief seemed immeasurable against time.

Reagan still heard things at night, when she should have been sleeping. The squeal of brakes. The yell from George in the front seat.

Feed her. Stop her screaming.

The splitting of the sky.

Carve me out and throw me in a ditch, she silently pleaded with the one-eyed guy staring down at her. She handed him his pencil. *Kill me after class, deal?*

He seemed the sort. Dressed in dirty jeans and a dirty white shirt. A broken but well-shaped nose. Dark, longish hair. That one eye staring out of an angular face that might have been handsome, had he not looked like he'd murdered a few people in his time.

His one eye was dark blue, and it seemed to understand her. A hint of a smile grazed his full lips. And Reagan understood.

He pities me!

Did he know, too? Everyone else in Travis County knew, he could very well know too.

I should never have come here, Reagan thought, while she sat up straight again and looked forward at the blackboard.

No, she corrected herself. *It is right that I am here. There was no other place to start.*

Brookhaven College was a place where she had signed on only after she'd lost everything else. Before, her life seemed to be in a permanent layaway, a pause for which there was no "play" button. After she had signed up for school again, a glimmer of hope emerged. It had only been two and a half years since she had left. And she was smart. Everyone had always told her so. She'd made good grades in high school, and later, college. If she hadn't met George, she might have finished college the first time.

Reagan registered for Texas History because it had sounded interesting, because she'd always felt like she didn't know enough about her home state.

And wasn't it true, as someone had once said, that those who do not know history are doomed to repeat it?

Tonight's subject truly bothered her, however. She didn't understand history's insistence on retelling stories of mass murderers, glorifying violence and murder when there were plenty of people out there who had done so much good and deserved their place in history.

It was the difference between knowing Florence Nightingale and Jack the Ripper.

The man Reagan had read about last night was worse than Jack the Ripper. He was worse than anyone she had ever read about before.

Mack "Mad" Maron.

Reagan inwardly shivered.

Reagan hated the assignment. She'd heard of Mad Maron before, but had never read in detail what he had done. Last night in bed she had read about the Fredericksburg Massacre. After she turned out the light, the serial killer and his three henchmen invaded her dreams. It was a marked change from what her dreams usually encompassed.

Celeste, Celeste . . .

Reagan turned her head and stared out the caged window. Through the glass she could see night had finally settled, and only the half moon exposed the currents of the nearby lake.

Gossamer Hall was a distance away from the rest of campus. Reagan didn't know enough about the school's history to know if it was intentional or not. The other buildings were lined up in structured, land-scaped rows within the campus, but Gossamer Hall was lost beside a tree-strewn dirt path that stretched along Lake Travis. At its best, it gave the impression of a massive castle lost in the woods. At its worst . . .

Reagan frowned. She couldn't even put a name to what she felt when she walked away from the building after class—only that every time she stuck her key into the door of her Honda Civic, it was like she had once again defeated the forces of evil.

Maybe it wasn't Gossamer Hall's fault. Reagan admitted to herself that she had felt doomed for a long time.

In this nothingness.

In the endless, empty hole.

In this death.

Her heart was still beating, but Reagan had learned two years ago on a road trip back from San Antonio— death was not the only way to die.

George had a bad temper. Reagan knew this when she married him, but at the time she had not cared. He was arrogant and witty, confident and strong. Reagan's father had died from colon cancer six years ago, and ever since she'd been in need of a dominant male figure, or at least that's what her mother's friend, a self-credited psychologist, had told her. George had fit the bill to the T.

Reagan met George her junior year at UT. Reagan liked his smile, the way he wore a tie to class. His expensive polished shoes, his impassioned knowledge of politics. On their first meeting outside English class, George took a loose eyelash from her cheek and told her to make a wish and blow. Reagan made a wish, not really knowing what she was getting into. It just seemed natural to want to know him better.

The first time Reagan witnessed George's temper was in his dorm room. His roommate—a faceless, droopy computer dork Reagan no longer attached a name to—had spilled Starbucks on George's keyboard, and George cursed like a madman, scaring the wits out of his roommate and everyone else on the floor.

Reagan sat there and listened and wondered if the day would come when George would yell at her that way. And of course it did.

Not long before their wedding day, Reagan had changed the bridesmaids' flowers from yellow and pink to violet and pink. She had forgotten to tell George, and he had no way of knowing to change the boutonnieres he and the groomsmen would wear on their coats.

It was the night before the wedding, and Reagan was in the kitchen of their new home examining the champagne flutes for the next day's festivities when she heard George calling her from the other room.

"Reagan . . . honey . . ." His voice was soft. Reagan later discovered that his voice was often soft just before the explosion, the way the tides rolled back into the sea just before a tsunami. "Reagan, may I talk to you for a minute?"

She sensed the danger when she entered the room, though she could not pinpoint its source.

"George?"

"You wouldn't happen to know why the boutonnieres and bouquets are different flowers, different colors, would you?"

Reagan knew, but she did not say. George's fiery eyes spoke of an insurmountable rage that chilled her to the bone.

Careful, careful, she told herself. "I can't say that I do, sweetheart," she finally answered. "Perhaps the florist messed up."

George tilted his head, a joyless grin marring his face. "That's not really the case, is it, Reagan, sweetie?"

His voice felt like winter on her skin. Goose bumps formed along her arms and legs. Reagan looked up to the ceiling and prayed.

Careful, careful.

"I don't know what you mean," she said.

"Reagan, I talked to the florist."

Such a simple sentence, but George might as well have said he'd murdered her mother. Color drained from Reagan's face. Her legs turn to jelly. "And?" she asked, forcing her voice to stay steady.

Oh, so careful.

"And he said you changed the color of the bouquets a month ago. He said he talked to you himself. Come here, take a look at this." George yanked out one bouquet and one boutonniere off the chair. "You see this, Reagan? Do you?" His cheeks reddened while his voice became louder. "Take a fucking look at this!" he screamed.

And Reagan saw it. The ever-so-evident color differentiations. The yellow and pink boutonnieres. The lavender and pink bouquet. The little earthquakes that were bound to devour her one day.

"George, I'm sorry—"

He didn't give her a chance to finish. His hand hit her face with such rage that she reeled backward and fell to the ground, banging her knees against the bed's footboard on the way down, the champagne flutes slipping from her hands and shattering in a million pieces around her.

"What are we going to do now, Reagan? Have you thought of that? WHAT THE FUCK ARE WE GOING TO DO NOW?"

"They're just flowers," Reagan whispered and placed her hand against her burning cheek. "Perhaps he can change—"

"The wedding's tomorrow, you stupid bitch! You fucked up, stupid idiot—"

"It was a simple mistake," she said.

But who are you and who am I marrying, and what happened just now?

George looked like a rabid dog with shots of spittle jumping from his lips. He screamed, "All I've heard since we started planning for this fucking wedding was assurance from you that every base was covered! I thought this wedding was a closed deal!"

George was a law student and enjoyed the idea of "closed deals."

"And look at this shit," he said, raising the flowers up high enough so their stems were pressed against the top of his head. "Flowers that don't match."

They're just flowers, you stupid bastard, Reagan thought, but her voice did not follow her thoughts, and instead she picked herself up from the floor and limped into the kitchen. She spent the rest of the night pouring glasses of gin and listening to George break things in the next room.

They went ahead with the wedding anyway, Reagan's mistake aside. She made an emergency run to the grocery store and bought yellow flowers to stuff with the pink ones in her bouquet. She held a bag of ice to her face the entire night so the next morning her cheek was clear of her lover's rage. She did not look George in the eye during the entire ceremony, not even when he leaned down to kiss her.

Reagan did not finish college because soon after the wedding, somewhere between George's temper tantrums and law classes, she became pregnant with Celeste. The pregnancy was not easy, the labor hard, the delivery harder. But when Celeste arrived, Reagan cherished her. She was a porcelain portrait of gorgeous blue eyes; soft, dark hair; and two chubby, perfect cheeks. Reagan thought her daughter was heaven in human form. She inhaled her like a scent. Everything wonderful in life resembled her baby, and when Reagan looked at her daughter, she could see nothing but good in the world, and there was nothing that could be unsolved in a place holding all that beauty.

Even George seemed to stabilize under the weight of his love for his daughter. Her baby giggles were the antidote to his poison. A world shattered and another was reborn.

Then one day, when the baby was five months old, George decided to take his family to San Antonio for a shopping trip. On the way home, Celeste started crying.

"Reagan, shut her up."

"She's just hungry."

"Then feed her," he demanded.

"I can't pull her out of her baby seat to feed her."

"You can feed her from the bottle."

"I don't have any water to mix with the formula."

"What?" George glanced away from the road long enough to scowl at his wife. "What the hell? Are you stupid, Reagan? Do you have no fucking sense?"

Reagan knew where this was going. "There was no hot water in the bathroom at the restaurant," she explained.

"You could have asked the waitress."

"I forgot."

"Well, great, you fucking idiot. Now we have to hear her scream the whole way home."

"I'm sorry."

"*I'm sorry, I'm sorry*," George mimicked. "That's all I fucking hear is how sorry you are. Why don't you get your head out of your ass? Damn it. I feel like I'm the only adult here."

George pulled over, and Reagan jumped out and got into the backseat while both her husband and her baby continued their frenzied screaming.

"It's okay, my angel," Reagan murmured to Celeste. "It's okay, baby."

George hollered from the front seat, "Feed her, you sorry excuse for a fucking woman. You pathetic. . ."

Reagan fumbled for the belt, unlocking the buckle. The baby's head fell sideways while she was pulled her from the seat, her loud cries subsiding when she realized food was nearby, and George steered back on the road and gunned it.

Reagan breathed in the lilac scent of her daughter's neck while Celeste's lips touched her nipple and the car went silent.

Reagan remembered her last thought before the accident.

I hope George is happy.

Reagan awoke in the hospital a day later. She had suffered major head injuries, a fractured wrist. George had barely a scratch.

Celeste's fate had not been so kind.

"She should never have taken the baby out of her car seat," she heard George's mother say in the kitchen while Reagan was in the bedroom sitting at the edge of the bed, contemplating killing herself.

And so it was, days upon weeks upon months of waking up or not waking up, depending whether she slept the night before. A shower, followed by bouts of crying. Contemplating suicide over eggs and orange juice. Sitting very still in the dark living room. Crying. More contemplation. Lunch and crying. Watching TV and contemplating. Preparing steak and potatoes for George's Atkins Diet. TV. Contemplation and crying, and only sometimes afterward, sleep.

On a morning in mid-December, when time had stretched far enough for Reagan to feel something other than suicidal grief, she stood at the kitchen counter and watched George at the breakfast table and realized she hated her perfect husband.

Reagan stared at his polished shoes and Ralph Lauren suit, his hair combed back to disguise his receding hairline, his head bent over the business section of the *Austin American-Statesman* while he stirred his routine twelve packets of sugar in his coffee, and felt an almost uncontrollable desire to hurl the bread knife at his eye. With each annoying clearing of his throat, with each tap of his spoon against the cup, Reagan made a list of everything she despised about him, and when she was done there was nothing left. His words, his gestures, his Rolex, his prized high-school soccer trophy. His stupid polished shoes. The razor by the sink with his hair lying beside it. His tone of voice when he asked what was for dinner that night.

But especially, Reagan thought, was the way he never blinked when he passed Celeste's nursery.

And Reagan asked herself the inevitable question:

would she have taken Celeste out of the car seat had it not been for George?

And the answer, of course, was no.

The marriage ended on the first anniversary of their daughter's death. Reagan was outside drinking Nescafe from her World's Greatest Mommy mug, watching the hummingbirds buzz around a feeder left by the house's previous owners. George walked outside with the divorce papers in his hands, his heavy-footed steps unmistakable against the deck's rotted wood.

She saw the papers before she saw him. He handed them over her shoulder while he stood behind her and whistled a Broadway tune apathetically. Reagan clutched them with one defeated hand. She listened to his footsteps while he walked back into the house and thought, *In one year he went from hot- to cold-blooded.*

Reagan did not know what to make of the new, emotionless George. She had walked through the inferno, had felt its burning fire. She knew what to expect in hell.

She had never known the Antarctic. She could handle George's anger, his rage. But she could not swallow his cold indifference.

Reagan signed the papers without a fight, leaving everything to him and moving into a one-bedroom apartment near the city limit of Lakeway, where her family was from. *I hope George is happy,* she mused whenever her thoughts steered to the what-could-have-beens.

Death is not the only way to die.

Reagan looked back at the one-eyed guy and smiled to herself. He reminded her of the men she had dated before George. The dangerous types who never said phrases like "closed deals." Thinking about it, she kind of missed those manly beasts.

At least you know what you're getting into, she thought.

A sound like thunder shuddered from outside. Its loud, intense rage jolted everyone, including Reagan, in their desks. One of the jocks in the back whistled.

"No one's ever heard a storm before?" Dr. Hastings asked.

A moment later and Reagan could hear the pounding of the rain on the roof. Had they been in another building it might not have been loud, but Gossamer Hall's roof was old and in need of repair. Reagan remembered reading in the Brookhaven College newsletter about a car wash for the reconstruction of "our most beloved building on campus." She guessed the roof hadn't been repaired, and the building wasn't as loved as the newsletter supposed it to be.

"Ignore the rain. It's only rain," Dr. Hastings said, his scowl deepening in a face that was used to scowling.

But am I imagining this, Reagan thought, *or is Dr. Hastings glowing a little, like a new bride?*

No, she decided. She was just seeing things. A man like the professor probably thought any sign of happiness was a form of weakness. Reagan knew the type.

Dr. Hastings cleared his throat while more thunder roared through the night like a train storming through a tunnel. "As for class . . . tonight, we will try something different," he said. "Prepare yourselves."

CHAPTER FIVE

SOMETHING WAS WRONG.

Juan looked down at his hand. His fingers were flapping back and forth furiously. His hand never shook that way unless it was about to *make*. Juan looked back up at the professor. Dr. Hastings was watching him. A faint smile brushed the corners of the man's lips.

Juan had never seen Dr. Hastings smile before.

Something was wrong, wrong, wrong. A shaking hand and a smiling teacher who never smiled.

It occurred to Juan that it was Dr. Hastings who had been watching him earlier outside.

But why?

Juan took a deep breath while the rain continued to pound the roof, while the thunder roared through the October night, while lightning struck like a bizarre fireworks display through the Texas hill country.

Nothing to be afraid of. Just forces of nature at work.

But Juan could not shake off Dr. Hastings's horrible smile. *He's working for me,* Dr. Hastings thought. He turned around and faced the chalkboard, holding his hand up to cover his widening grin.

I got him, I got him.

It was time for Phase II of his plan. Dr. Hastings turned back around and faced his students. The two athletes; the grungy, one-eyed freak; the quiet redhead; the knockout princess; the smart kid taking in every word.

And Juan. Priceless, talented Juan.

"Class," Dr. Hastings began, "I want all of you to stand up and create a circle with your desks."

Lars sat in the circle between the redhead and the Hispanic kid.

The redheaded girl glanced Lars's way. Her sad, brown eyes reflected a mixture of interest and uncertainty. She seemed to be thinking the same thing Lars was.

What the hell is going on here?

In some ways the redhead reminded Lars of

Heather—the familiar never-ending grief that dressed her face like a translucent veil. Lars wondered what her story was.

If I asked her out, what would she say?

It occurred to him that he hadn't had sex in over a year, not since Heather died. It wasn't intentional. After the initial pain had subsided, a lack of self-confidence followed, mostly stemming from his lack of a left eye.

But maybe it is time to meet someone.

(If I get outta this class alive tonight.)

Lars wasn't sure from where the thought came. It was silly to think that he would not survive Texas History. It was a stupid history class at a gung ho Christian college. Nothing bad could happen here other than a bad grade or some name-calling from Dr. Hastings when he was in that shitty mood of his.

And yet Lars's instinct told him he had every right to feel funny about this evening.

Do yourself a favor and trust your instinct.

That was Mickey's sage advice. Lars had met the bastard on a dirt road past Juarez—this was after Heather had her head blown off, after the Mexican mafia had left him alive but dying and with only one eye. Lars was in hate with the world and needed a punching bag. Mickey was it.

The air had smelled like fresh roadkill while Lars

walked toward Mickey under a sky thick with clouds. Dust kicked up under his shoes with each calculated step.

"You piece of shit!" Lars screamed, and Mickey started walking backward.

"What, no poetry?" Mickey asked, followed by a nervous giggle. "You pseudo-intellectual prick. You were always one for the sonnets. At least that's what Heather said."

"Fuck you."

Mickey's smile grew crooked; his shoulders slumped forward. "How'd you find me?" he asked.

Lars got the word from the guys at a local bar that Mickey was in Juarez pulling a heist. After hearing the news, it wasn't hard to find him. Mickey was an easy one to spot, especially around Mexicans. His hair was red, and he wore it pulled back in a greasy ponytail. His skin was the color of paste. His was the antithesis of Mexican DNA.

The dusty road seemed a whole lot dirtier with Mickey on it. Lars kept reaching out to give Mickey a nice knock on the noggin, but his sight wasn't what it used to be. Losing an eye took some getting used to.

"What happened to your eye?" Mickey asked when his foot caught the side of a stunted cactus, nearly tripping him.

"Fuck my eye. Heather's dead."

Mickey slowed down. "Wait, wait a second. Did

you say Heather was dead? You're kidding, right? How?" He had the nerve to look surprised.

"Shot. In the head."

"Damn. Who?"

"You know who."

Mickey's face turned as red as his hair. "Why?"

"She took a bag from them."

"And you let her?"

"I didn't know . . . she said they owed her a favor."

"And you believed her?"

"I didn't know what to believe. My instinct . . ." Lars's words trailed off. He had made progress. Mickey was closer now. Lars could smell the crystal meth on him.

"Your instinct?" Mickey shook his head and reached into his coat pocket, lighting up a Marlboro. "Next time, do yourself a favor and trust your instinct."

They were Mickey's last words. Lars found the courage to trust his one eye and threw a punch. Mickey's cigarette flew out of his mouth and into the dust.

One punch was all it took for Lars to go crazy. He totally went for it, hitting, kicking, whatever it took to bring Mickey down. When it was all over, Mickey lay on the ground just like the dog Lars believed he was, bloodied and battered in the sand, his red ponytail bubbling up over a motionless, collapsed head. Lars reached down to feel his pulse and realized there was none.

Lars stood for a long minute and mulled over his feelings. He tried to feel something, tried to look at Mickey's pale eyes staring up at the sky and feel some kind of guilt that whatever chance the guy had to redeem himself was forever lost, but all Lars could think about was Heather dead on the floor, caped in her blood-drenched yellow dress.

"Jesus," Lars muttered to himself and bent down, taking Mickey's fallen cigarette, putting it to his lips and sucking in the cancer.

Lars hadn't meant to kill the guy, but here's the thing: it happened.

He decided, in the end, he was only doing what Mickey had told him to do. He had followed his instinct, and his instinct said Mickey deserved a first-class ticket to hell, and Lars was the pilot.

Instinct. Trust it now. Something's up.

Lars's mind settled back in the present day, back to Dr. Hastings and the ridiculous circle they had made. Dr. Hastings looked like he had just had the best shit of his life. All smiles, all posture. Even his eyes appeared to warm to the color of cinnamon.

Outside, lightning and thunder terrorized the sky. An unfamiliar tingle of dread started at the bottom of Lars's spine and crawled upward like a spider with a thousand legs. He remembered Gene Wilder in *Charlie and the Chocolate Factory*, on the boat through the chocolate river:

There's no earthly way of knowing which direction we are going . . .

"I put us in this circle so we can have absolute focus on our lesson this evening," Dr. Hastings explained. "It's very important you hear every word I'm saying because you're all going to be tested on it."

Lars sniffed bullshit. He wasn't sure exactly why Dr. Hastings wanted them in a circle, but it had to be more than just the attention factor.

The Hispanic kid looked dubious, too. He glanced over in Lars's direction and Lars shrugged his shoulders.

The skinny bespectacled kid named Mark raised his hand. Dr. Hastings placed his hands on his hips. "What is it?" he growled.

"Sir, it's actually been proven that students learn better in straight and parallel lines as opposed to circles."

One of the jocks chuckled.

Dr. Hastings snorted. "I don't care what studies have said. I teach this way from time to time, and since this is my classroom, we're going to do what I want to do. Got it? Now, what we are about to do, boys and girls," he began, "is experience something that was once used in the universities back during the Enlightenment Period. Does anyone know about the Enlightenment Period?"

Mark raised his hand.

"All right, Mr. Green, go ahead," said Dr. Hastings.

Mark cleared his throat. "It was a term used to describe a time when the world's intellectuals got together and pulled civilization out of the Dark Ages."

"There's more to it than that, Mr. Green."

"I know, but that's the starting point, right?"

"Yes."

"The Enlightenment took place in the eighteenth century. It inspired a framework for the American and French Revolutions, as well as the rise of capitalism and the birth of communism."

"Socialism, but close enough."

Mark paused, looking momentarily unsure of himself before continuing, "It got people to think about spirituality, not just in a religious sense, but in an individual sense, and there was a lot of progress in science, mathematics, and the arts."

"Very good, Mr. Green. I am impressed. Would you like to further this discussion by explaining the Hume Method?"

Mark swallowed hard. Lars could tell the kid didn't know the answer but didn't want to admit to it. Guys like him were use to knowing everything.

"I guess," he began, "I don't think I know enough to explain it."

Dr. Hastings flashed a triumphant smile. "Fine. Let me give it a try." The professor inhaled deeply, looking very self-important. "The Hume Method was named after David Hume, one of the great thinkers of the Enlightenment Period. One of his biggest studies was the relationship between being and perception."

"Are we learning history or philosophy here?" one of the jocks asked.

Dr. Hastings narrowed his eyes. "All will be explained in time, Mr. Jacobs. Now, where was I? Oh, yes. The Hume Method is when members of a class would learn about a historic period by pretending they were back in that era. Usually this meant that each student would take on a character in this historical document and go about acting it out in their mind, but within a circle of people, almost like a play, but more inclusive. This method had a rebirth back in the '60s when New Age became popular. Has anyone heard of past-life regression?"

One of the jocks raised his hand and without Dr. Hastings acknowledging him, he asked, "Is that like what that John Edwards dude does?"

Dr. Hastings shook his head. "No. John Edwards claims to speak to the dead. Past-life regression is when a person meditates to go back in time, back when they were another person."

"What a crock of—"

"Careful, Mr. Herzig. We are at a Presbyterian school. There is no cussing here."

The beautiful girl with the black hair raised her hand. "So, what are you proposing?" she asked. "That one of us pretends to be Mad Maron?"

"If the shoe fits, Ms. Blythe."

The girl's face screwed up. Lars could tell she wasn't a believer. He felt the same way. Whoever heard of such a thing? *The Presbyterian Church would go nuts if they knew about Dr. Hastings's scheme,* he thought.

"I don't think my pastor would agree to me doing this," Mark said.

"Your pastor isn't grading you on it," Dr. Hastings replied sharply. "I am."

The lights flickered inside, back and forth from light to dark, and finally darkness stretched over the room like a long arm. Lars heard someone gasp. He thought it might've been the redheaded girl.

"I think it's time to go home," suggested a voice that sounded like Mark.

"We're not going anywhere," Dr. Hastings growled. "The only way I can dismiss class is if there's a blizzard. And since this is Texas and October, I can assure you the probability is almost zilch. I have some candles I brought especially for our séance." Lars heard the desk drawer open, followed by a lighter igniting, and he watched Dr. Hastings pass out lit candles to the class. The candles rotated around the circle, each person receiving one.

Lars turned to the side and saw that the Hispanic kid had dropped his candle and was out of sorts, shaking around like there were electric currents moving through him. Lars looked closer. The kid's hand was the real diva. It looked like it had a mind of its own, the way it was thrashing back and forth. The only time Lars had seen a person in worse shape was when he had visited Heather's job at the retirement home and met a woman suffering from Parkinson's.

Parkinson's is an old-person's disease, isn't it?

The Hispanic kid doesn't look a day over eighteen.

"It's better that the lights are out," Dr. Hastings said. "I think it will get us more in the mood."

"Hey! My cell phone is dead!" yelled a voice from the darkness. One of the jocks stood up from his desk. "This is bullshit!" he exclaimed. "I'm going home."

Dr. Hastings inhaled sharply. "Out of the question," he said. "We are here until 9:45 p.m. That's final."

"Dude, I don't give a shit." The jock stuffed his *Playboy* magazine into his backpack.

"You leave and you fail this class." Dr. Hastings's voice was ice cold. "I mean it, Mr. Jacobs. You've already been absent twice. One more absence and you automatically fail this class."

A pause followed while everyone held their breath, waiting to see what the jock would do. Finally, he dumped his backpack to the floor and fell back into the desk.

"Nice of you to comply, Mr. Jacobs," Dr. Hastings said, clearing his throat. "Now, shall we get started?"

CHAPTER SIX

CALEB JACOBS HAD MAILED OUT A REPLY TO AN E-MAIL someone had sent him a month ago, and since then there'd been hell to pay. It wasn't even a good e-mail either, definitely not worth getting in trouble for. If he hadn't been drinking Red Bull, staying up late, and spending the night in the dorm for once, he probably would never have answered it.

Here was the subject:

What is your porn name?

The text followed: *Your porn name goes like this: the first name is the name of your pet, the second name is that of your street. Once you figure it out, write it down and send it to ten people.*

The kid who had sent Lars the e-mail wrote down his name:

Spot Mulberry.

Caleb could do much better.

He started typing, and since he was alone and had a lot of time on his hands, it ended up being a lot longer than he had planned.

So, what would my name be? Well, my porn name could be a whole bunch of shit. Bear with me. There's Jax Crepe Myrtle, Bernie Mimosa, Felix Coker, Babe Mimosa (even though that one sounds like a girl), Chance Bradford, or how about Lucky Saint Oak Wood? Bailey Oak Wood? Jax Crepe Myrtle is the most old-school.

At this point Caleb had reached a flow. Blame it on the Red Bull, the Energizer bunny of drinks. He thought about it, and wrote some more.

How about Coco Riser? Or maybe Hank South Fifth? Hank South Nineteenth? Or out of respect for my favorite dog, Gordy Coker.

Red Bull again. Nostalgia was feeling good. Plus he missed Gordy. It had been too long since he'd had a dog like that.

Gordy was the coolest. I found him dead in the driveway one teenage morning after driving home from some late fucking party. I had to bury this dog. He was a seventy-pound Catahoula-Aussie Shepherd badass that didn't get out of some car's way. He was my other dog Bailey's muscle in the neighborhood. Bailey could pick on and mount any dog at the lake because Gordy was backing him up. The two dogs were connected.

Gordy was a badass on the run. My mom met Gordy one time at the lake. She was up early to guzzle coffee and figure out how to raise two boys with a third husband. Then she heard a gunshot.

Mom went outside to check it out. Within minutes, there was a buckshot-riddled, heavily panting, very scared, multicolored dog hiding beneath her Saturn minivan. After a couple of weeks, with a little dog nursing from a human nurse, Gordy was part of the gang. It was like he swore an oath to Mom. Gordy was protector, injector, and your own soul reflector. To be as cool as Gordy, you would have to stop a skyjacking, you would have to hate the common man, you would have to take steroids and run through a baseball field buck naked, which, by the way, I have done, and trust me, it's the coolest shit ever.

It was the last line that sang out. How it got back to the school's dean, Caleb didn't know, though he suspected Ryan Gaskins, the second-string linebacker.

So, old Dr. Kurcan and her tight, hadn't-gotten-laid-since-the-Reagan-administration ass went on a rampage, calling the athletics department and all of Caleb's teachers and even his parents in Florida. "No 'roids at Brookhaven," she said in a meeting in the boys' locker room. "This is a Christian-friendly school. Drugs kill, Jesus heals."

They all got tested—every athlete from the football team to the girls' ping-pong club. They got their blood drawn and their balls poked and their hearts checked and their urine sampled. Ten kids were dismissed right away, most of them athletes who had landed in Brookhaven from a scholarship.

Caleb was safe, because it was a flaw of his to brag about the drugs he hadn't done and the wild times he hadn't had.

Dr. Kurcan was furious enough to ask Caleb be re-tested. He agreed. And so it went again. Blood, balls, heart, urine. Another negative test.

"I don't know what you're doing," she said the last time she saw him in the parking lot, "but you better watch your back, mister." She raised her fingers and pointed them at her eyes and back at Caleb, telling him, *I see you.*

Of course, Caleb wasn't worried about getting caught with something he had never taken to begin with. His main concern was the football players' reactions. How would they treat him?

Like horseshit, Caleb soon realized.

He had a standard issue response going out when his teammates picked on him:

Look, it wasn't like I was planning on Dr. Kurcan seeing my e-mail. What you should be concerned with is who forwarded her my e-mail.

And his eyes would dart to Ryan Gaskins if Ryan was around, but no one ever took the bait, and Caleb was reduced to being the bad guy.

Josh Herzig tapped Caleb on the shoulder. "This is bullshit," he said, pointing at Dr. Hastings. "We should get the hell out of here."

Josh was one of the only football players still talking to him. It was luck they had the same shitty night class together. He was good company. Coincidentally, he came out of a little crocodile town just miles from Caleb on the Florida panhandle.

"We should go down to Sixth Street after this,"

Caleb suggested.

Josh snorted. "Ha. Not in this weather."

"The rain will have stopped in an hour."

"Or maybe not."

Their professor, Dr. Hastings—or Dr. Fuckings, as Josh and Caleb liked to call him— marched over to where Caleb sat and flattened his palms on the desk. He leaned over and sneered.

"Would you like to tell the rest of the class your conversation, Mr. Jacobs?"

"No."

"Are you sure? Because if you're finished with your conversation, the rest of the class and I can continue. Would that be all right with you, Mr. Jacobs?"

"Sure." *You asshole.*

"Good." Dr. Hastings leaned up once again and turned around to speak to the rest of the class. "Everyone has an assigned person who they will be in this special—shall we say, for lack of a better word— séance. And I have already assigned them to you." The professor walked to his desk and took the class roster.

"Lillian Blythe." Dr. Hastings's gaze turned to Lily, who sat between Josh and Mark. "You'll be Brianna Davenport. Lars Case. You're Mad Maron. Josh and Mark and Caleb, you're his three cousins and henchmen: Zachary Maron, Andrew 'Flat Shot' Maron, and Bezus Smith. Reagan Tanner, you're Sara Parker, the wife of the bank owner. And Juan Fuentes, you're the map."

Thunder struck outside while the class seemed to mull over what being a "map" entailed. The Hispanic kid raised his hand. "Excuse me, sir, but the map?"

Dr. Hastings nodded, a smile cracking through the cold marble of his face. "Absolutely. In every séance during the Enlightenment Period, there was always one person who was an inanimate object. It was considered a control object. If the others got too into their characters, the person playing the object could control them."

"I've never heard such a thing," Lily mumbled.

"There you go. You learn something new every day," Dr. Hastings shot back. "Let's proceed."

CHAPTER
SEVEN

JUAN FELT SICK, LIKE THE TIME HE'D HAD THREE MAR-
garitas at Chile's with a couple of guys from his biology
class, except without the nice side effect, the feeling of
exhilaration and fearlessness. His sickness was scary
and all-consuming. He wanted to vomit and pass out
at the same time.

If Dr. Hastings noticed that one of his students
was falling apart, he did not say anything.

"Close your eyes," he ordered, "and listen."

He began, "Lars, this is for your benefit. This is
to help you imagine yourself as Mad Maron. He was
six-foot-two, with black, stringy hair. He never wore

anything but black."

"Many people don't know this, but Mad Maron was a schoolteacher before he started robbing banks. I guess there's a small irony there, considering the salary we schoolteachers make." Dr. Hastings's attempted joke faded in the laughless silence of the classroom.

But he remained unswayed, and continued, "Maron was a schoolteacher when he originally met Brianna Davenport. That's you, Lillian. Imagine a woman, dark hair, over six feet tall, very thin. She was thought to be very beautiful in her time.

"On the morning of the Fredericksburg Massacre, Mad Maron was sleeping with Brianna in the Fredericksburg Lounge. No one knew he was there. Brianna and her maidservant had rented the room the night before. There were whispers that the mayor's daughter was sleeping with the bandit, but there was no hard evidence. Brianna, like many women from high-class backgrounds, had a penchant for bad men. Excuse me, Mr. Case, did you say something?"

"Was Brianna in on it? The robberies?" Lars asked.

"It is not clear that Brianna knew Mad Maron's plans. If she had, she never spoke to anyone in the days leading up to the event." Dr. Hastings cleared his throat and continued, "Lillian, you are Brianna. Lars, you are Mad Maron. It is important that you visualize what the morning felt like. You wake up from your bed. You are arguing. What are you arguing about? We have never clearly understood the condition of Maron and Brianna's relationship, there has never been evidence of what went wrong, only the brief and vague testimony of the maidservant who swore they were fighting that morning." Dr. Hastings coughed. "Though we have hardly gotten to that part yet.

"Now, stay on that wavelength. Caleb, Josh, Mark, it's your turn. You are Mad Maron's right-hand men. You've been with him since he started his rampage. Let me give you some background on these three men. Josh, Zachary is your character. At six-foot-four, he is larger than the other men, with the same long black hair as his cousin. He had a crooked spine and often walked hunched over. Smoked three packs a day. Reports say he was never without a cigarette. He wasn't all there, if you know what I mean. Borderline retarded. But he could shoot a string from a mile away, or at least that's what they used to say. Zachary, all and all, had more brawn than brains.

"Mark, your character is Flat Shot. He did not have the best aim of the group, as you can guess by his name. He was the shortest of the men, at five-foot-eight. His hair was described as orangey-red, and his eyes were gray, like Maron's. He was Maron's second-in-command, a sort-of lackey. It was legendary that he rhymed whenever he talked, a quirk of his.

"Caleb, your character is Bezus Smith. He was often described as handsome, standing just over six feet, his hair was dark, his eyes blue. He was educated in the East, and joined Maron's group last. He was known for reciting Shakespeare while he was killing, I don't know why. Jesse James was the same way. Bezus had a penchant for beautiful women, and beautiful women liked him—a real ladies' man. Now, as for the outfits—think of yourselves in leather pants and long-sleeved shirts, two guns at your hip, boots, hats, the works. Have you ever seen *Tombstone*? Just think of that.

"The three of you are waiting at the edge of Fredericksburg, in a little shack owned by former slaves. You came in with your knives and pressed your weapons against their throats, you told them they were going to die if they did not give you shelter. In the morning you killed them anyway. Can you see it? It was a family of three, a mother, a father, a son. All dead. You get on your horses and ride away. I'll get back to you in a second.

"Sara Parker, it is your turn. Your husband is out of town—it is your duty to run the Fredericksburg Bank. You run the bank together with your husband, and you know what you are doing. You are a petite blonde, in your mid-forties. You set about your day as planned—rise from bed, dress, comb your hair, order the farm boys to slaughter a pig. You ask your foreman to take you to the bank. He obliges, looking kindly at you. You are a good, respectable woman. You have a daughter, and her name is Hannah."

Juan heard a sharp intake of breath from the other side of Lars. Dr. Hastings must have heard the sound, too, because he paused and asked, "Ms. Tanner, are you all right? Do you need water?"

The redhead shook her head. "No, thank you."

"Fine, I will continue. Please get back into character. You are Sara Parker. You bring your daughter with you on this day because the schoolteacher is sick with fever. You don't mind because Hannah is a lovely child, and customers are happy to see her when they walk into the bank.

"Juan, I will be with you in a moment. Remember, you are the map. You are the control.

"All characters collide now. Let's come together. It is noon in Fredericksburg, a quiet day, by all accounts. The Fredericksburg Bank is having its usual stream of business during lunch hour.

"Brianna Davenport sees her lover ride away on his horse. She follows him, for whatever reason, we never really know. She has never followed Maron before on any of his other robberies. Mad Maron makes a stop at Burt's Brewery and waits for his henchmen. The four ride off into the distance. Brianna sees them

81

and follows.

"Everyone, see the clock in the bank? It is high noon. Mad Maron and his three henchmen see it from outside. Sara looks at it from her place at the front desk. She glances over and sees her daughter skipping rope in the bank. She is impressing the customers. Sara tells her to stop—there is no jumping rope inside the bank. Sara turns her head for a moment. Just a moment. And then she hears a shot.

"She turns back around. Her daughter is lying on the floor, in a pool of her own blood."

The redhead—Dr. Hastings had called her by her last name, Tanner—cried out into the room. Juan and the rest of the class looked at her just as a slash of lightning cut through the sky. Juan saw what the darkness had been hiding all along.

Tears. The redhead was crying.

"Ms. Tanner, are you okay?" Dr. Hastings sounded more annoyed than concerned. "We are just visualizing this. If you are finding yourself too close to your character, you are welcome to leave the room until we finish."

"I'd like to leave the room," Juan heard one of the jocks say.

"I'll pretend I didn't hear that," Dr. Hastings retorted stiffly.

"I'm fine," the redhead whispered through sniffles. "Really."

Anyone with half a conscience knew she wasn't fine, but no one had ever accused Dr. Hastings of having a conscience. "Okay, then, let's continue," he said.

"Sara screams. She rushes to her daughter's side. Mad Maron takes a hold of Sara and pushes her away. He says to her, 'Give me the gold and you can live.'

"His men follow suit, moving through the bank, their guns drawn. The bank tellers load up bags of gold. Four sacks, one for each horse. Sara stares at the mayhem from under Mad Maron's iron clasp. She watches her daughter dying. She watches her husband's dream turn to dust. She watches as her customers get robbed, one after another. Sara tells Maron, 'You didn't have to kill her.'

"No one knows what Maron says to this. People are shouting, the henchmen are shooting guns in the air.

"Then Sara makes a fatal mistake. She thinks she can overcome Mad Maron. She miscalculates how strong he is. Or maybe she just wants to die. She looks down at his hip, where a holstered gun sits. She thinks maybe she can get to it. Her reflexes were quicker than most women's. Most men's, in fact. She'd had a lot of practice on the ranch.

"Sara reaches down and manages to get the gun out of the holster, but Mad Maron stops her just before she can aim the gun at him. He pushes the gun away from her in a death struggle, and the gun goes off, and there is Sara, lying on the floor not too far away from her daughter.

"The henchmen, believing the gunfire came from someone other than Mad Maron, think they are being attacked. They open fire in the bank. Bodies fall, smoke forms, a death toll is born.

"Mad Maron orders them to get out of there. The four men scatter from the premises. They jump on their horses. Can you see it? The bank is pandemonium. There are screams and people running this way and that. A fire has broken out. The day turns into a perpetual night.

"The sound of Mad Maron and his clan echoes through the hills while they make their escape, shooting everyone on the street who happens to be in their way. Meanwhile, Mad Maron has no way of knowing that Brianna is following behind them.

"They reach a place—can you see it? No one knows where this secret place is, not even me. It is a place where the men bury their gold. Mad Maron draws a map. Brianna sees it from a distance. She rides back to town. All experts agree, me included, and yes, I am the most informed expert out there, that Brianna never had a problem with Mad Maron's career before, but seeing the child shot to death in the bank has changed her view of him.

"Mad Maron sees Brianna watching him and follows her on his horse. Brianna gets to the motel just in time to tell her maidservant what has happened. She tells her everything she saw, including details about where they buried the gold, and the map. Maron walks into the room and, knowing that Brianna has betrayed him, shoots her. The maidservant rushes out of the room and jumps on the horse, racing into the town square.

"Mad Maron chases behind her. The townsfolk spot Maron, and a lynch mob forms. They follow him, and one of the bereaved men shoots him in the heart, or so it is said. As I have mentioned before, no one has ever seen the body. Anyway, they kill the other three men, as well. It was a stupid move on the towns-people's part, really, because Maron's three cousins could have told them where the gold was." Dr. Hastings paused, and turned to Juan. "The maidservant tries to tell the governing officials what Brianna had described to her, about where the gold was buried, but when they go look for it, they cannot find it. The maidservant also tells them about the map, but since no one can find Maron's body, no one has the map, either. One big conundrum, wouldn't you say, class?" he asked, and chuckled to himself.

Dr. Hastings's eye landed on Juan, and when the old man spoke, his tone was grave and serious. "Finally," he continued, "Juan, I come to you. Do you see the map, Juan? You are the map. Try to imagine. There are hills and mountains, directions and footprints. It is signed MM for Mad Maron. Do you see it?"

The classroom waited for Juan to answer.

Juan shivered in his desk.

Yes, I see it.

He saw it too well, actually. His hand saw it, too, which was why it was shaking.

It wanted to *make* it.

No, that could not happen.

He could not let the others know what he could do.

You'll be a freak show, Juan thought.

Yet there was no holding back. He felt like a car losing its parts. The wheels, the transmission, the brakes. All gone. His senses were boiling over like oil from a broken tank. His hearing gone, his sight leaving, taste and smells hitting the ground and running.

The map was growing out of his palm. It would *make* right there.

Stop, please, God, stop . . .

CHAPTER EIGHT

LARS COULD SEE HIS RIDE AS MAD MARON CLEARER than day. He saw himself waking up next to a beautiful lady, arguing with her (although his imagination would not extend to what they were arguing about), and walking out of the hotel dressed all in black. He saw everything, every little detail—robbing the bank, killing Sara, firing through the streets of Fredericksburg, riding through the hill country with bags of gold.

He could see the green grass flying past, and the sun, and the sky. The sand dunes in the distance, the rolling hills, the lakes. He felt the wind raging past him, trying to capture him, blowing his hair back.

Maybe Dr. Hastings had a good thing going, this Hume Method.

If Lars really wanted to be honest, he had to admit it was not a far stretch from ex-junkie murderer to bank robber murderer. Hell, no. Sins—the big ones, the shit people got lethal injected for—were well related.

Lars was coming to the home front. The images were sinking in, one by one, in frames pushing through, eclipsing one another. For the first time in a long time, he did not hate himself. For the first time in a long time, he was free of his sins.

The clouds, the dust, the vast open sky . . .

A resounding crash broke through his inertia.

Lars opened his eyes. He was back in Dr. Hastings's room. The Hispanic kid who had been sitting next to him was wallowing and shaking on the floor.

Lars jumped out of his desk and kneeled down before him.

"Hey . . ." Lars's voice stumbled, unable to remember the kid's name. "Hey, buddy. This isn't real, you know?" His hands reached down and gripped the kid's shoulders.

Wasn't he supposed to be the map? Wasn't he supposed to be the *control*?

The kid didn't even look like he was in the here-and-now. His eyes were darting back and forth like he was in a deep stage of REM. Lars tried to hold him down, but in a split second, the kid reached up and ripped out a piece of Lars's hair.

"Make it stop," the kid begged, his knuckles tightening around Lars's hair.

"Make what stop?" Lars asked. The kid didn't answer. Lars looked up at Dr. Hastings standing several feet away. "I thought you said he was the control," Lars accused. "What the hell is happening?"

"He is the control. I can't explain his condition." Yet the tone of Dr. Hastings's voice told Lars he knew exactly what was happening.

"Make it stop," the kid repeated.

Mark kneeled down next to Lars. "What's happening to him?" he asked, pushing up his glasses to have a better look. "Juan?"

"He's a little too into this," Dr. Hastings said, shrugging his shoulders. "It will stop in a minute."

"The hell it will," Lars growled. "He's having a fucking seizure."

"May I remind you, Mr. Case, that cursing on Brookhaven property is subject to suspension? This is a Christian school; we do not condone obscenities."

"All right, dude, I'm out of here. This is too freaky for me." It was one of the jocks speaking. Whichever one it was, Lars could not tell. To him they seemed interchangeable.

"I'm following," said the other one.

"We should call 911," Lars heard the redhead say.

"The phones are down, remember?" he answered, perhaps too harshly.

"Stop . . . it . . ." the kid said.

"Juan, Juan, what's happening?" Mark asked, leaning over his friend. He looked up at Lars. "He's been acting funny all night," he said.

Lars had had enough. He reached under Juan's frame and pulled the kid up, capturing him in a cradle hold. It was harder than he thought it would be. Juan was shaking violently, wiggling out of Lars's hands like Jell-O.

"Open the door for me," Lars ordered through clenched teeth.

The redhead was the recipient of his determination. Their eyes met in a gaze of mutual understanding while she reached back and pulled the handle of the door. "Yes," she said and she moved away to let him pass.

Dr. Hastings walked over and stood at the entrance just in time to stop Lars. "I wouldn't do that," he warned, pushing the redhead to the side.

"What the hell is the matter with you?" Lars screamed. "Can't you see this kid needs help?"

Lily stood behind him, her hands on her hips. An angry scowl marred her perfect face. "Let him pass!" she hollered. "He's dying. Can't you see that? He's fucking dying."

"He. Is. Not. Dying," Dr. Hastings announced in a voice that chilled like winter. "Put him down. All of you go back to your seats. Where are the football players?"

"They went out through the other door," Mark said.

"Go and get them. Bring them back. We will all remain calm. Juan's condition will be better in a few minutes. Seats. Now."

CHAPTER NINE

Dr. Hastings had first seen Juan *make* in the classroom, during their Alamo test the first week in September.

Dr. Hastings observed the pathetic frowns on his students' faces. *You'd think I'd given them grim death instead of a simple discussion test*, he thought.

The Juan kid had stuck out from the rest of them because he was not writing anything. He sat looking at the sheet of paper in front of him with a jaded expression on his face, like he was trying to solve a puzzle that involved no words or numbers.

Dr. Hastings noticed a moment later that the kid

didn't have a pen or pencil. *Ah ha*, he thought smugly and sat back in his chair. *I've got you now, you little shit.*

Dr. Hastings opened his mouth, ready to belt out a sermon about how students needed to come to class prepared, and if they didn't, they had to face the consequences of their irresponsibility, and if that meant not taking a test on test day, so be it.

The first word didn't fall out of his mouth before Juan did a very strange thing, even for a Christian university.

The kid bent over and prayed.

Well, not really. It only looked like he was praying . . . a deep meditation of some sort. His eyes were squeezed shut, and his hands were shaking uncontrollably.

When Juan finally lifted his head and opened his hands, a pencil lay in his palm.

At first Dr. Hastings did not believe what he'd seen. *Who has the power to make something out of thin air?* It only occurred to him later, while he lay in bed exhausted from class, that there were Monhu medicine men who could do just what Juan did.

They could *make*.

The next morning Dr. Hastings started his research. There was a friend of his, some faggot he and Dr. Kurcan both knew, who had done some major research on the Monhu tribe years ago but had never done anything with all his research. Dr. Hastings gave him a call and milked his brain for everything it was worth.

"Well, Killian Hastings," Sam said. "To what do I owe the pleasure of your phone call?"

"Hi, Sam. I'll cut to the chase."

"You always do."

Dr. Hastings ignored the comment. "Tell me what you know about the Monhu tribe."

"Christ, Killian, that would take me hours. The Monhu for me is like Mad Maron for you, get it?"

"Fine." said Dr. Hastings. "Tell me something specific, like something about the Monhu medicine men and their Wjurnu ritual."

"You know your Monhu," Sam said with a trace of respect.

I know my gifted students, Dr. Hastings thought.

"Well, what can I tell you? The Monhu clan, as you already know, was once an overpopulated and flourishing tribe in the southeast corner of Mexico. Their numbers, however, have dropped dramatically over the last century because of war, famine, and white men's diseases. The only survivors were said to have crossed the Mexican border in the late 1800s and mixed with the Hispanic populations of major American cities.

"But, as you also know, Killian," he continued, "while you were doing your Mad Maron research, I was searching down there east of Mexico City looking for any of the remaining members."

"And they exist?" Dr. Hastings interrupted.

"Of course," Sam replied with a spark of pride. "I found them."

"And you saw the Wjurnu ritual?" Dr. Hastings asked.

Sam cleared his throat. "I saw an example of it, yes."

"What do you mean, an 'example'?"

"You have to understand, Killian. The Wjurnu is ancient. No one practices it anymore. The Monhu put on a play for me, that's all."

"So, today's Monhu don't do it anymore?"

"No."

Dr. Hastings inhaled a lengthy breath, his impatience growing by the minute. "I guess what I'm trying to ask, Sam, is if the shit really happens, you know, where the old men sit in a circle and something forms out of nowhere."

"It's been historically documented," Sam said. "The ritual, translated into English, means 'Birth of the New.' It involves the tribe's medicine men—there are four of them, one for each element, who sit in their ancient thrones and meditate for eight hours straight in dead silence. At the end of the eight hours, whatever the men were able to create is deemed the item of spirituality for that year, you know, like the Chinese have the astrology thing, year of the donkey, year of the roach, whatever."

"And what do they usually create?"

"Oh, it can be anything. Plates, bread, trees. Say, why such interest all of sudden?"

"Oh, it's just curiosity getting the best of me."

When the conversation ended, Dr. Hastings stared reflectively for a long time at the computer screen in front of him, his nerves jumping with excitement.

Juan had to descend from the Monhu, Dr. Hastings was fairly certain. Over the next couple of weeks, his conviction turned to obsession, and just browsing Web sites and calling old friends wasn't enough. Dr. Hastings started following Juan.

His research, as corrupt as it was, had remarkable results. Not long ago, in downtown off Lamar Street, close to midnight, Dr. Hastings watched in the shadows while Juan *made* a leather jacket for a homeless man lying on the street. And only this morning, Dr. Hastings had watched from his parked car as Juan sat on the sidewalk and meditated until something that looked like salt poured from his hands.

Dr. Hastings's call to Juan's mother in San Antonio only confirmed his suspicions.

"Hello, is this Mrs. Fuentes?"

"Yes, it is," she replied. "Who is speaking?"

"Hi, Mrs. Fuentes, this is Dr. Killian Hastings. I'm head of the history department here at Brookhaven College. I'm one of your son's professors. May I speak with you for a second?" Dr. Hastings worked to make his voice sound as sympathetic as possible.

"Is Juan okay?"

"Juan's fine, Mrs. Fuentes . . . for the most part. See, I haven't spoken to Juan yet because I wanted to discuss it with you first. It has come to our attention that Juan has a very special gift. Do you know what I mean when I say Juan has a special gift?"

A long paused followed before Mrs. Fuentes replied, "I do not know if I follow you, sir."

You know damn well what I'm talking about, Dr. Hastings thought.

"It appears to me, Mrs. Fuentes, that your son has the gift of . . . I'm not sure how to say this correctly . . . but it appears he can *make* things."

The woman gasped into the receiver. "It's true," she cried between sniffles. "Oh, Mary, mother of God. I didn't think he still used his gift."

Checkmate, Dr. Hastings thought.

Mrs. Fuentes went on to explain that Juan's "gift" was what made her give up her beautiful son to begin with. It was her belief that her mother, an unusually holy woman, could knock the devil's gift out of his body and send it straight back to hell where it belonged.

"I am sad to know he is still using his gift," she said in a way that reminded Dr. Hastings of a mother discussing her child's drug habit.

"I can help," Dr. Hastings lied. "If you'll give me a chance to work with him, Mrs. Fuentes, I'll knock that evil right out of him. Promise."

His mother agreed. She had no way of knowing that Dr. Hastings had absolutely no intention of helping her son lose his talent. If anything, he wanted to see it manifest.

Watching Juan struggle with *making* the map that would turn Dr. Hastings into a rich man, the professor couldn't help but congratulate himself on being the luckiest son of a bitch on earth.

CHAPTER TEN

MARK TOOK OFF HIS SWEATY GLASSES. HE HAD NO use for them. There was nothing to see, just darkness stacked onto more darkness. His candlelight reflected the bodies of the jocks ahead of him, but truth be told, it was easier to hear than to see them. The collective sound of two football players walking down the hall reminded Mark of rhinos rampaging through the Sahara.

"So, what about Sixth Street, dude?" one of them asked.

"Fuuuck that, dude. Crazy Eight is off the hizzle tonight."

"Is that off Fourth?"

"Hell, yeah. Warehouse District. Dollar mugs all night long."

"Oh, dude, I'm so there."

'*Roid heads*, Mark thought. He'd heard all the rumors, and he saw Dr. Kurcan in her office a few days ago handing Caleb's ass to him. It was only a matter of time before the loser got kicked out of school, as losers often did. Mark was glad. Caleb was a punk. Josh was a punk. All jocks were punks, at least to guys like him. It was the same crap he had experienced in high school. His parents said college would be a different experience.

Wrong.

Mark applied for Brookhaven College not only because it was a Presbyterian school and he was a Presbyterian and a devout one at that, but also because he thought in a Christian atmosphere guys like him wouldn't get picked on. Guys like him wouldn't get wedgies or have boogers flown at them like at Cedar Park High School. Sometimes Mark wished he was more like the jocks. Hip idiots without a clue. The world was an easier place to live when you didn't know anything about it.

Mark held his candle higher. "Why isn't this thing moving?" Mark heard Caleb ask.

"Because it runs from electricity, dumb ass."

"Yeah, but it should have a separate power source."

"Not in a building this old."

"Fine. Where's the stairs?"

Mark sucked in his chest and raised his voice, "Stop! You guys can't go anywhere."

"Is that the little Mexican dude?" Josh asked.

"No. It's Mark. Dr. Hastings said you couldn't leave."

"Screw Dr. Hastings. The man's crazy."

"Don't—"

But his words were interrupted by the squeaking sound of the stairwell door opening, and the *thump thump* of the jocks' footsteps hitting the stairs.

Mark stood in the hallway frozen, unsure of his next move. If he didn't bring the jocks back, there would be hell to pay. Dr. Hastings didn't mess around, that was a rule. Like the Theory of Gravity, some things were purely scientific. He'd probably give Mark a bad grade for his failure. Mark had never received a bad grade in his life.

So it was his academic future, if nothing else that got him moving.

Mark started walking to the stairwell. "Losers," he muttered to himself.

The door opened and slammed behind him, and Mark was suddenly cloaked in more darkness than he had ever known. He could hear the jocks slamming down the steps in front of him.

"Wait," he called out, and his echo called back.

The jocks did not answer back.

Mark walked faster until out of nowhere, the ground awoke with a monstrous tremble.

CHAPTER ELEVEN

Juan lay on the floor in a heavy sweat. Black and white and black again, over and over, pounding through his eyes and skull. His head jiggled with the waves of earth moving underneath him. It felt like a subway train was coursing through the building, only louder, and with a cracking, brutal force.

This is no map I'm making, he thought while the world shuddered and cried underneath him.

Just when everything was going right, something seemed to be going very wrong.

Dr. Hastings stepped back. His mind slipped back to the Monhu books he had gathered over the last weeks. None of them had said anything about the medicine men having full-on seizures, and certainly there was nothing about earthquakes.

He was about to suggest class dismissal *(fuck the map, I just want to get out of here alive)* when his legs wobbled underneath him. The earthquake had come and gone, but the cracks on the floor were still splitting, slicing the room into halves.

Dr. Hastings and his students fell to the floor, landing like a castle of dominoes.

Then the floor split open and ate Dr. Hastings whole.

CHAPTER TWELVE

THE EARTHQUAKE HAD SNUFFED OUT ALL THE CANDLES, and Lars was sightless and crushed on the ground, but when a banging sound erupted like thunder throughout the building, Lars knew it was his teacher's body hitting the next floor down.

"Professor!" Lars heard the redhead cry. He listened to the woman's footsteps creeping to the hole in the floor. "Professor!" she cried again.

Lars stood up. He looked over at where he thought the redheaded woman might be. "Is he alive?" he asked into the darkness.

"I can't see anything!" she answered. "It's too dark."

Lars couldn't get to the hole. Not right away, anyway. He searched the darkness with his hands and realized quickly the earthquake had knocked over a series of desks that now acted as a barricade between him and the hole.

Lars heard a rattling sound. He turned around to see the sliver of moon outlining a frantic Lily standing over him, going through her purse.

"What the hell are you doing?" he asked. "You have a flashlight in there?"

"Yeah, and a sledgehammer," she answered, her words dripping with sarcasm. "I'm looking for my cell phone, for your information."

"Your cell phone doesn't work."

"But what about the light?"

She was right. In the absence of a flashlight, the glow from a cell phone's screen might be the only light they had.

Lily pressed something on the phone to make it light up and handed it to Lars. He took it with a strong grip and breathed deeply, deciding his next move. The dilemma was getting a cell phone to a girl he couldn't see. If he threw it too close, it would fall in the hole. If he threw it too far, it might break against the wall, and they'd be in complete darkness again.

"Describe to me where you are," he ordered.

Funny about the dark, he thought. *You didn't*

really need two eyes anymore. Just instinct.

"I can't. I don't know where I am. Wait." There was a pause while Lars heard her fiddling around. "I think I feel the chalkboard. Do you remember where it was?"

"Kinda."

"I think . . . I feel . . . Dr. Hastings's desk. His chair. His briefcase. Do you remember where he set his briefcase? It's in the middle of his desk."

Lars followed the direction of her voice. In his mind's eye he could see everything like it was an hour ago, before the séance, before the seizure, before the earthquake.

What was next, he thought. *Locusts?*

Lars felt aligned with the redhead. His hearing had strangely become superpowered since the Mexican gangsters incident. Perhaps there was something to be said for being a modern-day Cyclops.

"Get ready," he warned, rearing his arm back.

"I'm ready," she answered.

He threw it. The phone sailed through the air, and Lars's breath held in his chest until he heard her cry out, "I've got it!"

He could vaguely make out the phone's light while the redhead crawled over to the hole and leaned the phone over the edge. "I still can't see him. Oh, wait, I see him. Dr. Hastings!" she called. "Dr. Hastings!

Wave something if you can hear me!" The silence that followed was the loudest sound Lars had ever heard. He could hear the second hand clicking on his wristwatch, and the sky above them rumbling with the threat of fresh thunder.

"He's unconscious," the redhead finally said.

"If he's not dead," Lars mumbled under his breath, shaking his head.

"Think cheerful thoughts, okay?" Lily said beside him. "Let's just assume he's alive for right now."

"I'm only being realistic," Lars answered, and his voice was not without sadness. "I mean, the man fell ten feet."

"What about Juan?" Lily asked. "Where is he?"

Yes, Juan, Lars remembered. He had forgotten about the kid during all the drama. It was his freakout that, in a way, began this whole crazy night. Lars knelt and started searching with his hands. When his right palm slid against the lace of a shoe, Lars smiled, relieved. The kid was exactly where he had left him. Lars leaned over and touched his shoulders. Where there was once shaking and trembling, there was now absolute stillness. Lars lightly patted his cheek. "Hey, Juan! Can you hear me?" He received no answer. Lars pressed two fingers onto his neck. "He's got a pulse," he said.

He could hear Lily starting to pace behind him.

"What just happened?" she asked. "And where did all the candles go? I can't see a damn thing."

"If you can't see anything, I suggest you stop pacing," said Lars.

Lily stopped walking and stood in place. "I can't see anything," she said simply. "You threw our only source of light to that woman."

The redhead cleared her throat. "There's a candle beside me. I feel it. Where's Dr. Hastings's lighter?" she asked.

"On Dr. Hastings," Lily replied.

"Lucky for us, I smoke," Lars said. "I have a Zippo in my backpack, if I can find it." Lars searched the cracked floor for his familiar leather bag. He heard Lily on the ground searching for it, too.

"Does it have three pockets, one with a pack of cigarettes inside?" Lily asked after a few minutes.

"That would be it," Lars said and held out his hands when Lily tossed his bag to him. He took out the Zippo and ignited it. "Do you see me, Redhead?" he asked.

"Yes, and the name's Reagan." She threw the candle and Lars caught it. "Two for two," she cried out.

Lars lit the candle, and the room was suddenly reborn with light. "Good," Lars said. He turned to Lily. "Let's look for the other ones. Dr. Hastings passed one out to each of us, so there has to be some more lying around."

Lily saluted. "Aye, aye, sir," she said, and started her search.

Lars had a feeling they had a long night ahead of them.

CHAPTER THIRTEEN

MARK REACHED UP TO MASSAGE HIS POUNDING HEAD and felt the gooey liquid of blood. "Josh! Caleb!" he called out. The jocks couldn't have gotten out of the building before the earthquake. He had heard them right before the tremble, right before he had fallen God knows how many flights of stairs.

Funny. He had lived in Austin all his life, and had never experienced an earthquake before. He wasn't even sure Austin had ever had one. There were several hot-button plates in the earth's sphere, and Texas wasn't on any of them.

Mark tried to stand, but a sharp, violent pain

sprung up his legs and drove through his hips. His agony tightened around him, and he fell with a miserable yelp, squeezing shut his eyes and biting his mouth. His knee hit the floor again, and another surge of pain shot through him. He opened his mouth to cry for help, but the pain made it impossible for words to push through. His misery left his body a prisoner.

Mark was not sure how much time passed before the pain subsided and he was able to breathe normally. Slowly he reached down to touch his legs. His hand squeezed on the lower part of his right thigh, where the pain thickened like a cord around his muscle.

A broken leg, he surmised.

"Help!" he screamed. "Please, help me! Josh! Caleb! Somebody!"

Silence was his only answer.

CHAPTER FOURTEEN

JOSH SURVEYED THE DAMAGE AND REALIZED HE WASN'T hurt. *Praise the Lord,* he thought. He had a game this weekend. Coach said recruits were coming from the minor leagues. If he'd had to sit out the game . . .

I'd be royally screwed, he thought.

Josh didn't want to go back to Florida and work at his dad's hardware store. He didn't want to see the same people walk in and out every day. He didn't want to work the register and count dollars and answer stupid questions about plumbing.

Playing football for Brookhaven College wasn't the same as playing for UT, but just living in Austin made up for the mediocrity of his football career. Austin was like Babylon for a boy from a Bible-beating, southern Podunk town in the middle of Sticksville. Austin was rock 'n' roll and hot girls, drunken nights, and three-dollar shots. Austin was the place to surrender to sin, beg God for forgiveness later. Josh loved it all, loved every piece of it. If he could go somewhere like it with the minor leagues, even if it was up north and cold as the devil, he would take it. Florida and his father's hardware store was a choice he'd make only if everything else failed.

But I'd better get out of this mess first . . .

And what mess was this, exactly? *An earthquake,* he thought. *That's what this mess is.*

He had a brother out in liberal California who talked of earthquakes all the time, but Josh had never experienced one himself.

Until now, he thought, lifting his closely shaven head from the floor's surface and rising, feeling for the first time that he and Caleb were all alone on the ground floor in the shit hole called Gossamer Hall.

It was dark but Josh could make out Caleb lying by a garbage bin near the wall. The surprise of seeing his fallen comrade left him momentarily frozen. Josh stared at him for a long time the way a child stared at a magician pulling a rabbit out of his hat. *Big, tough Caleb down for the count.* Finally, Josh blinked back his shocked wonder and began walking in his direction.

"You better be all right, dude," he called out.

Caleb wasn't a bad kid, not in the way that everyone thought he was. Josh had received the e-mail, too. Everyone had. And it was funny. Porn names and dogs humping. Caleb was a funny guy, a good guy. Steroids snitching aside, Josh was glad they'd had this class together—otherwise he would have been bored to pieces sitting around with those two spastic nerd fags and the uppity girl with a thumb up her ass.

And what was up with that dude with one eye, anyway?

"Hey, Caleb, dude, you gotta wake up, man."

Josh reached down and tried to shake Caleb awake. "Dude, come on, don't play possum."

Josh leaned down and listened for his friend's breath. An inhale, an exhale, and Josh grinned, shaking his friend again. "Hey, man, everything's cool. We just experienced an earthquake."

Caleb did not stir, but something else did. Josh leaned up, his back erect. He could hear footsteps walking toward him. One step, two steps, three steps, moving ever so slowly in their purpose.

"That you, dipshit?" Josh asked, thinking it was the nerdy kid who had been following Caleb and him down the stairs.

He received no answer.

A smell gathered in the corridor. *To say it smelled like a wet garbage can*, Josh thought, *was an insult to wet garbage cans everywhere*. Josh had to shield his nose; it was that toxic. It reminded him of the first—and last—time his father took him deer hunting. For his first kill, his father and friends poured blood all over his face and camouflage clothes. "It's tradition," his dad had said.

Josh had hated it. He took shower after shower but the smell never lifted. At night he went to bed and dreamed the deer was in bed with him like a wife next to her husband, only it was spilling its blood out onto the covers, the mattress, over Josh's body all over again.

Josh hadn't hunted since, even though his father and his brothers called him a pussy. The smell of bleeding organs was too high a cost, and there were far too many other things in life to prove your manhood, like living wild and drinking beer and chasing pretty Austin tail.

Whatever he smelled in the hallway was ten times worse than the deer guts. And when the smell really hit, when whatever or whoever it was had closed the distance, Josh could no longer hold his nose to keep the stench at bay. It was Barf City, USA. Josh reeled over and gagged up everything he'd had in the last twenty-four hours—pizza, beer, chicken wings, Twizzlers, those cheap pigskins you get at 7-11s that are just so damn gross they taste good.

No Sixth Street for me tonight, he thought. No clubs, no drinking. It was straight home to bed. He had to get ready for that game on Friday. There was no way he would risk getting sick.

Josh's mind was married to his thoughts when the smell took over once more. Josh would have thrown up again but there was nothing left inside of him. It was all dry gagging, and he made it an Olympic event, dramatically bending over and heaving into the hallway.

It was kind of an afterthought, while he half kneeled on the ground with nausea, that it might not be the nerdy kid in the hallway with him after all.

Of course, by the time he'd reached this conclusion, it was too late.

A voice Caleb had never heard before sang out with its filthy breath into the darkness: "Look at what we have here."

CHAPTER FIFTEEN

Lily sat beside three strangers in a room with four lit candles and wondered how she'd gotten there.

While she thought about it, she remembered something she had heard on Dr. Phil the other day about "inciting incidents." Dr. Phil, in a speech given to an adulterous woman and her wimpy, beaten-down husband, said there were ten "inciting incidents" in a person's life that made them who they were.

Lily, turning away from the death-and-doom conversation between Reagan and Lars, mentally counted hers. Call it a defense mechanism, something to keep her mind off the current unbelievable events, whatever. Lily wanted to go there, and so she did.

Inciting Incidents Top Ten List

1. My parents' divorce.

2. Giving up beauty pageants (indicating the desire to be loved and cherished for who I am, not for what I look like).

3. Voice lessons (foreshadowing the journalism career that I would one day aspire to obtain).

4. Breaking up with my first love (indicating strength of character).

5. Reporting my rape (indicating courage).

6. Choosing not to press charges (indicating compassion for friend's dad).

7. Foregoing scholarship to party-hardy UT to take journalism classes at a religious school for Bible nuts (indicating seriousness of future profession).

8. Admitting to my father that I never felt he loved me (indicating my honesty and ability to seek closure).

9. Saving an injured squirrel on Guadalupe Street (indicating desire to heal and nurture).

10. Not sure yet. Should know by the end of the night.

Lily had a choice. Inciting incident Number 10 could be the earthquake, the séance that made a boy freeze like a slush puppy, or the death of her college professor right in front of her. Any of these were strong candidates.

Possibly, however, would be the inciting incident of staying alive. The walls were crumbled on both sides of the entranceways. There was no way out of the room.

Lily and Lars had worked at moving the desks away so all three of them presently stood at the hole in the floor, peering over at a possibly dead teacher below them.

"We can crawl through the hole," Reagan suggested softly—although, Lily noted, her voice had become more confident in the last hour.

"We need a rope to pull us through," Lars answered. "It's a ten-foot drop, at least."

"I have an idea," Lily said. "I'm not sure if it will work."

"Shoot," Lars said while another series of thunder rolls crackled through the night.

"We can throw down Dr. Hastings's desk. That would be—what, four and a half feet? If we throw it directly above the other desk downstairs—"

"Dr. Hastings is lying next to that desk," Reagan interjected. "We'll be throwing that desk too close to him."

"But he's dead, isn't he?"

"We don't *know* that," Reagan said. "He could just be unconscious."

"The desk is a good idea," Lars said. "If we can get it down there, it should be enough for me to drop without breaking anything. And I can help you guys down."

"But," Lily began, "what if the walls are crumbled down there, too? Then what do we do?"

"It's not like we have any other options, do we?"

"We can wait for the cell phones to come back on," Lily suggested.

"And how long do you suppose that will be? I don't even have a cell phone. Do you?" Lars asked Reagan.

"No."

Lily's eyes widened. "Are you guys serious? Where do you live, a cave?"

Reagan shrugged, throwing the phone back to Lily. "I don't have anyone to call. Anymore," she added gently.

"I second that," Lars said.

It was a clue to Lily that both these cats had fallen on hard times. She looked at her phone. "I don't have much battery left," she sighed.

"Then turn it off," Lars ordered. "Who knows how long the fucking poles will be down? We have to think."

"We have to act," Lily corrected. She nodded at a seemingly sleeping Juan. "We have got to get him to a hospital and maybe Dr. Hastings, too. And what about Josh and Caleb, and that other kid? Maybe they're hurt, as well."

"The cell phones are down, but what about the regular phones?" Lars asked.

"I know there's one in Dr. Hastings's office," Reagan said.

The three of them simultaneously leaned over the hole, looking down into the darkness below. Lily knew what the others were thinking.

They had to get down there.

CHAPTER
SIXTEEN

JUAN WOKE UP IN THE DESERT. AT LEAST THAT'S WHAT
it looked like at first, like a place he had seen in movies where Clint Eastwood draws a pistol and dares a
couple of scoundrels to make his day.

He looked up at the endless blue sky, with sand
dunes in the distance, and down below where cacti
scattered along the floor of sun-baked earth.

Juan rose, expecting to feel as heavy as lead, but instead felt featherlight, like he was weightless in space.
He cupped his hands over his eyes and studied the dead
land, trying to make sense of his surroundings.

A hot wind wrapped around him and caught his

shirt, flapping it against his back. Juan pulled his hands away from his eyes and inspected them.

They're no longer shaking!

It did not occur to him at first why he thought they should be shaking. The events that preceded his trip to this unknown place did not immediately come forth. Still, he felt, for whatever reason, the last time he had been conscious, his hands had been shaking.

Remember, remember . . .

His memories appeared like obscure acrobats, tumbling through his head in no particular sequence, like images after a night of heavy drinking. A candle. A map. A lightbulb flickering. Thunder and lightning. An old man daring him to use the gift which he was forbidden to use.

It dawned on him. He had been at school.

At Gossamer Hall.

I should not be here, he realized, and despite the heat, a chill reached inside of him and clutched his heart with an iron grip.

"How did I get here?" he screamed at the dust and clouds. Nature gave him no answer.

Juan started walking. *What else can I do?* Perhaps he was only dreaming. If he walked, maybe he would wake up after his mind ran out of imagination.

He was not in a desert, he soon decided. When he walked farther, he saw there were trees up ahead, a house or two, and what appeared to be a road. Not a cement road or anything so high-tech, but it was a road all the same . . . a sign of civilization.

He saw the girl on the horse once he had crossed over a hill. It seemed like she was waiting for him. Her face was turned his way, her eyes boring a hole into him. When he walked closer, he saw the dark braids pinned above her head. She wore a hooped dress similar to the ones he'd seen before in a—well, in a Clint Eastwood movie.

The closer he came, the more he realized she was not pleased to see him. On an otherwise beautiful face, her jaw was clenched tight like a boxer preparing to fight. A scowl of disapproval darkened her brow. She ran a delicate hand over her forehead, and shook her head.

A long sigh rose from her throat when he walked up close to the brown speckled horse. "Well, Juan," she said, "you've done it now," and reached down, dragging Juan onto the horse with her.

CHAPTER SEVENTEEN

A FLASH OF LIGHTNING FILLED THE SKY, AND FOR A moment the corridor where Josh and the stranger stood was filled with light, and Josh could see the stranger's face.

He screamed, jumping back and hitting the wall.

Once upon a time during Josh's senior year in high school, a friend and fellow football player brought a disease book to practice, just for kicks. Apparently his dad was a doctor or nurse or something like that. So they were sitting in the locker room flipping through it when Josh saw what had to be the most horrific thing he'd ever seen.

It might have been Eric Stoltz in *Mask*, but the face was rotted at the hairline, and the nose had collapsed into the skull. The skin was green and peeling in the cheeks and forehead, the lips were two scales of rotted flesh dipped to the sides like two collapsed parentheses.

"Shit!" Josh had yelled. "What the hell is that?"

"Leprosy," his friend had answered. "Pretty fucked up, huh?"

"Oh, yeah," Josh replied.

But whatever was presently standing before him, whatever this thing was, had the leper beat, hands down.

"That's a mask, right, buddy?" Josh asked. "An early Halloween gig?"

Thunder struck before the stranger answered, "Ain't right for a man to say things like that to another man." The man had a strong Texan accent, stronger than the most backward country boy Josh knew.

"Look at what we have here," he said again. "*Look at. What. We have. Here.*" He spoke in slow motion, drawing out every syllable. Josh pictured the man rubbing his hand over his crotch while he spoke, as if he was getting off on his own words.

Who the hell am I dealing with? Josh wondered.

Josh stared ahead with a wide-eyed face of disbelieving alarm. It was dark, but he could swear the man's face was glowing. Or maybe it was too ugly for the dark to erase.

Had to be a Halloween mask, Josh decided.

"I don't remember seein' something like you before," the stranger said.

For the first time Josh felt like laughing. There was no reason to be afraid. It was just a Halloween mask and some asshole making a joke out of a bad situation.

"I don't really remember seeing anything like you either, dude," Josh said, playing along with what had to be the worst joke ever.

Doesn't he see Caleb knocked out on the floor?

"Duuuuude," the man mimicked. "Duuuuude. . ."

Caleb moaned behind him. Josh quickly turned around. "Caleb?"

"That . . . smell . . ." Caleb coughed. "What happened . . .?"

"Don't move. Me and . . . uh . . . this guy are gonna help you." Josh looked in the man's direction. "Hey, dude, you want to help me and my buddy? That earthquake knocked him out pretty hard."

"I heard you callin' me," the stranger said. His Texas drawl was drenched with the throaty, low tone of a heavy smoker.

"Yeah, I called you," Josh said. "I need someone to help me carry him. I don't think he can walk." Josh looked over at Caleb. "Can you walk, buddy?"

"That . . . smell . . ."

"Forget the smell, dude. Can you walk?"

When Caleb didn't say anything, Josh turned to the stranger. "He's got a point. You could use a bath, dude. No offense. I barfed my brains out when you first came around the corner. I mean, it could be a concussion, too, but the truth is, your ass fucking stinks. You been eatin' Mexican?"

"Mexican," the stranger repeated.

Josh waited. And waited. The man said nothing else. The odor was gaining momentum with each passing minute. Josh covered his nose with his shirt. Caleb kept moaning about the smell.

All right, enough of this shit.

"Forget it," he said to the stranger. "I can help my buddy by myself. You just go on doing whatever it is you were doing." He added, "We're all supposed to be Christians here, you know. You and your Halloween mask can go party somewhere else."

"You weren't the one callin' me," the man grumbled. "You don't sound the same."

Josh opened his mouth for a smart-ass retort—something along the lines of, "Well, I'm the only person here, aren't I?"—when the lightning struck again.

The second round of lightning did the trick. Josh saw it all. *The whole shebang*, as his father would say.

The man in front of him wasn't wearing a Halloween mask. The man in front of him wasn't even really human, or if he had been, he wasn't anymore.

The stranger wore boots, and there were spurs on his boots, and on his spurs there was blood and what looked like severed flesh dangling from the spiked part. His clothes were old, at least by a century. Leather chaps and a high collared shirt splashed with blood and mud.

Josh thought a getup like that could be bought at that Party Pig out on Highway 183. But then again, something told him the clothes were as genuine as the non-Halloween mask he wore on his face.

Josh stepped back. Caleb was still on the floor, calling out to him, but Josh didn't hear a word.

"What are you?" he asked the man-thing. He could feel the stranger smiling at him in the dark.

A third series of lightning bolts struck, and Josh was left with the same impressions he had before—a freak-show face, an authentic cowboy costume drenched in blood. Only this time he saw something else.

He saw a gun.

CHAPTER EIGHTEEN

DR. GRETCHEN KURCAN CURSED UNDER HER BREATH, felt guilty immediately afterward, and prayed.

Dear Heavenly Father, stop me from killing this man.

She took a deep breath and tried to clear her head. There were factors to weigh before deciding on murder. On the one hand, if she did the deed, her career in higher education, for which she had worked hard all her life, would be kaput. There wasn't a great need for a forty-eight-year-old college dean in prison. Her knowledge of education wasn't very likely to serve a purpose.

And I might get raped with a broomstick nightly just like in that Linda Blair movie, she thought, and shivered.

But on the other hand, it might be worth it just to see that old fart begging for mercy. Gretchen smiled when the image popped in her mind, and again felt guilty.

Dear Lord, hear my prayer.

Her motive for murder sat in front of her, blinking on the screen of her ancient Mac laptop. Her school's e-mail page was exposed, and her cursor pointed to an e-mail sent by Dr. Killian Hastings with the subject line, "Quitting."

Gretchen read and reread the text, hoping she might have misread something. But the text stayed the same:

Dear Dr. Kurcan, I regret to inform you that after ten years of working at Brookhaven College, I have accepted another position at a better, more distinguished school. This is my resignation letter, effective immediately.

Not if I have anything to say about it, Gretchen thought.

Who did Dr. Hastings think he was, anyway?

Lord, give me strength.

Gretchen drummed her fingers nervously on her desk. *"Better, more distinguished school,"* my ass, she thought while she reached up and slammed the laptop shut.

"Bullocks!" Gretchen yelled, her fists punching

the air. She flew out of her chair and stomped the ground, the curlers in her graying brown hair bouncing along in her rage.

Gretchen paced back and forth along her genuine Turkish rug. "Lord, I want to kill him. So help me God, I want to kill him! Grrr!" she snarled, and her two long-haired tabby cats scattered to the other end of the house. "I'm not mad at you!" she yelled after them as she entered the hallway, but just when she did, her robe's sash caught the doorknob and she went crashing onto the hardwood floor.

"Fuck! Oh, hell, I'm sorry, Jesus," she said as she undid the rollers from her hair and threw them across the room.

Gretchen recalled a psalm that always made her feel better in times of crisis. "Lord, remind me how brief my time on earth will be," she recited Psalm 39:4 from the *Bible*. "Remind me that my days are numbered, and that my life is fleeing away."

Gretchen waited for the usual calm to wash over her, but nothing happened. She sighed and ran a tired hand over her forehead. Being a good Christian soldier was damn hard work, and she was finding the older she got, the harder it became. In her twenties, she had lived with her parents' harsh Southern Baptist values still morphing in her blood like a mutating virus, set to destroy her desire to sin at any time, any place, on any occasion. In her thirties, being one with Jesus was the only needed ingredient while being married to a closet homosexual politician in a Brady Bunch neighborhood of Cleveland.

But the forties—what a pain! One divorce, three houses, and two cities later. No kids and two stupid cats and SPAM every time she checked her e-mail, not to mention the growing suspicion that she was reaching menopause.

To make matters worse, Gretchen had reached the top of her field in shorter time than most, and anyone with half a brain knew there was only one way to go from there, and it was down. Add to that the handful of men who looked at Gretchen as if to say, "I should have your job," and Gretchen had one hell of a time being the godly person Jesus meant for her to be.

So, no, she wasn't in the spirit of Christian godliness and, frankly, had not been in it for some time. Lately she had found that her stash of student-apprehended marijuana made a better savior.

Maybe, that's exactly what I need, she thought as she made her way into the kitchen.

It began stupidly, as stupid habits often did. Gretchen was sitting in her office when the campus patrol knocked on the door. "More pot," Pat, the head of security, mumbled when he walked in. "Found it in the grass. Some punk must have dropped it."

Gretchen rolled her eyes and pointed at her desk. "Put it there," she said. It wasn't a usual practice for the dean to keep the confiscated weed, but at last week's chapel (a mandatory part of attending Brookhaven College), Gretchen had stood up in front of the faculty, student body, and staff and swore that with each illegal narcotic found on campus, there would be thirty extra minutes added to the next chapel. The entire room had groaned.

"So tell your friends, the ones you know who bring drugs onto this campus" (she had looked at Caleb Jacobs at this point), "that we will not tolerate drugs at Brookhaven College, and that's final. This begins a series of interventions I like to call, 'Drugs Kill, Jesus Heals.'"

For whatever reason, maybe it was because she was dog tired, Gretchen forgot about the weed and stuck it with everything else in her briefcase before leaving her office and driving home.

Gretchen had promised to cook lasagna for an old friend that night. Sam was an acquaintance from somewhere in her higher-education past (which part, exactly, Gretchen could not totally recall). He was as queer as a three-dollar bill and as broke as a church mouse (one of those artsy-fartsy types who never live up their potential), but he somehow knew all the guys who had made millions off Dell stock in the late nineties. The name for those guys was Dellionaires, and the name for the people who followed them was Dellionaire Heads. Sam bragged he was the biggest Dellionaire Head of them all.

Gretchen enjoyed Sam's company because he was wild and freethinking where she was stuffy and withdrawn. His stories were the stuff gossip columns were made of.

Gretchen was in the kitchen chopping onions when she heard him yell from the living room. "Hey, Gretchen! Get in here!"

"Just a second!" Gretchen yelled back, and put down the knife. She swayed back and forth to the background music of Paul Simon's *Graceland* as she moved through her swinging kitchen door and into the wood-floor entrance of her buttery-yellow living room. There she found her friend standing over her briefcase, the bag of weed in his hands.

"What is this?" the little man asked, his gray eyes narrowing. "Dr. Gretchen Kurcan, what is this in your briefcase?" he asked again, raising his voice like Dana Carvey's in his SNL church-lady skits.

"Pot," Gretchen answered. "I told you about the mandate I gave my school, didn't I?"

"No."

Gretchen waved her hand. "It's a long story."

"But, Gretchen." A smile stretched across his

elfin face. "You have pot!"

"I know, and it's going back to Brookhaven College first thing tomorrow. I was so tired when I left school today," and Gretchen yawned, as if to prove her point, "that I must have mistakenly put it in there."

"Mistakenly, my ass. Who was the philosopher who said there were no mistakes?"

"Nietzsche. I hate Nietzsche. He was wrong about everything. A godless man." Gretchen started walking back into the kitchen. She turned around and shook her finger at Sam. "Put the pot back, Sam, or else!'

Gretchen was over the stove again, when she was overcome with a wave of heat. "Whoosh," she cried, and started fanning her face. It was only getting hotter, and she reached up to feel a thick film of sweat over her forehead. Her breath left while the heat took over, and she knelt to the floor, gasping for air.

"Gretchen, what's going on?" Sam was at the door, and Gretchen could vaguely hear him walk over and reach his arms around her shoulders. "Hey, girl, what's happening?"

"Hot . . . flash . . ."

"Oh, heavens to Betsy, you are getting old, aren't you?"

"Shut . . . up."

"Come up, girlfriend," Sam said, putting his hands under her arms and lifting her. To Gretchen's surprise, because Sam wasn't the largest of men (he was constantly mistaken for Elijah Wood despite a twenty-year age difference), he was able to pick her up and carry her out to the gazebo, where the fresh night air began cooling her heated limbs.

"Feeling better?" Sam asked after a time.

Gretchen sat in her patio chair, looking up at the moon. "A little."

"You scared me."

"The Lord doesn't give us what we can't handle."

"I hate it when you get biblical."

"I hate it when you hate it when I get biblical." Gretchen released a long, hard sigh. "I'm the dean of a Christian college, Sam."

"And I hang out with millionaires. It doesn't mean I am one."

"I feel old."

"You know what you need?"

Gretchen turned to him. His eyes glittered with mischief. She shook her head. "No. Absolutely, unequivocally out of the question."

"Why not?"

"I don't do pot."

"Okay, first of all, you don't *do* pot. You *smoke* pot. And secondly, if you smoke it once, it's not going to hurt anything. No one will know, and it will help those hot flashes of yours. Promise."

"It's not in God's plans for me."

"You're absolutely wrong! In Romans 11, verse 36 of the *Bible,* it reads: 'Everything comes from God alone, everything lives by His power, and everything is for His glory.' You see, Gretch? Jesus wants you to smoke pot."

Gretchen laughed despite herself. "Sam, is that the only Bible verse you know?"

"I might know two more. So, what do you say?"

"I say you are the devil. I say I have to hold that bag up to the student body Tuesday morning."

"You have catnip, right? It looks like the same damn thing."

Gretchen rolled her eyes and gave in. "Fine. Go to the Super Stop and get some paper and a lighter."

Her first encounter with pot was a good one. She couldn't remember a time when she had laughed so hard, or when the food had tasted so good. The conversation had flowed, and when she went to bed that night, she slept better than she had in years.

The next night, and the night after, however, she did some heavy praying.

But, Gretchen thought, when she looked at the kitchen cabinet where the rest of the weed was stashed (the bag of catnip had done the trick that Tuesday morning), *even saints have their off days.*

A little more wouldn't hurt, she told herself.

Fine, it was decided. Gretchen marched to the kitchen cabinet with her terry-cloth robe billowing around her. Opening up the cabinet, she started her search. Her hand passed the half-empty bottle of Seagram's vodka, a bottle of Benedictine, three chardonnays, and finally, in the very back, her fingers grazed the little bag of happy grass.

"Ha!" Gretchen reached in closer and grabbed it.

"Do everything on your part to live in peace with everybody," she recited the line from Romans 12:18 from the *Bible*, while she began rolling the joint the way Sam had shown her.

Well, this is me making peace, she thought while she lit up. An image of Dr. Hastings surfaced when she inhaled. *I hate him, I hate him, I hate him.*

What school, exactly, wanted the damn fool? Everyone knew Dr. Hastings was a tired old fart whose favorite topic—Mad Maron—was dated, even in the subject of history. The books had been printed; the pictures had been made. The History Channel had done its special. No one *cared* anymore.

The only reason Dr. Hastings had his job at Brookhaven College was because Sam, who knew him from Brown, had suggested the Mad Maron expert during a cocktail party in West Lake.

"He just moved to the Austin area because, you know, this was Mad Maron's launching pad. He'll add some spice to your curriculum," Sam had promised.

"Brookhaven is a Presbyterian college, Sam, we don't want spice. We need grace," Gretchen corrected, but she had agreed to meet up with him anyway because Sam had always been there for her, especially during her divorce.

Dr. Hastings was all sugar and smiles during his interview. He made himself out to be the perfect gentlemen teacher, giving Gretchen cheerful replies, asking about her personal life in a caring but unobtrusive way. She found the red bow tie he wore charming. She saw him as the grandfatherly type who would take students under his wing like Robin Williams in *Dead Poets Society.*

Looking back, maybe the truth was that Gretchen didn't want to have to deal with interviewing more history professors, and Dr. Hastings seemed harmless enough.

Was I fooled or what? she thought while she sat at the kitchen table and took another drag of her joint.

Yes, you were fooled, and yes, you had better put down that joint now, get into your car, and give that man a piece of your mind.

"Yes!" Gretchen cried and stood up. "Thank you, Jesus! That's exactly what I will do!"

She knew where he was. It was Wednesday night. Dr. Hastings had Texas History on Wednesday night.

Gretchen had scheduled the class herself.

She took off her robe and wrapped her long, black coat around her thin frame. She reached for her nearest shoes—a pair of Ann Taylor's she had bid for and won off eBay. They were high heeled and uncomfortable, but they would do just fine for kicking the sense into an arrogant old schoolteacher.

Just before Gretchen walked out the door, the phone rang. *Let it ring*, she thought, but changed her mind when she saw the name flashing on her caller ID.

She yanked the receiver off the phone and held it up to her ear. "Hello, Sam?"

"Hey, Gretch." She could hear a party in the background . . . another one of Sam's endless Dellionaire social functions.

"Did you see *American Idol* last night?" Sam asked. "I think that fat guy's leaving tonight."

Gretchen sucked in her breath. "I did not watch *American Idol*, Sam. And I can't watch it tonight because, as a matter of fact, something has come up with Dr. Hastings."

"Again?"

"Yes, again." Gretchen went on to explain the e-mail she received.

"That son of a bitch," Sam said when she was finished.

"My thoughts exactly."

"He can't do that, can he? He's under contract."

"Yes, but in the end, he can do whatever he wants. I'm not going to waste thousands of dollars on legal help when I can spend it on new tables in the cafeteria. The appropriations committee wouldn't let me anyway, even if I wanted to. We're running on a tight budget as it is."

"I'm damn sorry," Sam said. "I didn't know this side of him, I swear it."

"I believe you."

"Do you think his quitting has anything to do with his newfound interest in the Monhu tribe?"

Gretchen paused. "What? What are you talking about?"

"Dr. Hastings called me a month ago, wanted to know about my visit with the Monhu tribe out in Mexico."

Gretchen reflected back. She knew something about the Monhu tribe, but she didn't want to ask Sam for further details. She didn't want him to think she hadn't been paying attention all these years. From what Gretchen remembered, the Monhu tribe was unique in that the medicine men were said to *make* things out of thin air.

"It's not about the *making*, is it?" Gretchen asked.

"Yes, it was. He wanted to know every detail. I'm telling you, Gretch, the guy gets weirder every time we talk. I'm sorry I ever recommended him to you."

"That's okay. You didn't know."

Why did Dr. Hastings want to know about the Monhu tribe?

Sam kept talking. "Look, we're having a party out here at Maude's. Want to drop by and say hello?" And he added with a whisper, "Mitchell Jackson is here."

Mitchell Jackson was the OB/GYN Sam had been trying to pair Gretchen with for the last month. Whenever Sam met a single, successful man who wasn't gay, he handed him her way. "Thanks, but no thanks," Gretchen said. "I've got to hightail it up to Gossamer Hall before that old fool finishes his night class. Drink a sour apple martini for me, okay?"

"Okay. Hey, Gretch? Do some of that praying of yours before you leave the house. The weather is pretty miserable."

"Yeah, thanks."

Gretchen hung up the phone and looked out the window. The storm was, as Sam had suggested, taking its toll outside. Gretchen glanced at her wristwatch. The storm had been raging for almost an hour. It was nine o'clock. It took her thirty minutes to drive to Brookhaven College. The class let out at nine forty-five, but if Dr. Hastings was like most college professors, he let his class out a little early, against Brookhaven rules.

Gretchen watched while the rain pounded her

swimming pool. She'd have to drive down Highway 2222 to get there. It'd be a hell of a trip.

But what would happen tomorrow if all the history students didn't have a teacher?

Help me out here, Jesus, she thought, and reached for her umbrella.

CHAPTER NINETEEN

Josh stood in the hallway and listened to a deranged cowboy mispronounce his name.

"Get back, Jack," the cowboy sang-said. "What do you think I is? I'm a man, just like you. Just like your friend over there on the floor. The three of us are on track, Jack."

Josh swallowed. "My name's Josh."

"Josh is for queers," the cowboy said. "You're Jack to me, Jack."

Lightning struck, and Josh saw yet another little detail —closed, rotted sockets where eyes should have been.

Josh ground his teeth together. He didn't believe

in monsters—no way, no how. Someone was just trying to scare him. It was a mask, it was a rented suit, it was a water gun. It was just a frat brother playing a prank, or maybe someone getting Caleb back for the whole steroids incident.

But that's not really happening here, is it? an inner voice asked him.

The cowboy was part of the air. He *was* the stench. He was the drippity, slippery wetness of a body melted away. The crackety-crack-crack of decomposed bones holding threads of muscle together, the sickety-moldy stench of decayed flesh buried years and years in a grave.

No, Josh finally decided. This was far from being a prank.

"Now," said the cowboy. "Was it you a-callin' me? Was it you, partner?"

The man's voice was like arsenic. Josh saw the image of the gun in his mind. "I don't think so," Josh said.

Run, run, fucking run. Get out of here!

But what about Caleb? What would the monster do to him if Josh left him behind?

"You seemed pretty darn certain a minute ago it was you that's been callin'," the stranger said.

"I made a mistake," Josh whispered.

Get out, get out, get out.

The stranger snorted while thunder pounded through the sky. "I don't like mistakes, partner," he said.

"Josh, help me," Caleb howled from the floor. "That smell . . ."

The smell should be the least of your worries now, dude.

"Listen here," Josh began, "my friend and me don't want any trouble. My friend's hurt, and I have to get him to a hospital. So, if you don't mind, let us do what we have to do, and you go about your own business as usual."

"My business is killin' people," the stranger said. Lightning struck, and Josh saw the spurs again—the skin dangling off them as if he'd used his boots to rip apart someone's insides.

I don't want to be that next someone, he thought.

Another flash of lightning, and Josh saw the cowboy was closer than before. Everything went dark again, but Josh could still hear his footsteps, the clunk of his heels hitting the marble floor.

A gurgled laugh erupted from the cowboy's throat.

"Business has been slow lately," he said. "Time for me to catch up, Jack."

Whatever doubts Josh had that this experience wasn't real suddenly dispersed. It no longer mattered that his legs were half-asleep. It didn't matter that his friend was lying nearby, crying for help. In times of survival, self-preservation was key.

Josh started running. Running hard. He forgot it

was dark. He forgot he couldn't tell a wall from a door. He only knew to run.

He could hear the man behind him, running with him, trying to catch him. He imagined the putrid condition of his face, the blood on his clothes, the skin hanging off his spurs like clothes on a clothesline.

He imagined the gun.

"Now stop running, Jack," he heard the stranger say. "You're gonna make these old legs of mine get tired real quick."

Josh stumbled over a mound of open floor left over from the earthquake, and his legs went flying in the air. His head hit the floor when he landed somewhere between the entrance of a classroom and the hall. He looked up, unsure of his next move, when a strike of lightning revealed the door just to the right.

Josh lurched up and slammed the door behind him, knocking the man-creature in the face and forcing him to the ground. A growl emerged from the man's lips.

"Not playing nice there, Jack," he called.

Josh reached out and made contact with the nearest desk. He lifted it and threw it against the door. He grabbed another desk, and another, throwing one on top of the other, using every muscle he had ever spent a gym afternoon working on.

"That ain't gonna help, partner. I'm comin' through."

Josh looked into the darkness.

A window. There had to be a window in this room.

He could make it out, just barely. A shade of light from the cloudy moon above revealed the trim and glass of a series of windows on the opposite wall.

Josh limped his way across the room.

The cowboy was up again, smashing the door's window with a fist. His feet were punching through the door, the wood flying in every direction.

"Get back on track, Jack!" the man screamed.

The cowboy's progress sent Josh into a frenzy. He leaped to the other wall, tripping over desks on his way. "Fuck!" he yelled when his ankle twisted around the leg of a bookcase. The shelf fell, and the books followed, one after another into a pile by Josh's feet.

"I hear ya, Jack!" the cowboy yelled. "I'm comin' for ya, just you wait."

Move. Get going.

He couldn't. His ankle was down for the count. The books had beaten the rest of his resistance.

But I have to, but I have to.

If I don't, he's going rip me apart with those spurs.

Josh picked the books off his torso, throwing them to the side. He could hear the cowboy battling the walls of desks. He could hear the clunk of the man's boots and the thunder outside like the background music to an apocalypse.

Josh twisted so he was crawling up to the wall.

His palms hit the surface, searching for the window. A bang and a punch, a scrape and a slap, and finally, his knuckles made a small crack into the glass.

Bingo.

"You're not tryin' to get out of here, are ya, Jack?"

Hell, yes.

Josh could almost stand. His hands gripped the window's ledge, and he forced his legs to straighten. His elbows punched into the glass once more, but he was met with more resistance than he was expecting.

What the—

Josh lifted his hand to his face and inspected the smidgen of something mossy and green along his fingers. He reached up again and touched it, looking for an answer to what was keeping him prisoner in Gossamer Hall.

"Elephant moss," the man said, as if he was reading Josh's thoughts. "You ain't gonna pry through it, boy. It's hard as nails. I'd know; I've been buried in it for a hundred years."

Whatever the stuff was, elephant moss or not, Josh knew it was still growing. It hadn't taken over the window yet. *I have a fighting chance*, he thought, and with that last bit of hope, he raised his arm back and threw the hardest blow he'd ever thrown, and the glass shattered around him.

Rain was beating hard outside, lubricating Josh's

crushed fingers. He took a deep breath and closed his eyes before his fists punched through the remaining glass. He let out a harsh cry when he lifted one leg over the frame and hit iron.

He looked outside and saw the cages that famously guarded the windows of Gossamer Hall. *Fuck*, he thought. He had forgotten about the cages.

Josh could see the gray moon and the river nearby. He could hear the cars roll by on 360. Behind him, the cowboy was still fighting desks to get to him, and Josh knew he was running out of time.

Josh didn't even know he had been shot until a warm, thick liquid flowed down his face, dripping past his eye. He reached up and touched it, bringing his fingers to his lips.

He cringed when the taste dissolved on his tongue.

Blood.

His blood.

"Just hold it right there, partner," he heard the cowboy say. "We can do this the hard way or we can do this the easy way, but either way it's gonna get done."

My head. He shot me in my fucking head, Josh thought. Waves of nausea washed over him. His breath grew rapid with panic. He turned around, his body half-in, half-out of the window. "Leave me the fuck alone!" he screamed at the man in the darkness. "Whoever you are, leave me alone!"

"That ain't the way to talk to a man, Jack."

Josh looked around the room, searching for the deranged cowboy.

"The way I see it, you owe me somethin'. Callin' me, gettin' me outta of my home," the cowboy said.

"I didn't call you," Josh said, his words slurred.

I can make it, he thought. *I can get over this window. Just another leg and I'll be free.*

"Now, Jack. We all know you're a pussy. Ain't that what your daddy calls you?" The cowboy howled with laughter. "Why don't you prove yourself, buddy? Why don't you show them all you can hunt like a real man?"

A boom filled the room, followed by the moan of a wild animal. A four-legged creature galloped toward Josh, its hooves hitting the marble floor with loud clackety clacks, turning the room into a virtual noise machine.

Josh squinted, looking closer.

A deer, he thought.

The animal's eyes were yellow flashlights blazing through the darkness as its four legs rushed toward him.

I'm about to get trampled by fucking Bambi.

When he felt the impact, however, it was not an animal running over him, but a single bullet that sent him tumbling to the ground.

CHAPTER TWENTY

"DID YOU HEAR THAT?" REAGAN ASKED.

The trio of students stood at the edge of the hole with Hastings's desk beside them. They had dragged it from its position beside the chalkboard and were preparing to drop it to the next floor.

"Yeah, I heard it," Lars answered. He flashed Reagan a worried frown.

"It sounded like a gunshot," Lily said.

"That's because it was," Lars replied.

"It couldn't be. Why would someone have a gun in Gossamer Hall?"

"As far as I'm concerned, after tonight, anything is

possible," Lars said, shaking his head. "Are we ready or what?"

"Are you sure about this?" Reagan asked. She looked down at the floor below them, where the silhouette of their candles revealed the body of Dr. Killian Hastings. "It's a long way down," she murmured.

"Again, do we have a choice?" Lars snapped.

Reagan shifted her slender shoulders. "Maybe we haven't looked at all the options . . ."

"Juan's messed up," Lily reminded Reagan. "And look down there at Dr. Hastings. If the man isn't dead, he will be soon."

"There. You see? We have no choice. Okay, here we go," Lars said, wiping sweat from his brow. "I'll count. We push it on three. Okay?"

"Okay," the girls said in unison.

It was a daring move. Just underneath them lay the body of a professor who might be dead or alive. If they threw the desk too far, it was likely to land on Dr. Hastings, and if that happened, there would be no doubt about the condition of their professor.

"One," Lars began, "two . . . three . . ."

Reagan felt her arms move without the permission of her mind. She pushed, and a second later a series of noisy, continuous crashes followed, one after the other.

"Damn, that's loud," Lily said.

Reagan looked over the side. The good news was that the desk hadn't hit Dr. Hastings. The bad news was that it hadn't landed only on that floor, either. Instead, it hit the floor just a yard away from Dr. Hastings and fell through, and through to the next floor, and the next, until it landed on the ground level.

The students had created a hole that went straight through Gossamer Hall.

"Holy shit," Lily whispered. "Can't say I was expecting that to happen."

"I hope they don't put this on my transcript," Lars said. "The job market's already shit."

"Whoever thought the floor was so weak?" Reagan asked, more to herself than to anyone else.

"It's over a hundred years old," Lily said, shrugging. She glanced at Lars and Reagan. "So, what's Plan B, friends?"

"Plan B," Lars began, "is that I jump down there onto the desk and pray I don't break my leg, fall through the hole, or hurt Dr. Hastings . . . if he can still be hurt, that is."

"We'll lower you down," Reagan suggested.

Lars shook his head. "You're not strong enough."

"If we had a leveler."

"Like what?"

"I don't know. It was merely a suggestion."

Frustration eased over Reagan like a contagious

rash. She looked down at Juan unconscious on the floor and felt the first familiar tingles of loss prickle along her back.

He has a mother, she thought. *He has a mother who loves him. For some woman out there, he is her Celeste.*

"We have to do something before he dies," Reagan said. She looked at Lars with pleading eyes. "Please," she begged. "I'm not good with thinking in a crisis."

Lars looked at her as if to say, *And you think I am?*

Yes, as a matter of fact, Reagan's unwavering gaze answered back.

Lars looked like he wanted to say something else, but stopped short. The look in her eyes must have told him Reagan was working on a different level than he, or even Lily, could ever know.

Finally, he nodded. "If we take off some clothes, shred our backpacks, whatever else we can find, we may be able to lower Juan to the desk below. As for us," Lars paused, looking down at the hole and the floor where their fallen teacher lay, "we're gonna have to take our chances."

CHAPTER TWENTY-ONE

THINK HAN SOLO.

Think Luke Skywalker.

Think Captain Kirk.

What would they do?

They would remain brave in the face of danger, Mark told himself. *They would not overreact. They would do what needed to be done.*

Mark opened his eyes and stared into the darkness. He waited for sounds, voices, movements, *something* that would signal that he was not the only one to survive the earthquake.

The sound of a gunshot wasn't what he was expecting.

Was it really a gunshot? Mark was dubious. Not even the hood with the one eye looked the type to bring a gun to class.

But something made that noise.

Seconds later, another sound followed. It was not a gunshot, but more like a crashing of metal against something else. *A deep impact,* Mark thought.

He continued waiting, hoping voices might follow the two suspicious noises, but nothing was forthcoming until finally he heard the stairway door open and close with a loud slam.

Mark could hear footsteps approaching and the low hum of a person's nearby breathing moving closer.

That was all. Nothing else. Footsteps, breathing, and the sound of Mark's heart beating out of his chest.

"Hello?" Mark called. His voice echoed through the stairwell. "Can you help me, please? I think I broke my leg in the earthquake."

Silence.

Mark cleared his throat. "My name is Mark Green. I'm a student of Dr. Hastings. We have a class on the top floor. I'm not sure who else is hurt."

Or if anyone else survived, he silently added.

The smell was his only answer. *That awful, cruddy smell.* If Mark didn't have a sturdy constitution—if he wasn't used to the quirky scents of chemical gases compounding together in Mrs. Norton's chemistry class—he would have passed out a long time ago from that god-awful smell.

The darkness seemed to thicken, and the silence deepened, and Mark felt the throbbing of his leg grow worse. He straightened his back, waiting for an answer from the unseen stranger.

Why isn't this person saying anything?

"Hello?" he yelled. "Please say something. My name is Mark Green . . ."

The footsteps were coming closer. It seemed to Mark like the person, he or she, should be beside him any minute.

Mark felt something hard against his side.

"What do we have here?" the stranger asked.

CHAPTER
TWENTY-TWO

Juan rode with the strange woman through the prairie, past the cows and sheep and horses, past the chicken coop and windmill, through the streets of a town that seemed somehow familiar and all at once alien.

"Where am I?" he asked. They were his first words since beginning the journey with the woman.

"Where do you think you are, Juan? You and that gift of yours," she replied over her shoulder.

Did she say "my gift"?

"Last I knew, I was in Gossamer Hall," he said.

"Gossamer Hall," she repeated. "Gossamer Hall."

"In Brookhaven College. You know, off 360, near

Lakeway."

She said nothing. Juan leaned back and let the wind pound against his face while the sun's hot rays burned down on him.

This is just a dream, he thought. *In a minute I will wake up, and it will all have been a dream.*

Just when Juan thought the journey would never end, the woman stopped at a dark building that looked like a house on the outskirts of town.

But it's not a house, Juan realized when he looked up at the sign on the door.

Fredericksburg Motel.

"You'll be safe here," the woman said as she pulled her leg over to the other side of the horse and dismounted.

"Safe from what?" Juan asked. The woman grabbed his hands, and with their combined strength, Juan jumped off the horse with little difficulty.

"All the trouble you can handle, plus some change," the woman said. She stared at Juan with an emotion bordering on pity. She had dark eyes he knew he had seen before.

Juan gulped. He felt his heart racing his chest. "What kind of trouble?"

"You'll see," she said, and she turned and headed for the hotel with Juan straggling along behind her.

CHAPTER TWENTY-THREE

Four yards of fabric held Juan by his arms and legs while he dangled from the hole in the floor. Lily was down to her camisole and skirt; Reagan had taken off her sweater and coat. She wore only a ribbed undershirt. Lars had taken off his shirt and was down to his jeans. They had used a knife Lars had in his back pocket ("In case of emergencies," he'd said) to rip open their backpacks.

How'd I know a guy like Lars would be carrying a knife? Lily wondered to herself.

All in all, the fabric was just enough to get Juan a foot over the floor.

Time froze while the three of them sat in a circle around the hole, musing over their dilemma. "We'll have to drop him," Lars finally said.

"Yes," Lily agreed. "We don't have enough to lower him all the way."

"What if it hurts him?" Reagan asked, her gaze going back and forth between Lars and Lily. "What if he gets a concussion?"

"What do *you* want to do?" Lars asked, sounding tired.

Reagan gulped. She reached down and pulled her shirt over her head. "Don't ever say I never gave you the shirt off my back," she attempted to joke, and passed her shirt to Lars.

Lars looked at her with newfound respect. "You sure?"

Reagan nodded. "Go ahead."

"Wait," Lily said. She began unbuttoning her camisole. "At the risk of making this look like a *Girls Gone Wild* video . . ."

"Well, since you two are sacrificing," Lars said and unbuttoned his pants. "I hope you guys don't mind a guy in his boxers."

"Nothing I haven't seen before," Lily said.

Lily watched while Lars tied the legs of his jeans to Juan's ankles before adding her and Regan's contributions around the boy's wrists. "Ready?" Lars asked.

They nodded.

They cautiously lowered Juan onto the floor with barely any slack left. He and the professor's body lay side by side, two seemingly still corpses in the coffin of a dark room.

"Now," Lars said, "one of you needs to use it like a rope and crawl down." He looked at Reagan. "You're tiny. Try it first. Lily and I will hold on up here."

Reagan wasn't a risk-taking kind of girl by Lily's estimation, but to her surprise the redhead nodded and reached over for the cloth rope.

"Here goes nothing. It's not like descending the Empire State Building, right?" Reagan joked.

"Hardly," Lily answered in her most encouraging voice.

"You'll have to blow out your candle," Lars said apologetically. "Otherwise it might start a fire if it gets too close to the rope."

Reagan looked at her candle one last time as if it were the Holy Grail before she leaned over, puckered her lips, and blew it out. The room became a little darker. Lily watched while the woman stuffed the candle into her pocket and made the sign of the cross.

Lily held on tightly, her teeth clenching as Reagan descended into the hole. It wasn't as easy as she thought it was going to be. It didn't matter how small the woman was—weight was weight. Lily looked over at Lars to see if he was having the same problem, but he was holding steady like he had done this kind of thing a hundred times before.

Maybe he has, Lily thought. There was no telling what a guy like Lars had done in his past.

"Be careful. Don't land on Juan. Or Dr. Hastings," Lars called out.

Lily heard the sound of Reagan's shoes hitting the desk. "I'm here," she called. "I'm here," she whispered again, just loud enough for Lily to hear her.

"Good," Lars said. He looked at Lily. "You're next."

Lily was unconvinced. "Are you sure you can hold me?"

"I'm counting on it."

Lily was preparing herself for the trip down when a smell entered the room—just a whiff of something at first, followed by a more potent stench, as if it were being blown in by a massive fan like the ones directors used to create thunderstorms on movie sets.

Lily started coughing. She turned to Lars. "Do you smell that?" she asked between coughs.

"Yes," he answered, sniffing the room. "Jesus, it smells like a—"

"Graveyard?" Lily finished for him. She suddenly had a terrible thought. "You don't think that's Hastings smelling, do you?"

Lars shook his head. "If he was dead, his body

wouldn't be decomposing yet. Not for a while."

"He's not dead!" Reagan yelled up to them. "He's got a pulse."

Lily bent over, her mouth opening on dry gags. Saliva was building at the base of her throat and pushing up through her mouth. "I can't take it. It's horrible," she whimpered as spit dribbled over her lips.

Lars, too, was having a tough time. "Don't think about it," he advised, patting her on the back. "Just start down."

Lily tried. She reached over to the rope and placed both hands around it. Taking a deep breath, she prepared herself for the voyage down. *Forget the smell, forget the smell, forget the smell. Most people's pain is psychosomatic. Remember what Dr. Phil said. Change your internal dialogue.*

It does not smell bad in here, Lily deluded herself. *It smells like roses, like a basket of Chanel.*

Lily looked up. Lars was giving her the thumbs-up sign. His face was green with disgust, but Lily could tell he was making an effort, for her sake.

A basket of Chanel . . .

(But it's death I smell, it's death.)

"If you can't do it, Lily, we'll find another way," Lars said.

"I can do it," Lily promised. "I can do it," she said again to herself.

But that smell . . .

It wasn't until her hand slid down the rope that she heard the door opening to the room downstairs, and the sinister laugh that followed.

CHAPTER TWENTY-FOUR

MARK SAID THE FIRST WORDS THAT POPPED IN HIS head. "You're an idiot!" he shouted, and then winced because he had never said anything like that to a guy twice *(okay, three times)* his size before.

Caleb reached down and picked Mark up off the floor, throwing him over his shoulder. Mark grimaced when a sharp pain exploded through his leg. "Be careful," he said. "I think my leg's broken."

"Holy shit, thank God mine's fine. I have a game on Saturday," Caleb said, and he snickered. "Come on, admit it, you were scared."

"Of course I was scared! I thought you were some . . ."

Mark searched for a word that might impress the jock, "fucking rapist or some shit." There. He had cussed. Caleb should feel at home. Jesus might be a little pissed, but He'd get over it. Mark looked up at the ceiling. *Sorry, there, old buddy, old pal.* He sometimes wished the Son of God had more of a sense of humor.

Caleb laughed. "Dude, if I was a serial rapist, I wouldn't be after your scrawny ass. I'd be trailing Miss Lily Blythe, that's where I'd be. Did you check out her ass in those pants last week?" Caleb let out a low whistle.

"I heard a gunshot," Mark said, not convinced everything was hunky-dory. "It made me nervous."

"Me, too. It was probably Josh. He has one of those old Mustangs that kick a fit every time you start the engine." Caleb paused before adding, "You know what that jackass did? He left me on the floor to die. Just walked away and left me like nothing happened."

"Why would he do that?" Mark thought it was harsh, even for a jerk like Josh Herzig.

"Hell if I know." Caleb snorted.

"The steroids thing?"

Mark felt Caleb flinch underneath him. "Don't bring up shit you don't know about," he warned. An uncomfortable pause followed. Mark felt Caleb might throw him on the ground and leave, but a second later the jock spoke up again. "So, your leg is broken?" he asked in a kinder voice.

Mark tried again to move his leg. All he got in return was pain, pain, and more pain. He bit back a scream. "I think it's broken. I'm not doctor. Yet," he added. "What about you?"

"Concussion, I guess. I was out of it for a bit."

"We're lucky," Mark said. "With a tremor like that, it's a good thing Gossamer Hall didn't fall to the ground."

"Word, dude. Word. I can tell you now, though, if I have to smell whatever this crap is a second longer, I am gonna die. It's awful."

"The earthquake may have damaged the plumbing," Mark suggested.

"You mean there's a pool of shit somewhere in here?"

"It's a possibility."

"Fuck me."

Mark's thoughts turned to Juan, and he shot his eyes upward, as if he could see the condition of his friend through the ceiling. *What happened to him*? Mark wondered. He had freaked out before the earthquake, during the séance. Mark wondered if he had recovered.

I won't leave Gossamer Hall until I know he's okay.

Juan was a big mystery to him. Mark considered him a friend, but the truth was, there wasn't a lot he knew about him. They'd spent a lot of time together, mainly because they had the same classes, and they had hung out together downtown once or twice. Juan had even joined Mark for his fifth viewing of *Star Wars: Episode III.*

Mark thought about the strange conversation he'd had with Juan when the movie was over.

"How do you justify Star Wars and God existing in the same place?" Juan had asked. They were sitting at Amy's Ice Cream across from the Alamo Drafthouse, Juan with a vanilla cone, Mark with concoction of strawberry and butterscotch ice cream mixed with Gummy Bears and raspberry syrup.

"What do you mean?" Mark asked. "Are you saying I can't like one without loving the other?"

"No," Juan said, shaking his head. "It's just—well, remember a few years ago when a bunch of Christian groups picketed Harry Potter because it had witches and warlocks?"

"Yeah, but that was extreme. Even Brookhaven College sent out a newsletter admitting those people were nuts."

"Okay. But you have to agree there is no evidence of God in any of the *Star Wars* movies," Juan argued. "I mean, I haven't seen the films as many times as you have, but wouldn't you agree that there's a lack of God there? Princess Leia didn't cry out for God to help her; she called out to Obi-Wan."

Mark thought about it. "Maybe, Juan, but it's just a movie. It's just Hollywood."

"But you admit to enjoying it, right?"

"Of course." Mark took a lick from his vanilla ice cream as a group of drunken UT students entered the store, their loud voices and laughter echoing off the cotton-candy-colored walls. Mark suddenly felt like a homosexual sharing ice cream with another guy on a Friday night after going to the movies.

Juan didn't seem troubled by the students. He stared out the window with eyes no longer seeing the present. Mark looked down and saw Juan's right ring finger was tapping to a rhythm of its own making.

"I guess what I'm trying to say," Juan began once the students had left, "is that just because you enjoy *Star Wars*, something that isn't in the Bible, something that makes no reference to God, a Hollywood confection to the extreme—just because you like *Star Wars*, doesn't make you a bad person, doesn't make you evil."

"Of course not!" Mark exclaimed.

"Right," Juan said, nodding. "Right." Juan didn't say anything after that, and while Mark wanted to discuss it in further detail—he enjoyed a good debate about anything, he couldn't help himself, he had a wealth of knowledge to pull from—he decided, using intuition he'd never thought he'd had in him, to remain quiet and never bring it up again.

"We're almost there." Caleb's voice penetrated

Mark's thoughts.

"What?" Mark asked and looked around. He didn't know how he had done it, but he had managed to block out the moment. The horror of it. Even the disgusting smell.

We're going down, Mark thought when he felt Caleb's feet descending the stairs. *We're headed for the front door.*

"What are you doing?" Mark asked. "We have to go upstairs, not down."

"I'm not going upstairs. I'm getting us the hell out of here," Caleb replied. "Does that make sense to you, dude?"

"You can't leave!" Mark cried. "What about the others?"

"Screw the others. They can fend for themselves."

Mark cleared his throat. "Look, you didn't like it when Josh left you in the lurch, yeah? Come on, we got to go up there. It's the Christian thing to do." He thought if there was ever a time to stand up to a guy like Caleb, it was now.

"I didn't come to this school because I was a Christian," Caleb replied. "I came to this school because I had a scholarship."

But there was hesitation in Caleb's steps, Mark could feel it. He heard the football player sigh dramatically. Finally, Caleb stopped on the stairs next to the EXIT sign.

"It was a shitty thing for him to do," the jock mumbled.

"Yeah," Mark agreed.

"But it had nothing to do with the steroids!" Caleb exclaimed in a voice that told Mark he was trying to convince himself more than anyone else.

"Okay," Mark said. "Let's go."

Caleb turned around and began walking in the opposite direction with Mark tucked over his shoulder. Together, David and Goliath made their way up to the top floor of Gossamer Hall.

CHAPTER TWENTY-FIVE

WHERE'S THE SECURITY? GRETCHEN WONDERED WHEN she pulled onto the Brookhaven campus. There was supposed to be someone at the entrance, no matter what hour, but when she looked into the security booth, no one was there.

Gretchen cracked her knuckles against the steering wheel. *Someone's head is going to roll.* Brookhaven College spent a lot of money on security, more than she thought they should. To see it go to waste really pushed her buttons.

The board will be hearing about this.

After driving to the far end of campus, Gretchen

pulled her car in next to Hastings's Volvo. It was the nearest parking lot to Gossamer Hall, but because the building was in the back of the school, it was a long walk no matter where someone parked.

Gretchen reached into the backseat and angrily snatched her purse, umbrella, and flashlight. *Hastings being a dick, and now security missing.* "What else, Jesus?" she asked, looking up. "What the fuck else?"

Gretchen jumped out of her car and opened her umbrella in record time. She closed her car door and journeyed up the unpaved sidewalk leading to Gossamer Hall, her flashlight beaming ahead of her. Raindrops torpedoed from the sky around her, millions at a time. Her Ann Taylor shoes stuck into the soft mud with every step she took, and after a while, she reached down and ripped off the heels, soldiering on with bare feet and mud clinging to her pantyhose.

Just you wait, Professor Hastings, just you wait, Gretchen sang to herself—Eliza Doolittle singing to Henry Higgins.

Just you wait.

He wasn't worth weathering this storm. No one was. But what was her other option? What would she tell the school board? Hastings had been *her* call. It was her ass on the line.

Gossamer Hall appeared around the corner, lit only by the moon, and while most people would have run to escape the rain, Gretchen found herself slowing down, each step a calculated move to postpone her arrival. It wasn't intentional, but the truth was, she hated Gossamer Hall. *It's such a morose-looking building,* she thought. Gretchen didn't understand why it had been built in the first place. The Gothic style had long been outdated, even while it was being built. It was ugly, and if she had her say, if the board let her *(and God forbid the board let me do anything)*, she'd rip it all down and start anew. History be damned.

Gretchen wasn't alone in her feeling. Almost everyone who had any association with Brookhaven College hated the building. Everyone, that was, but Hastings. He had even *insisted* on having his office there.

"Good vibes," he had told Gretchen ten years earlier, when he had first come to Brookhaven College. "The building is as haunted as I am," he'd said.

Gretchen didn't doubt that—she didn't doubt that one damn bit.

Her gaze was unwavering as she moved closer and closer to it. The roar of thunder overhead, the flash of lightning, the never-ending rain and mud puddles gathered around the stairs only added to its dark luster.

And there was something else Gretchen noticed as she climbed the stairs in her bare feet.

Is Gossamer Hall sinking? she wondered, looking wide-eyed at the cracked staircase that no longer went directly to the entrance but appeared to stop just above the front door.

Gretchen shook her head. Maybe it had always been that way, and she was just noticing it for the first time. No one had ever accused her of visiting Gossamer Hall regularly.

Gretchen stared at the strange architecture for another moment before opening the door and stepping inside.

The stench was the first thing to hit, followed by darkness.

Gretchen cringed. A line from Shakespeare's *Macbeth* slipped like a snowflake inside her head.

Things bad begun make strong themselves by ill.

Gretchen was prepared to take another step when the earth suddenly trembled beneath her. A slow growl came from the sky, and the earth shook harder still as if in answer. Gretchen tried to lock her legs, but the night had turned into a pinball machine of sounds and shakes, rattles, and flashes of light.

"No!" Gretchen screamed into the laughing darkness. Her legs collapsed, the left and then the right, and her back gave way, and she fell through the door and outside, into the rain, the night, the devilish storm, where her body twisted and turned down the marble steps leading to Gossamer Hall.

CHAPTER TWENTY-SIX

THE GREEN-FLOWERED WALLPAPER WAS THE SINGLE decoration in what was otherwise a plain room furnished only with a bed, a side table, and a ratty stool.

Juan sat at the edge of the bed and studied the woman who shared the room with him.

"Lily."

Her name arose on Juan's voice like a dove batting its wings through a moonlit forest. He watched while the woman turned from the window and looked at him, her amethyst eyes emotionless in the shadows.

"Call me Lily if that is what you wish," she said.

Juan gulped. *But she is Lily. Isn't she?*

She looked like Lily. The dark, wavy hair, the slender shoulders. The violet eyes and sand-colored skin.

"But you are her," Juan insisted, his voice rising with conviction. "You can't be anyone else. You look exactly like her."

"What is it about a beautiful woman that drives a man insane?" the woman Juan now thought of as Lily asked, folding her arms over her chest.

Juan did not know how to answer. Lily waited for another moment before turning around and watching the window once more. After a period of silence, she said in a voice as soft as silk and as definite as death, "I only look like her because it is how you imagined I would look. Remember, Juan, you can only *make* what you have seen, what you have felt."

Juan's breath caught in his chest. "How did you know . . ." he began.

"Erase that question from your vocabulary," she interrupted. "*How did I know, how did I know?* Erase it or else it will be the only question you ever ask. And there is so much more for you to know than *how did I know*." She pointed a long, thin finger at the window. "Listen now." She inhaled and said, "You'll see one soon, I can feel it. And there's only one way to un*make* them. The one who plays them has to die. Do you understand, Juan? Souls don't replace one another. They eat one another. Eye for an eye, tooth for a . . . well, you've read the Old Testament, haven't you, Juan? You *are* a student at Brookhaven College."

Juan went still as he registered Lily's words. It all seemed like insanity.

Was Lily a crackhead? he wondered. Juan looked closely at the woman in front of him. She didn't look like a crackhead, but then, what did a crackhead look like? Oprah had admitted to smoking crack before, and so had Juan's great-aunt who, for the last two years, had played the organ at her Baptist church.

"I'm not a crackhead," Lily said, looking over at him with fire in her eyes. "Whatever 'crack' is."

"Wait a minute," Juan said, his breath caught in his throat. "How did you—?"

"Here he comes," Lily said abruptly, waving her hand to silence Juan.

Juan looked over to the window where Lily was pointing. In the distance, a lone figure galloped toward them, the dust kicking up from the horse's hooves. Juan watched the rider approach and wondered, *Is he a husband, a lover, a friend?*

When the rider closed the remaining distance, Juan had his answer. "Josh," Juan whispered. He looked at Lily. "That's Josh Herzig, from Dr. Hastings's class."

The closely cropped brown hair, the goofy face, the bulk of his athletic body—it was him all right. The only difference was that Josh was not dressed in his usual frat boy Abercrombie & Fitch garb. He looked more like a cowboy than a football player, dressed in jeans and leather chaps, his feet clad in rough, brown cowboy boots with silver spurs. A red scarf was tied around his thick neck, and a brown hat sat on his head.

"Why is Josh dressed that way?" Juan wondered aloud.

"He's not Josh Herzig anymore," Lily said matter-of-factly.

"I don't understand," Juan whispered. He felt his heart pump hard in his chest. It was like learning a horrible secret. He compared it to the time he had heard his mother talking on the phone, telling some-one she thought her son was dangerous.

Juan looked at Lily. "Why is Josh out there?" he asked.

Am I in the twilight zone or what?

"I don't know what the twilight zone is, but I can guarantee you're not in it," Lily answered.

Josh shook his head, disbelieving. "How do you keep—?"

"I told you to stop asking how I know things."

"Okay. Then tell me why a boy from my history class is outside on a horse. And while you're at it, why don't you tell me why I'm here, with you, in a hotel room that looks like it should be in Deadwood?"

Lily didn't answer immediately. She watched the

183

rider slow down and stop in front of their door at the Fredericksburg Motel.

What is he waiting for? Josh wondered.

"He wants to kill us," Lily answered. When Juan gasped, she turned and looked at him. "Yes, I can read your thoughts. Some of the time, anyway. And, yes, he really wants to kill us." She paused and placed a thoughtful hand to her cheek. "You don't know what that man did, Juan. You have no idea what he has unleashed."

"What man?"

Lily cocked her head. "You know," she answered.

Juan flinched. Yes, he did, indeed, for whatever reason, know to whom she referred. Dr. Killian Hastings. The séance had been his idea. The Hume Method. All that shit, all Hastings's idea. And somehow Juan was trapped in this world, while Mad Maron—

No! It can't happen!

Juan shut his eyes. "How did he know I could *make*?" he asked.

Lily shrugged. "How should I know?"

"You seem to know everything."

"Not everything," Lily said.

"Why does Josh Herzig want to kill me?"

Lily looked at Juan again, her eyes narrowing. "You haven't listened to a word I've said, have you? Well, listen to me now," she said. "That's not Josh

Herzig on the horse out there, Juan. I'm not sure which one of Mad Maron's cousins it is, but it's not the guy you know. The guy you know is dead. Whoever that is," Lily pointed at the window, "has one purpose, and one purpose only. He wants to kill you, and he won't leave until he does."

CHAPTER
TWENTY-SEVEN

ANOTHER EARTHQUAKE, REAGAN THOUGHT. THAT WAS all, nothing more. The earth and the sky were at war, and she was just a bystander, and the evil laugh she thought she heard was nothing, just more collateral from Mother Nature's raging battle.

Reagan did her best to ignore the moldy stench in the air while she moved soundlessly through the room.

"Can you hear me? Are you there?" she heard Lars yell.

"I'm right here," she called. "I'm fine. Just a little shaken."

"I thought I heard someone else down there," Lars

said.

"No," Reagan said. "I'm alone."

"Another damn earthquake," she heard Lily mutter. "Hold on, Reagan, I'm coming down."

Reagan cleared her throat to answer, but stopped short when she heard a sound from the other side of the room.

A laugh. Well, not just *a* laugh, but *the* laugh—the one she'd thought she heard before. It rolled like slow thunder into the room, a low, lingering chuckle that aimed to alarm, echoing and amplifying all at once.

"Celeste."

Reagan stalled in place. It felt like worms were crawling through her veins and arteries. Her stomach sank to the pit of her gut, her heart beating a million times per minute.

He said her name!

Reagan squeezed her shoulders and looked around at the blackness, expecting some spark of light somewhere to reveal who occupied the room with her.

She waited hopefully, and there was nothing.

Reagan was scared to speak or stay quiet, she was scared to move, and she was scared to stand. The mouse her husband had married and divorced was returning, little Reagan Tanner with a cork where her voice should be and a pounding heart that felt too much and said too little.

The stranger in the darkness spoke, his words like cancer. "Where do you think that daughter of yours is now, my pretty, little frilly thing?" His voice was rough and clearly Texan, and he spoke with a light slur. Reagan was close enough that she could smell the whiskey on his breath.

"What's happening down there?" Lars called in a concerned voice. "Lily's coming down."

Reagan finally opened her mouth and words tumbled out. "Don't bring Lily down!" she screamed.

"Why? Who's there?" he asked.

With each word the stranger spoke, the smell in the room thickened with its dreadful sickness. "Pretty little Reagan," he said. "Ol' Flat Shot here could use some of you real bad. It's a shame you're so sad. Let me make you glad."

Reagan flinched, not sure if she should laugh or cry. The stranger was a rhymer, and a terrible one at that. *I've written third-grade sonnets with more creative flare.* "Whatever you're offering, I'm not accepting," Reagan said.

Don't let your voice shake. Don't let him know how scared you really are.

Reagan bit her lips while she nervously moved her fingers along the strap of her bra. *God, if ever there was time to be half-naked!*

"Is it Josh or Caleb?" Lars asked.

"Maybe it's that skinny kid," Reagan heard Lily whisper.

"Mark?" Lars asked.

"Please . . . please," Reagan said softly. Her eyes darted from right to left. "Whoever you are, leave me alone." *And leave my daughter alone*, she silently added. "Don't hurt me."

She must have been speaking loud enough for Lars and Lily to hear, for the next thing Lars said was, "No one's going to hurt you. It's just the jocks or someone trying to scare you."

I don't think so, Reagan thought as she felt the man's hand reach out and grab her around the hips.

"No!" Reagan screamed. She turned and slapped the hands away, and clawed at his face, digging her fingernails into skin that felt more like cream cheese than flesh.

"Bitch!" the man spat. He reared back and threw her away from him, and Reagan went flying across the room. A flat surface hit the side of her head where she landed, sobering her with tingling pain.

"Reagan!" Lily screamed.

Don't stop. Keep moving. No matter what.

Where her will came from, Reagan did not know. She rose from the floor with her hands flailing around her, searching for the door that would be her escape. Her knuckles hit chairs, her feet tripped over desks.

Finally her palms came in contact with something that felt like a doorknob.

She grabbed the knob and twisted, only to find resistance. "No!" she protested wildly, pulling at it. "No, no, no, no . . ." she cried over and over.

"I hear a pretty, little frilly thing, sing for me, oh, won't you sing . . ." the man chanted in a low, sinister voice. "Come on, Ray-gon."

"No, no, no . . ."

"Now, I'm sorry what I said back there," he said. "A bitch ain't nothin' to call but a dog. You far better than that, sweetie pie. You and me, we're friends tonight."

After a pause, an invisible question hissed through the darkness:

Don't you want to see Celeste again?

They were words that seemed more material than audible, as if they had formed a physical appearance in the room.

Don't you want . . .?

Reagan shook her head, blocking out the sound—the shape—of it.

Celeste is gone. He's only trying to trick me.

I
(don't you want)
have
(to see)
to get out

(Celeste)
of this room!

A frustrated cry rose from Reagan's throat as she kicked and punched the unyielding door. Blood poured from her knuckles, darkening the wedding ring she still wore. "I hate you!" she screamed, and whether she was yelling at the maniac, the door, or the wedding ring that still held her prisoner, she did not know.

"I HATE YOU!"

This room will kill me.

He will

She smelled him before she felt his hand encircle her neck.

kill me.

"Pretty fillies don't fight like that," he said, his grip tightening. "Pretty fillies sit there and smile, smile away, night and day, they're just that way. Now, won't you smile for Flat Shot, sugar?"

Reagan turned to look at her captor just as Lars jumped down onto the floor with Lily's glowing cell phone in hand.

Just a little light, but, oh, what a little light could do. For the first time, Reagan had a chance to see the man's face.

Or what was left of his face, she corrected herself, and let out a blood-curdling yell.

He cupped his hand over her mouth, forcing her

words to waste away into silence. The taste and texture of his flesh reminded Reagan of raw meat.

"Don't scream now, darlin', ol' Flat Shot here will take care of you real good-like. My missus done gone and left me, and I ain't had nothin' soft to cuddle with in a long time," he said with poisonous breath.

Reagan escaped his hand and vomited in his arms. Her mind, her body, her self was spinning out of control, held together by only the simplest of ideas.

Must. Get out. Have to. Get out.

"Oh, what's the problem now, sweet thing? Flat Shot knows what haunts you." He leaned closer and breathed one word, "*Celesteeee . . .*"

The man suddenly lost his grip on her neck. "Fuckin' damn shit!" he cried as he flew in the air, landing in a pile of fallen desks.

Reagan looked up to see Lars standing over the man with the cell phone in his hand. The man was hunched over on the floor, moaning, while Lars kicked him over and over in the gut.

"Lars!" Lily shouted from the floor above. "Don't kill him!"

"Why not?" Lars shouted back.

Reagan sank into a puddle on the floor. "She's right. You can't—"

But before she could finish, Lars delivered a blow to the side of the man's head, and he let out a faint gasp, like a balloon losing air, before his head fell backward against the floor.

The room went silent, filled only with the cobalt blue of lightning striking outside. Reagan could hear the wispy sound of Lars trying to catch his breath. "What did you want me to do, girls?" Lars asked, exasperated, looking up at Lily then down at Reagan. "Take him to the movies? In case you didn't realize it, Ronald, he was going to rape you first and kill you later."

"My name's Reagan," she whispered, and even softer, "I was named after my grandmother, not the president." She put her hands to her head.

My brain is going to explode. This is too much for me. I'm Reagan Tanner. I come from a shit stick town in Texas. I'm a nobody. Things like this only happen to somebodies. I'm nothing. I'm a ghost.

Then Reagan's attention zoomed out like a camera lens, and she saw Lars's face again, every dark and dangerous part of him.

I could never bring him home to meet my mother, Reagan thought. *She'd have a heart attack.*

Reagan shook her head, disbelieving she would have a thought like that under these circumstances. She closed her hands over her face once more, blinding her eyes to Lars.

"This is not happening," she mumbled. "This is not happening."

Minutes formed and fell away before Reagan felt Lars's hands touch the top of her head with the gentleness of a father consoling his child. "It'll be okay," Lars said. "I don't know what happened but—"

"That's right," Reagan agreed. "You don't know what happened." She looked up from her hands. "But neither do I."

"He must have been juiced up on something," Lars suggested.

"Juiced up?"

"Yeah, like he got a God complex. Umm . . . I can't really explain it. It can happen with some kinds of pills."

Reagan snorted. "And I suppose you know what that feels like?"

She saw Lars flinch in the cell phone's light. "I don't apologize for anything I've ever done," he said defensively, but with a trace of sadness.

Reagan looked away. "Then that makes one of us," she said. "It seems I never stop apologizing." She looked at him again and tried to smile, but it was fake, and from the pitying look Lars gave her in return, she knew he knew it was phony.

"Will someone clue me in on what's happening?" Lily called down. "I feel like you're in the orchestra and I'm in the balcony."

"Nothing," Lars answered, looking up. "We'll get

you down."

"How, exactly? No one's here to hold me."

"You jump. I'll catch," Lars said.

"Oh, hell," Lily mumbled. "Fine."

Suddenly Reagan heard Lars inhale a sharp breath.

"What is it?" she asked.

Lars glanced up at her. "Have you seen what you were fighting?" he asked.

"Sort of. He's definitely not Jude Law. Please, I don't want to see him again," Reagan said, waving her hand.

"I think you should," Lars said, motioning for her to come over.

With great trepidation, Reagan rose and walked over to where Lars stood. Her eyes searched and found the body of the man who had attacked her.

Not really a man. More like a creature, Reagan thought as she worked at keeping whatever food she had left in her stomach. She stared at the man, wide-eyed, holding her hand over her mouth.

He had no eyes, no nose. His ears were ripped flesh dangling from the sides of his head. His skin was a mesh of green gook and gelled red blood.

Reagan's gaze lowered to view the rest of him. She trembled when she saw what he was wearing: boots with spurs, and leather pants like the ones cowboys used to wear.

"What is going on here?"
And how does this monster know Celeste?

CHAPTER TWENTY-EIGHT

"THAT WAS A SCREAM," CALEB SAID MATTER-OF-FACTLY as he adjusted Mark on his shoulder. "Did you hear it?"

"Yep," Mark answered. "But it's possibly a good thing."

"How is that a good thing?"

"It means we're not the only ones who survived the earthquake."

"Oh."

Caleb had to admit, the kid was right. He suddenly felt ashamed he had wanted to leave without checking on the others. He wasn't Josh.

And I thought he was my friend, Caleb thought,

shaking his head.

He paced himself while he climbed the stairs. Each step was a calculated move to keep him and the kid from falling on their asses. A sense of balance had never been one of his assets, and had always been his Achilles' heel in football.

Caleb couldn't keep his mind from wandering back to Josh. *Screw him,* he thought. He shook his head. Whatever did he do to deserve that kind of treatment? What kind of passive-aggressive bullshit was he harboring anyway, leaving him barely conscious on the floor like that? No way would Caleb have done the same thing. Not even to his worst enemy. Not even to Ryan Gaskins.

His head didn't feel too bad, but Caleb decided he must have hit it pretty hard because he vaguely remembered Josh talking to someone. But who? Dr. Hastings's class was the only one in the building, and the rest of the class members, except for Mark, were still on the sixth floor.

Was it someone from outside maybe?

But who would have let Josh walk off without helping him?

Could it have been another football player?

Caleb snorted. *Better not be,* he thought, *or someone's ass was grass.*

"Gossamer Hall's a little far from the parking lot,"

Mark said out of nowhere.

Caleb shook his head. "What do you mean?" he asked.

"I mean, Gossamer Hall's a little far away to hear that big of a bang from someone's car starting up, even if it is an old Mustang."

Caleb paused at the door to the sixth floor. He wasn't used to being around someone who knew so much crap about everything. "So what?" he said. "You think that was an actual gunshot we heard?"

"It sounded like it."

"Not even a crazy dude like Dr. Hastings would bring a gun into Gossamer Hall."

"What about that one-eyed thug?"

Caleb shrugged. "It's possible." Caleb pulled the doorknob, opening up to a world of continuing darkness. "Hell, when are the lights coming on?" he mumbled to himself.

"HELLO!" Caleb yelled. "Can anyone hear me?"

Time passed for what seemed like forever before Caleb heard a faint female voice yell back, "Caleb? Is that you?"

It sounded like Lily.

"Yeah, it's me!" Caleb cried. "Are you all right?"

Lily spoke again just as another surge of lightning and thunder threatened the sky.

"WHAT?" Caleb asked. "I can't hear you."

"We're not all right!" she screamed. "We are far from fucking all right!"

"That was what I was afraid of," Mark mumbled, adjusting himself on Caleb's shoulder. "Ask her who's hurt."

Caleb placed his hands like a horn around his mouth while continuing to balance Mark on his shoulder. "Who's hurt?" he yelled.

"You're gonna be, fella," said a voice in a heavy Texan drawl.

Caleb heard the voice clearly, like the man was standing next to him. "Josh?" Caleb asked. "Is that you?"

"That didn't sound like Josh to me," Mark said.

Lily shouted again, "Caleb! Help us! Someone just attacked . . ." Her voice faded away, but it didn't matter because Caleb was no longer listening. The slowly growing stench around them had become awfully strong in the last minute. It was as if it had swallowed all the air and had become its own entity.

The owner of the mysterious words had moved close enough to Caleb and Mark that he could have reached out and touched them.

Caleb had the strange, unexplainable feeling that whoever it was wasn't there to help.

"Mark?"

"Yeah?"

"Mind if I put you down for a minute?"

"Go for it."

Caleb bent and lowered the boy to the ground. Just as he rose, a strong hand reached and grabbed his shoulder with brutal force. Caleb flinched and punched it away, walking backward while he pumped his fists into the air.

"I don't want no trouble from you, man," Caleb called out to the stranger.

"Trouble. You already got trouble, don't ya, Bro?"

The fist came out of the darkness like a rocket launching into space, and Caleb couldn't stop the man's knuckles from connecting with his cheek. He reeled back and grabbed his stinging face. When he looked up again, it no longer mattered that he couldn't see a thing, that the only light was Mark's puny BlackBerry with its miserable white light. The game was set.

"You're on," Caleb hissed, slinging his own fist and smashing it into the stranger's skull.

Caleb cringed when he felt his knuckles against the man's head. It wasn't that he'd hurt his fist. Far from it. The texture of the man's skull made Caleb feel like he was punching pudding.

It was enough for Caleb to pause, and enough time for the man to punch into his stomach twice before Caleb leaned over and grabbed him by his face, twisting him away.

His face is a fucking ice-cream cone.

What am I dealing with?

"You think you'd be punchin' so good if you ain't got them 'roids jacked up in ya?" the man asked.

Ah ha, Caleb thought. So this was what it was all about. The Steroid Issue. Some football player with an axe to grind.

That stupid, damn e-mail.

"I'm 'roid-free," Caleb said and flexed his fist, gearing up for another punch.

"Caleb?" It was Mark. "Maybe there's another way to pacify this situation . . ."

"Shut up," Caleb said. "Just lay there and shut the hell up. I've got the matter under control."

"Umm . . . okay," Mark said quietly. "Just trying to help."

The unknown man laughed with a crackling hiss. "Is that Mark there on the floor?" he asked.

Caleb straightened his back, his fist against his chest, ready to pounce. "Leave him alone, dipshit. This is between you and me."

"And Marky-boy," the man said, laughing again.

"Hey! I've never taken steroids in my life!" Mark cried.

The man's laugh became louder, and the stench was suddenly a bomb bursting into the room.

Caleb knelt on the floor, overcome with nausea. "You're the smell," he accused the stranger. "You're the fucking stench."

He could hear something click above him. It sounded like a gun.

He's gonna shoot me!

But whatever his intention, the man didn't have a chance. Below them, the earth shifted again, and Caleb, Mark, and the dangerous stranger all became prey to the ground's angry shake.

CHAPTER TWENTY-NINE

MARIJUANA HAD FORMED A BEAUTIFUL HAZE OF DISASsociation in the mind of Dr. Gretchen Kurcan. When she awoke on the steps of Gossamer Hall, it did not occur to her that she was in a very strange place at a very strange time of night.

Nor did she immediately think of the earthquake that had brought her to Gossamer Hall's bottom step, where her legs were tangled around a rail and bleeding, and her bare feet were twisted on the muddy grass. Her purse and umbrella had blown away to God-knowswhere in the midst of the storm, and she had only her flashlight dangling from her limp fingers.

Nothing broke through Gretchen's central point of focus. She imagined she could sit in Dante's Inferno and give birth to the Antichrist and there would still be only one thing on her mind.

Dr. Killian Hastings.

I hate you, Killian. I hate you. God help me, but it's true. If these were biblical times, I would tie your ankles together and throw you out into the middle of the street and stone you to death. You'd better believe it. And not a single person on this planet would blame me, because they loathe you, too.

Driven with pure, unadulterated hatred, Gretchen tried to stand, ignoring her scraped legs and the shock waves of pain moving up and down her back. She hardly winced when her feet felt the chill of the cement steps.

Slowly Gretchen limped up the stairs to the oddly set doors of Gossamer Hall, which were situated even farther below the top of the stairs.

The whole damn place is sinking. She paused and thought about what to do. The movement of the stairs and the door was a building-code violation, and attempting to go inside could be a risk to her safety. She reached into her coat and pulled out her cell phone. She looked at the screen where it said "No Service," then rolled her eyes and put the phone back in her coat. *I'm on my own*, she thought.

Gretchen bit her lip and looked around her while the lightning tore through the night and the rain continued to pound around her. It occurred to her that no matter how bad the conditions were inside Gossamer Hall, they couldn't be much worse than the conditions outside. *To hell with it*, Gretchen thought and opened the door, stepping inside.

Gossamer Hall was darker than it was outside, but at least it was dry. Gretchen squeezed the rain from her coat, and the drops leaked to the marble floor. *"The instrument of darkness tell us truths,"* she quoted from Shakespeare's *Macbeth* before yelling out into the hallway, "Hello? Killian?" She tried to remember some of the students in Dr. Hastings's class, and only one deviant name came to mind. "Caleb Jacobs?" she called. "Is anyone here?"

They're still in the classroom, Gretchen thought. It was just like Hastings to force his class to stay even when the lights had gone out. *Lord, forgive me, but what a bastard,* she thought while she proceeded down the hallway.

Only another minute passed before Gretchen realized there was something far more off about the building than stairs that didn't meet the door and a power outage.

What is that stench? she wondered, coughing loudly into her hand. The smell was a ball-breaking, kamikaze, throw-your-head-back-and-sink-the-dagger-into-your-ribs kind of funk that Gretchen had never experienced before.

Sewage, she thought automatically. It had to be. The earthquake must have busted up the pipes. It was going to cost a fortune to repair the place. *The appropriations committee is going to have a field day with this one.*

Gretchen walked farther down the hall and stopped only when she saw the pile of broken marble flooring. *And things just keep getting better and better.*

She was feeling her weed buzz dying away. There was something about seeing a hole in the ground, surrounded by a pile of marble, as if something had risen out of the ground, that finally knocked reason back into the heart of a woman who had built her life on brainpower.

Get the hell out of here. Don't stay here another minute. To hell with Dr. Hastings. Something bad has happened here.

But she couldn't move. Instead she raised her flashlight, first to the right, then to the left of the marble mound, looking for evidence of what had happened.

Run. Get out of here, she told herself again.

But she couldn't, not yet. It didn't matter what her instinct told her. Dr. Gretchen Kurcan was not the type of woman to leave without answers. She was used to getting to the bottom of things. It was how she had gotten this far in life—getting the job done and getting it done well, and God help the people who stood in her way.

Slowly and with great forethought, Gretchen stepped over the pile on the floor. She winced with pain when her bare feet made contact with the shards of marble, but after the first step there was no turning back.

On the other side of the rubble pile was something Gretchen would have never in a million years expected to be in the hallway. She staggered back when she saw it, touching her available hand to her forehead.

What is a teacher's desk doing in the middle of the hallway? And why is there ceiling dust surrounding it?

Gretchen's light moved upward to the ceiling, and there her puzzle was solved.

A hole had opened in the ceiling, and above that was another, and another until, as far as Gretchen could tell, the opening reached the sixth floor. She took a second step back, remembering who taught class on the sixth floor of Gossamer Hall.

That's Dr. Hastings's desk!

Her light would only go so far into the darkness above, but she could sense something, a little bit of movement far above her. "Hello?" Gretchen called out. "Is anyone up there?"

Her only answer was the thunder, which roared like a dragon from the depths of the enraged sky.

Gretchen inwardly shivered, and for the first time, fear trickled like drops of water in her heart and she no longer desired to discover the secrets of Gossamer Hall.

Time to get the hell out of Dodge. When she left Gossamer Hall, she would get help. She would find the security guard, wherever the heck he was.

Gretchen walked back to the marble pile, wincing when her feet touched the chips again, and headed to the door with the flashlight firmly in her hand. She looked behind her one last time before reaching for the doorknob. She turned it and, to her surprise, found resistance.

"Now what?" she thought aloud. She tugged harder on the knob, but it wouldn't budge. Gretchen held the flashlight up to the door latches, searching for answers.

She wasn't prepared for what she saw holding onto the door through the cracks.

Mary, mother of God, is that—

Gretchen threw out a number of different nouns: *slime, gook, spit, snot, boogers, green gelatin.*

Runny, watery, moldy . . .

Gretchen cringed when she reached up and touched it. She was prepared to feel something gooey, but instead her fingers touched something that felt like concrete. She exhaled a long breath. *You're really trying me now, aren't You, Lord?*

Gretchen moved to the side and worked with the latch on the window. When she tried opening it, it wouldn't budge. She held the flashlight up. Again, the green concrete thing.

Gretchen stepped back and held her flashlight up, moving the light along the tops and bottoms of windows.

Every single window, from glass to hinge, was covered with the stuff. Gretchen cringed.

I can't get out of here!

CHAPTER
THIRTY

I DON'T WANT TO MAKE *ANYMORE*, JUAN DECIDED WHEN he looked out onto the dry landscape of a place he identified as Fredericksburg, where a lone rider sat and waited to kill him.

"How did this happen?" he asked aloud.

Lily sat on the dingy stool in a corner of the room, swinging a bottle of a ginger-colored liquor from one hand to the other as if she were preparing to drink it. She had untied her hair from the cumbersome braids, and each tendril flowed along her shoulders, chest, and back like dark, glossy rivers.

Lily smiled at Juan, revealing the pearly whites of

her teeth. "You can't help who you *are*," she said, her mouth staying open on the last syllable.

"It's not who I am," Juan corrected. "It's only what I do."

"You are what you do."

"Okay," Juan said, gulping heavily. "I accept that." He paused before asking, "So, what is it that you do?"

Lily's smile brightened and darkened all at once. "You mean, who am I?" she asked.

Juan nodded. "Yes. Who are you?"

"When you ask that question, are you referring to who you think I am or who I really am?"

Juan inhaled and exhaled slowly, like he was smoking a very expensive cigar for the first time. "You remind me of a philosophy student," he said, and covered his mouth shamefully. "I mean that in a good way," he added.

This made Lily laugh.

"What I mean is," Juan continued, "they're always trying to twist their sentences around to appear deeper than they really are. You should see them on campus. They huddle in a circle around a tree. They don't talk to anybody but each other."

"Is that what you think I'm doing, Juan?" Lily asked. She opened the bottle and took a slow sip, closing her eyes while she savored the taste. "Mmm, it tastes exactly how I remembered it," she said, standing up and putting the bottle aside. "Let's see, where were we?" Her violet gaze stared up at Juan. "You think I'm a philosophy student, yes?"

"I think that you act *like* one."

"Is that better than being a crackhead?"

Juan laughed, despite himself. "Yes. It's way better than being a crackhead," he answered.

"Then we're making progress, aren't we? Now, what were we discussing? Ah, yes. Who I am. Let's see. I suppose you don't really care about me; I am, after all, over a hundred years old." She laughed hollowly and continued, "I guess you want to know about Lily. Lily Blythe. Lillian Franka Blythe. What can I tell you about her . . . I mean, me? I was born in October. That would make me a Libra, wouldn't it? If you believe in those things. Maron certainly did." She paused and took a deep breath.

"I was raised in Chicago until my parents were divorced, and then my mother moved me to Houston. Oh, I hated it there. I've never been partial to hot weather. And all the boys just stared at me like they'd never seen a beautiful girl before. The shopping was nice. The Galleria. Such beautiful things, when I could afford them. I used to sneak out on the roof of my mother's house to smoke cigarettes. Camels were my favorite. I stopped smoking when I decided I wanted to be the next Diane Sawyer. You can't be a news anchor with yellow teeth. I made that my goal. It was my climbing god, one that I could depend on. That's why I came to Brookhaven College. If I went to UT, I knew I would just get caught up in all things evil again.

"And what else?" Lily paused again, looking up to the ceiling, willing herself to remember. "Here's something terrible. Do you want to hear it?" Juan nodded. "Fine. I was raped when I was seventeen by my best friend's father. I'd always thought he was a pervert, and then one day he agreed to take us to San Diego for spring break, and while my friend was out with a boy she had met at the movies, I was in the room alone, and *voilà*, he came into the room and . . ."

Her voice trailed off, and after a short while, she continued, "Well, I decided not to press charges. I mean, it would have ruined my friend's life. She wasn't one of the strongest characters to begin with. Kind of like that Reagan girl in the history class, you know who I mean? The girl with the red hair. She was in love with a monster. But then again, so was I, and when I mean I this time, I don't mean Lily."

Lily's last words hung in the air like a cloud of smoke that refused to evaporate. She looked out of the window, her face sad, her eyes glazed over. When she finally looked back at Juan, her face was devoid of emotion. A smile once again tugged at the corners of her mouth. "Did that help at all, Juan?" she asked.

"That's very sad, but your troubles don't constitute who you are," Juan said.

Lily nodded. "You're right. I've been loved. I am very fortunate to be beautiful." She closed her eyes and turned to the window again. "Another one's coming, you know." Juan waited for her to explain, but she didn't.

"Another what?" Juan asked.

"You know. Another soul."

Juan coughed into his hand. "You mean another dead friend, don't you?" he asked, his voice betraying the sadness that grew in his heart.

Lily sighed. "Are any of them *really* your friends, Juan, really? You're not even friends with Lily, are you? Or none of what I've just told you about her would have come as a surprise."

"I have Mark."

"Mark. Yes. Mark." Lily opened her eyes and turned to look at him. Her eyes were the color of a stormy night. "When it is finished, you can go back," she said.

"You mean when everyone is dead?"

"I don't make the rules, Juan."

"So, I'm just supposed to sit around and let my classmates get picked off, one after another?"

"I don't make the rules," Lily repeated.

Juan swallowed hard. His head felt like it was imploding. "And until then?" he asked as a wave of helplessness washed over him.

Lily slowly walked toward him, her brown tendrils bouncing with every step. "You still want me to be Lily, don't you?" Her lips slid into a seductive grin. "Maybe I will be Lily for you. Maybe before you leave here, I'll make a man out of you. Do you like the sound of that, Juan?"

Juan didn't know what she was up to until Lily slid up right next to him. Her right hand moved around his waist; the other caressed his neck. She nibbled lightly at his chin, until her soft, pink tongue moved lower and probed his ear. Juan shuddered and moaned. Soon, her full, red mouth nibbled its way to Juan's lips. Juan slid backward onto the bed, and Lily lay across him, unbuttoning her blouse and guiding his hand to her breasts.

"I don't think I can do this," Juan said.

"How old are you? Eighteen and still a virgin? In my time, that would mean nothing; in your time, it means you're a late bloomer. Is that the term? 'Late bloomer'?"

"I'm not talking about that." Juan nodded to the window. "I don't think I can get in the mood when Josh—I mean, whoever that is—is outside the door, waiting to kill me."

Lily flashed him a slick smile. "Juan, honey, would it ease your mind if I told you that there was not a way in hell he could get in here and interrupt us?"

Juan held his breath. "Do you know anything

about the anatomy of a man?"

"I know enough."

"Okay, well, I can only, you know, rise for the occasion when I feel like it," he said. "Get it?"

"Oh," Lily laughed. "And you don't feel like it?"

"Not with Josh out there, no."

Lily's smile widened. "Juan," she said, leaning down to graze the buttons of his jeans with her tongue. "Baby, I will make you feel it. You can *make* a lot of things, but you can't *make* what I'm about to give you." And she started working on his belt.

CHAPTER THIRTY-ONE

POSSIBLE SUGGESTION FOR INCITING INCIDENT NUMBER 10:

Surviving four earthquakes in one night (indicating stealth).

The fourth earthquake rocked the ground with twice the power of the other three combined. The floorboards under Lily's feet quivered and then shook at full blast, and just before her legs were about to fall through, she bent down and jumped through the air at an Olympic height.

The burning wax from Lily's candle went flying across her face, hitting her on the cheek when she landed with a crash near the windows. Eyes squeezed shut, she listened to the series of banging and slamming and the shattering of glass around her.

The noise seemed never-ending, the earthquake eternal. Lily opened her eyes again, and she felt drops of water across her forehead and cheek, soothing the spot where the wax had burned. She felt the dense chill of night air around her bare arms and legs and slowly looked up and saw the sky above her.

I'm outside was her first impression, but when she looked closer, under the glow of the cloudy moon, it dawned on her that she was still on the sixth floor of Gossamer Hall.

The roof was gone!

"Tell me this didn't just happen," Lily said aloud in the strong voice she used as a self-defense mechanism when life became too tough to handle. "Tell me the damn roof didn't just crumble."

She could hear something—a voice below her. Someone calling her name.

"Lily! Lily!" It was Lars.

"I'm fine!" Lily cried in the loudest voice she could muster.

But tears welled up in the corners of her eyes, and she realized she was not fine after all. Her physical being was fine, but her nerves were near gone, and getting stuck on the highest floor of Gossamer Hall in the pounding rain with no roof over her head was going to take some getting used to.

She could hear Lars say something else from the floor below. Instead of maintaining contact, trying to yell something back over the thunder and the wind, Lily decided it was best to find shelter and work her way from there.

The moon gave more silver light to the sixth floor of Gossamer Hall than the floor had known in the past two hours. Lily cupped her hand over her eyes and looked around. She saw a piece of a roof still hanging onto part of the classroom where Dr. Hastings's desk used to be. She made a run for it.

It wasn't until she had made it to her shelter that she thought about Caleb.

Caleb and Mark! They were on the floor with me!

Lily's eyes started searching for some sign of the jock.

"Caleb? Mark?" she yelled. "Are you still here?"

They might not have survived the last earthquake!

The storm had blown the crumbles of wall, ceiling, and roof away with the wind, and Lily had a panoramic view of Dr. Hastings's classroom, plus remnants of the hallway and the two rooms on either side, and she looked around frantically, her eyes scanning every inch, every layer. There was no sign of Caleb or Mark.

"Caleb?" Lily called again. She shivered. Her

arms closed over her nearly naked torso.

The sudden beating on a nearby pile of rubble caught Lily's attention. "Caleb?" she called, stepping to the edge of the remaining roof. "Mark?"

The pile of rubble shook and moved, and the particles rolled forward. Some pieces blew away with the wind, but others remained like a warped yellow-brick road leading Lily to the pile.

Lily rushed forward and started helping whoever it was move the mass away. "I'm here," she consoled, ripping off the rubble layer by layer. "We'll get you out of here."

As the pile dissolved, Lily held her breath and waited for Caleb or Mark or some piece of them to emerge, but when a hand surged out of the rubble and grabbed on to Lily's wrist, she knew right away it wasn't the jock or the biology nerd.

Lily's breath caught in her throat, and she looked down at the mass of putrid flesh holding her arm prisoner. A scream started from the bottom of her throat and grew louder, until her voice was a roar that challenged the thunder.

Lily took her other hand and squeezed the stranger's fingers away. She was caught off guard by the mushiness of a hand that had no form, no bones, no muscles—just a wobbly bit of skin held together by empty veins.

Lily fell backward, her eyes widening with un-adulterated fear as the man crawled out of the rubble like a snake slithering from a hole.

"Lily?" She could hear Lars's voice from below. "What's happening up there?"

"Help me!" Lily screamed and sank to the floor, beginning a frantic search for Lars's knife.

It's got to be here somewhere.

Suggestion for Inciting Incident Number 10:

Surviving a sick, twisted pervert's attempt on my life (indicating courage and stamina).

Lightning scattered across the sky, followed by the roar of thunder, and the rain fell harder while Lily's fingers searched the debris for Lars's knife. Every system in her body, it seemed, was shutting down, and she could not breathe, it was hard to move, and her heart felt like it was about to burst out of her chest.

"Lily-cat, Lily-cat, is that you?"

He had a familiar voice, but it was not friendly. It was not someone she was pleased to recall.

But I've heard that voice before, she thought, and she began working through the corridors of her mind to discover the voice's owner.

A ghost from the past.

"Don't tell me you don't remember," the man said. "Come on, Lily-cat. Has your memory gotten bad at the ripe old age of nineteen?"

The voice struck the right nerve, and a name surfaced like a piece of shit to the toilet of her thoughts, and Lily shut her eyes to ward off the memory.

"Not you," she whispered, and she stumbled backward, feeling again like the teenage girl on spring break with her friend in San Diego. Feeling again like she was huddled in bed, listening to the door open. Feeling again like a hand was sliding down her back.

But how can it be? How did he know I'm here?

"Lily!" Lars screamed. "Jump!"

"That's right, Lily," the man said. "Jump. Run. Tell the police. Just like last time."

"You stay away from me," Lily hissed. "I don't know why you're here, but you'd better fucking believe you're not welcome."

The knife, the knife, the knife. Her fingers danced along the floor, searching. *Where could it be?*

"Let's not put up a fight again, Lily-cat. We're all friends here."

"I mean it," Lily said. "I have a restraining order against you."

"Restraining orders don't mean shit up here," he said in a threatening voice.

"Damn you!" Lily shouted.

She hated him like she had never hated anyone before. Her innocence had been stolen when her parents got their divorce, but when Dawson Alexander, the father of Lily's best friend, sneaked into the bedroom and stuck a middle-aged hand over her mouth, it was as if her desire to live had been taken away, too.

But the lesson from Inciting Incident Number 5 remained:

Courage was key.

It had taken three rape specialists, one psychologist, and bottles upon bottles of pills to get over the mess. Not to mention the follow-up sessions in the form of Dr. Phil, channel nine, two o'clock. Returning to the world of the living was not easy, but Lily was tough, and she had learned after her mother had left her father, and her father drank himself into a stupor and gambled all his money away, that death was not the only way to die, and Lily was not prepared to die in any form.

And I will not die now, she thought, as she found herself standing mere yards away from her rapist.

"Lily-cat," Dawson slurred. "You're one damn beautiful girl. I've missed you."

"Not again," she promised. "The day you do will be the day you die." As soon as the words flew out of her mouth, her hand flattened along the sharp edge of Lars's knife. She curled her fingers around the handle and lifted it up behind her back. "Come and get me, motherfucker."

Dawson laughed with such crackling disdain it

sounded more like a snarl. He stepped forward, and the click of his spurs scratched the ground.

Spurs, Lily thought with bewilderment and looked down at the floor where Dawson's boots were walking in her direction.

Lily's eyes widened, and her face tightened with more puzzlement than fear. Dawson Alexander was an accountant in a smug Houston finance company. The man didn't wear spurs. *Nor did he wear cowboy hats*, Lily noted when the shaded moon revealed a large hat on his head.

That's not Dawson Alexander, she realized, and her thoughts drifted back to the man who had attacked Reagan downstairs.

Were there two of them?

Well, what do you think, Lily? she chided herself. *Do you really think Dawson Alexander would have driven all the way from Houston to confront you during your night class at Gossamer Hall?*

It didn't add up, and it hit Lily like a bullet that it wasn't supposed to.

"You're not Dawson Alexander," she said, taking another step back.

He was so close. The gray moonlight lingered on the side of his mangled face, and Lily had to close her eyes to block the sight of the monster's face from permeating her mental vision forever.

"All men are the same. Ain't that what you say?" His voice was becoming more accented, more Texan, more country bumpkin. It was losing its Dawson Alexander, upper-middle-class snottiness and sinking into a sticky, redneck slur.

Lily's grip tightened around the knife. "What are you?" she asked.

The monster laughed.

"Lily!" Lars called.

"*Lily! Lily! Lily!*" the monster mimicked. "Now, who's that down there, girly? You're not cheatin' on me there, are ya, Lily-cat? Not when I treat you so good. Remember how it felt when I was inside you, beautiful girl? You tasted soooo nice." The monster stuck his tongue out and rolled it around in the air. "I need me another taste," he said decisively, and he lunged for her, the jelly flesh of his arms slinging across her side when she jumped away just in time to miss his grasp.

"Come on, Miss Lily, you're not playing fair," he growled.

Lily bellowed a war cry, and she launched herself forward, burying the knife in the monster's abdomen. She stuck Lars's knife far enough in she could feel the gook of his intestines.

The man grabbed her arms when she tried to pull away and flung her to the side. He leaned down, pressing all his weight on her, and she could smell the cemetery of his breath. Then he forced the knife out of her hand while she beat at his chest with her remaining strength.

"Just lay still, my Lily-cat. You're worth all this trouble," he said, and added, *"Did my heart love till now? Forswear it, sight! For I ne'er saw true beauty till this night."*

Lily cringed. *Did this crazy lunatic just quote* Romeo and Juliet *to me?*

She didn't have time to think about it. His mouth slammed down on her. The ropy flesh of his decomposed tongue deepened inside her throat, and she could taste the decay of teeth.

"No!" Lily shrieked when he let go of her mouth.

"What's the matter, Lily-cat?" He laughed and quoted Shakespeare again, this one from *Twelfth Night.* *"Love sought is good, but given unsought is better."*

"Okay, you creepy weirdo, how's this for ya?" Lily roared again and forced her leg into an arch, angled enough to knee him in the groin.

The monster bent over with a growl, and Lily had the time she needed to pull herself off the ground and grab the nearest object: Dr. Hastings's briefcase.

Oh, well, what the hell, got to do something, she thought, and swung it at the monster's head, over and over.

The monster covered his head and moaned. "Now,

Lily-cat, that's hurtin' ol' Bezus . . ."

Lily didn't see how. It was just a stupid brief-case. But on her tenth time knocking him in the head, the real force behind the briefcase-for-a-weapon appeared—Dr. Hastings's whiskey flask, which had always been talked about around Brookhaven College but never seen. *Until now*, Lily thought. The silver flask flew against a wall and landed on the floor, its KH initials glowing under the cloudy moonlight.

Lily hurled the briefcase across the room and made a run for it. She had no compass for where she was going, no destination, no sign. All she knew was that "ol' Bezus" wasn't through with her yet, and she didn't have the benefit of a proper weapon.

Where was that hole in the floor?

Possible Inciting Incident Number 10:

Finding the hole in the floor that saved my life (indicating finding and discover capabilities that I never thought I had).

"Lars!" she cried. "Yell so I can find you!"

She heard his voice to the left, where a pile of fallen roof lay.

"Lily-cat, Lily-cat, I'm comin' for you," the monster growled.

Not if I can help it, Lily thought as she furiously began throwing the debris away from the hole. She could see a light underneath. Lars's lighter, her cell phone. *Just a little more digging,* Lily thought.

He was behind her, moving closer. She could smell the rot on him; she could hear his spurs clicking the ground.

Just a minute more.

Lars was right under the hole, his one eye looking up at her. "I can see you, I can see you!" Lily cried as if somehow saying it aloud made her escape come quicker.

A sound like a low whistle sounded in the air, and Lily found herself falling over into the rubble. A liquid that was not rain ran down Lily's leg.

He shot me! The son of a bitch shot me!

"I don't see you gettin' away. It just ain't in the cards for ya," the monster said. Lily could feel his jelly hand crawl over the nakedness of her skin. "Yes, sir, ol' Bezus is gonna have some fun."

"Screw you!" Lily said hoarsely, and spit in the monster's face.

Lightning shot through the sky, and Lily could see the gun in the monster's hand. He was pointing it right at her.

"Jump!" she heard Lars yell.

"I can't!" Lily cried. "He's got me!"

Possible Inciting Incident Number 10:

My death (indicating mortality).

He was straddling her. "See how you like a piece of me," he said, and winked.

Oh, God, not again.

He held his pistol on her throat while he ripped off the straps of her bra. "Now, Lily-cat," he said, "you don't behave, you know what's goin' to happen to ya, don't ya?"

Lily squeezed her eyes shut.

Fall through. You can do it. Just lean back a little and let the debris take you down.

But if it doesn't work?

Remember what Dr. Phil says: if you don't even try, you're guaranteed 100 percent failure.

Oh, hell. What do I have to lose?

All it took was one last whiff of the monster's breath by her ear. The rotting stench of the grave. Lily opened her eyes and saw him for what he was—death waiting to eat her alive.

Lily was sure as hell not ready to die yet.

Inciting Incident Number 10:

Falling through a debris-covered hole to keep from getting raped and killed by a madman cowboy monster zombie thingy.

Lily closed her eyes and lunged backward, letting the darkness consume her.

CHAPTER THIRTY-TWO

GRETCHEN PICKED HERSELF UP FROM THE FLOOR AND cursed.

What in God's name has happened now? How many messed-up things can happen in one night?

Gretchen reached down and touched her scraped, bleeding calves. The rotten smell had grown in pungency, and the darkness remained a silent, unwavering beast that seemed intent to conquer all.

American Idol *looks pretty good about now,* Gretchen thought. She leaned against the wall and worked at trying to breathe. She had no anger anymore. All she felt was a vague sense of blankness, as if the last two earthquakes had swallowed the last of her resolve.

The earth was going mad. Was it Armageddon? Was the end here?

She thought about the green gook stuck to the windows and the door, keeping her prisoner in Gossamer Hall. She could still feel the hard texture of it against her fingertips.

You were wrong, T. S. Eliot. The world does not end with a whimper. It ends with four big earthquakes and green, indefinable snot-stuff. Sorry to prove you wrong there, friend.

The end of the world. Or maybe just the end of Gossamer Hall. *Well, that might be a blessing, wouldn't it?* But whatever it was, Gretchen had a decision to make. Not that there were a lot of options. She was locked inside Gossamer Hall, and she could choose to either sit on her ass and let another earthquake come or she could find a solution.

Gretchen knew what she had to do. She had to plow on. She had always been a solutions-oriented kind of gal. *To seek the impossible dream,* she thought. She bent down and grabbed her flashlight, lifting it up and examining the hallway, searching for a direction.

She discovered the elevator was right behind her. Gretchen leaned over and pressed the "up" button just when she remembered the power was out. *Duh,* she thought, slapping her hand to her head. *It just goes to show that even smart people have stupid thoughts.* She felt like the guy who tries to heat up a microwave dinner during a blackout.

There's more than one way to skin a cat, she thought as she opened the door to the stairwell and began climbing the stairs.

When she turned the corner, the light from her flashlight fell on something—or someone—in the center of the stairwell.

Gretchen faltered, surprised but unafraid. "Well, hello," she said automatically. Relief washed over her when she realized it was a student. *At least one person survived the quake.*

The kid wore sneakers and jeans and a letterman jacket. *A jock*, she thought. Maybe Caleb, the kid who had outsmarted Gretchen twice by passing a steroids test.

"What are you doing here in the stairwell?" Gretchen asked.

The kid said nothing. Gretchen held the flashlight up and walked closer, taking a better look. She couldn't see his face. His head was folded in his hands.

"Who are you? Is that you, Caleb?" Gretchen asked. He didn't answer. Gretchen sighed heavily. "What is your name, young man?" Again, no answer. "I've had enough," she said, and she meant it, in every way it could have possibly been taken. She'd had enough. She was sick of the night, of the earthquakes, of the storm, of the kid on the stairwell who wouldn't answer her, and most of all, she was sick of Dr. Hastings and Gossamer Hall.

"Did you hear me? I've had enough!"

She thought her shout would do the trick. No student wanted to be around an angry dean. But the kid still didn't budge.

"Listen here, buddy, if you don't answer me now . . ." Gretchen reached over and angrily tugged the kid's shoulder, and he fell over, his neck flipping his head back to stare at the ceiling. Gretchen pointed the light up, searching for the kid's face. And realized he didn't have one. There was only a giant hole where it should have been.

CHAPTER THIRTY-THREE

Juan leaned up and rested his head on his elbow, watching Lily retie the bow at the back of her dress. A slow smile spread across his face.

Lily looked up before he had time to turn away. "Ready for a second go?" she asked in a half-joking, half-serious voice.

He smiled. "Yes."

"Too bad. We can't. Not now, anyway."

"Okay." A silence fell over the room, and Juan reached over and pressed his hand against her back. "Do you know how long I've been *making*?" he asked.

Lily turned her head to stare at him. "No," she

replied.

"There's a long story behind it."

"We have time."

Juan's hand slid along the length of Lily's long, slender back. "I was four. I was in Walgreens with my mom, and there was this candy advertised at the cash register. I really, really, really wanted that candy. Begged and pleaded for it. My mom said no. She said she had four other kids to feed and wasn't about to spend her money on junk food."

"She made sense."

"Yeah, but it didn't make sense to me. I pitched a fit. Mom beat the hell out of me. I thought about it over and over in bed that night. It wasn't even about the candy; it was about being denied the candy. My mother spent half my childhood saying no to every-thing, and I mean everything, and it just seemed like one more thing she denied me.

"So, that night I'm in bed, and I just think about the candy. It was the kind that looked like it was in a tobacco bag, but it wasn't. Just grape gum, and there's a famous baseball player—Darryl Strawberry or someone—on the front, swinging a bat. And I could see it—every part of that stupid bag of candy. I didn't even realize my hand had started shaking until I felt something beside my leg."

"Let me guess," Lily interrupted. "It was the candy?"

Juan nodded. "Yeah. I was so shocked. I looked at it forever, wondering how it got there. I thought maybe my mom bought it for me after all and stuck into my bed when I wasn't looking. But I knew deep down that she hadn't. I was physically exhausted after I *made* the candy—like I am every time I *make*. So after I rested a while, I ripped the bag open and dug in, eating it to eat it, not really enjoying it. The next morning my mom saw the empty wrapper lying on the floor, and man, I got a beating. She thought I had stolen it. Little did she know." Juan laughed. He looked at Lily. She was smiling at him, but her eyes were serious.

"When did you know you could *make* big stuff?" she asked.

"You mean human beings?"

Lily nodded.

"Never," Juan answered. "I still don't know how it happened."

Lily cut her eyes away. Juan had the feeling she knew a lot more than she let on. He sat up and opened and closed his mouth several times, unwilling to ask the question.

"Go ahead," Lily said. "Ask."

Juan blanched. He had forgotten she could read his thoughts. "Who are you?" he asked. "Who are you really?"

"Who are *you* really?" Lily asked, her violet

eyes narrowing. "Who are any of us?" She laughed. "Those are questions Lily might think are cheesy. Do you understand *cheesy*?"

"Yes," Juan answered.

"Then tell me. It's her word, not mine. I don't know what it means."

"It means . . . I don't know . . . dorky."

"I don't know what *dorky* means, either. You're not helping me," she said, rolling her head forward. She stood up from the bed and walked toward the window, raising the curtains and looking outside. "They're still alive, you know," she said.

"Who?" Juan asked.

"Your friends. All except Josh, of course. But you already knew that."

"How do you know they are still alive?"

Lily turned around. "Because Mad Maron and the other two are still on the other side."

CHAPTER
THIRTY-FOUR

LARS DIPPED UNDER AND CAUGHT LILY RIGHT BEFORE
she hit the floor. His arms wrapped around her shaking body as he pulled her close, away from the hole.
Large raindrops splattered against his head, and he
looked up and saw the open sky with its imprisoned
stars and convicts of lightning escaping.

Mother Nature was a bitch, but it was the creature hovering above that locked into Lars's vision. The
thing was a replica of whatever had attacked Reagan.
Lars blinked hard, unbelieving what his eye told him.

"What are you?" Lars whispered.

The thing stared at him with its empty sockets.

"When sorrows come, they come not single spies, but in battalions," it muttered from Shakespeare's *Hamlet*, and Lars thought he heard a hint of annoyance in the creature's gurgled speech.

Lars stepped back, grabbing Reagan by the shoulder and pushing her forward with Lily still dangling from his arms. Every part of his body was twisted in different angles of obligation, and Lars wasn't sure how much more he could handle.

His eye glanced up again at the monster the moment the thing leaned over the hole, attempting to jump.

"Don't go too far!" the thing cried. "I WILL find you."

"You come down here, you're one dead motherfucker," Lars threatened. He breathed in, and the chilling feeling of indifference filtered through him like an old friend. *When you got nothing, you got nothing to lose.* A muscle twitched in his jaw, and he felt like smiling. The old Lars was coming back, the Lars who had murdered, the Lars who had murdered again, the Lars that could go for round three if called on to do so. *All for good causes*, he thought when the blur of his track record flashed before him.

He turned to Reagan. "Run!" he ordered. "I'll follow."

Another surge of lightning tore through the sky, and Lars saw Reagan was shaking her head. "We can't simply leave Juan and Dr. Hastings here!" she cried, and a growl of thunder answered.

Lars leaned forward on the balls of his feet, peering over at the two bodies lying on the floor. *She's right,* he thought. *Damn it, what to do?*

His arm loosened around Lily's waist. "Can I put you down?" he asked her.

"I can walk," she assured him, her voice quaking.

"Your leg is bleeding."

"I can walk," she insisted. She gave Lars a cold, hard, confident stare.

Lars nodded and gently placed her on the ground, his desire not to hurt her at war with his survival instinct. "Okay, here's the deal," he said as his one eye studied the hole. He could see the monster's shiny spurs with each dagger of lightning. Lars shook his head. "Dr. Hastings, Juan . . . I can't carry both of them."

Reagan nodded. "Lily and I can take Juan together."

"Yes," Lily agreed, though Lars was unsure. The blood gushing out of her right leg was looking pretty damn serious.

But it was worth a shot anyway. For what seemed like the hundredth time that evening, he asked himself, *What other choice do I have?*

Lars nodded and gave the thumbs-up sign to the two girls before he leaned down and picked up Dr. Hastings's limp frame. Lily and Reagan followed suit and picked up Juan, one girl at either side of his body.

Lars looked up and watched while the monster dangled above the floor. The creature's face turned suddenly and his no-eyes made contact with Lars's single eye. "You're next," he said, and Lars would be damned if the thing didn't wink at him with its sockets.

"The hell you say," Lars muttered, adjusting Dr. Hastings on his shoulder and making a run for it.

Lars was barely out of the door when he felt Dr. Hastings stir on his shoulder. The professor's steady, hollow breathing became wracked with coughs. "What's . . . the meaning of all this?" he heard Dr. Hastings ask.

"Oh, so you're awake now?" Lars grumbled. "Wait until we get out of this zombie motherfucker's way and I'll clue you in on a few things. Just stop moving."

The three of them ran down the hallway. Lars left the candles behind and had only Lily's cell phone, which was running low on battery, and his Zippo lighter, which was hard to keep lit under the circumstances.

A crash echoed through the building when the monster landed on the floor behind them.

"We gotta get to a safe place!" Lars yelled.

But what place was safe anymore?

"Lily-cat!" the monster cried. He was following right behind him; Lars could hear his spurs hitting the floor. "Don't run too far!"

With Hastings dangling from his shoulder, Lars

held his Zippo lighter in the air and waved it from right to left, looking for the exit to the stairwell.

"Where are we going?" Lily asked, breathless.

"The bottom floor," Lars said.

"Where are the stairs?"

"When I find out, I'll let you know."

"Look to your left!" Reagan exclaimed, and then she screamed, and the intensity of her fear raged through the hallway, over and over in violent echoes that froze Lars's heart in mid-beat.

Lars turned and held up his lighter. "Reagan!"

Reagan was no longer running, no longer holding Juan. She was standing straight in the center of the hall-way, the monster behind her, holding a gun to her head.

Lars took a step back. "What do you want?" he asked the monster.

Dr. Hastings must have thought Lars was talking to him and strung a slur of incomprehensible words together as he dangled over Lars's shoulders like a rag doll.

I'd better get an A for this, Lars thought wryly.

The monster laughed, his voice a dark, crackling hiss. "Stop running or the girl gets lead in her head," it threatened.

Lars stared ahead at it, unsure of his next move. Reagan's face was one of numb fear—Lars had seen that look before, years ago, in the car with Heather that fateful night when they had admitted their addiction.

243

Lars gulped hard. "What do you want from us?" he asked.

Thunder roared, the Zippo's flame blinked to near extinction, and for a second Lars lost sight of the monster. But when the flame arose once more, he saw the creature again, and it was no longer the cowboy zombie creature he was expecting, but someone terribly familiar.

Lars's breath caught in his throat. He felt the walls and floors of Gossamer Hall fade away, and he was once again on a dirt road by Juarez.

The man's red hair shined in the dim light of the Zippo's flame. "You know what I want," he hissed.

Lars stepped back. "Mickey. What are you doing here?"

"*Mickey?* His name is Mickey? You know this piece of shit?" Lily cried.

Lily. Lars had forgotten all about her. He looked over and saw the brunette was sliding against the wall with Juan sagging from her arms, her punctured leg dangling to the side like a broken marionette.

"An eye for an eye," Mickey called. Lars wasn't far away enough he couldn't see the miserable bastard's yellow teeth smiling at him.

"An eye for an eye?" Lars repeated. He laughed. "You have a lot of room to talk. Remember Heather?" Lars pointed at his chest and growled, "I loved her! You killed her! I thought you were dead!"

"Why, just because you killed me?" Mickey threw his head back with laughter. His shoved the barrel of the gun deeper in Reagan's temple. "A trade," he said. "The girl for you."

"Lars?" Lily was beside him, her violet eyes pleading with him. "Who is he?"

Lars glanced up at her. "Stay quiet," he ordered.

"You're dealing with the devil," she said.

Lars shut his eye and let the enormity of the situation wash over him. When he opened his eye again, he nodded. "You've got a deal," he said, and he flicked his Zippo off and stuck it in between his skin and the elastic of his plaid boxer shorts. He bent down and leaned his shoulder to the side, and Dr. Hastings slid off and hit the floor with hardly an altered breath.

"Good," Mickey said. "Walk this way."

Crossing the hallway took only a few seconds, but as he walked toward the man he had thought he'd killed a year ago, it felt like time itself had stopped, and Lars was plowing through the eternity of a single moment.

Mickey pushed Reagan away and grabbed Lars by the arm, pressing the gun to his temple. Lars closed his eye and waited. "Kill me."

"Don't!" Reagan yelled.

Lars tried moving his hand closer to his boxer shorts, close to where he knew he had his Zippo, but the smell of steel was enough to put the fear of God into him. His hand moved ever so slowly.

"Okay, wait a second, wait a second," Reagan said. Lars couldn't see the redhead but he sensed her anxiety, her fear, which had its own presence in the hallway like a fifth, invisible entity.

It was a shame, Lars thought idly, they would never have a chance to explore the strange spark that had grown between them in the last hours.

Reagan wiped her forehead and said, "There has to be something . . . some kind of an . . . I don't know . . . arrangement that can be made."

Mickey snickered. "This is the arrangement, darlin'. Just sit back, Miss Reagan, let me have some fun with your boyfriend first, and then I promise, it will be your turn."

A surprisingly logical thought occurred to Lars within the massive truckloads of incomprehension: *How did he know Reagan's name?*

It wasn't Mickey! Mickey wouldn't know Reagan. He wouldn't even know Lars had gone to Brookhaven College. *Hell, he wouldn't even know where to look for me! He doesn't even know my fake name!*

And Mickey had been dead a year—Lars had seen to it himself. Hell, he practically woke up every morning with the image of Mickey's body lying on the dirt road, engraved in his mind like an incurable case of brain maggots.

The Chocolate Factory song came back to him:

There's no earthly way of knowing which direction we are going . . .

Lars's breath stalled in his chest, and he fought to make sense of everything.

Is it
(not Mickey?)
the monster
or
Mickey
(just a hallucination)?
Am I mad?

It was hard to see the man standing next to him, hard because he was to the left of him and Lars only had his right eye, and his peripheral vision was screwed. He could feel the strain of his optical muscle while he fought for a glance—just a simple little taste of whatever was holding him hostage.

Finally, a reward. He had a quick glimpse of the man's profile.

Surprise, the man wasn't a man, and he certainly was not Mickey.

It was the monster, the eyeless, smelling, gooey cowboy. His hat was even in place again, and his cowboy boots, and the spurs that clicked on the floor like some sound track to the parade into hell.

"Easy, man, easy," Lily was saying.

"Lily-cat, don't think I've forgotten about you. I've missed you," the monster said and then quoted Shakespeare's *Hamlet*. "'Doubt that the sun doth move, doubt truth to be a liar, but never doubt I love.'"

Since when do cowboy zombies recite Shakespeare? Lars wondered.

"Just let the guy go," Lily said. "Whatever your deal is—"

"I don't think I made myself clear," the monster said. "I'm through with negotiations."

I'm here. See me.

Lars heard a whisper. The voice couldn't be real, but Lars opened his eye and there she was, to the right of him, coming closer. *Heather*. She was holding something behind her back and walking slowly, like a cat stalking a bird.

"Heather," Lars whispered. *It's good to see you again*, he thought, and waited for her to answer, forgetting that his words were only spoken in the privacy of his mind.

Heather pulled something from behind her back— Lars was guessing it was his knife, the one that had gone through the hole when Lily had fallen—and rounded her arms and thrust them forward into the monster's stomach.

Heather jumped back, and the monster lurched

after her. Lars took the opportunity to close the distance between his hand and his boxer shorts, and reached in, grabbing the Zippo. He lit it and held it against the monster's clothes.

The fire didn't start immediately. It was just a little flame at first, nothing to get excited about. But then the shit, as Lars's Uncle Frank would say, really hit the fan.

"He's a human fucking torch!" Lily exclaimed, pointing at the flame-engulfed monster.

Lars turned from the inferno and saw Dr. Hastings making snow angels on the marble. "Come on," he ordered, and picked up the old man by his shirtsleeve, slinging him over his shoulder again. Whatever protests the old codger made were lost in the moment of desperation.

The monster spun around, engulfed in flames, the smell of burning flesh mingling with the other foul stench. The hallway came alive with orange and yellow sparks shooting in every direction.

Lars looked over at Heather while she ran beside him. He reached over and touched her hand and she looked up, surprised. He smiled at her.

We're going to be all right, his smile said.

She smiled back, sort of. It was a hesitant half smile at best, but Lars took it as an endearment all the same. He thought about all their murky heroin fixes. They'd been through a lot of craziness together, dreamed up a lot of stuff while on the junk, like elephants forming out of subways, reptiles coming out of the floor, girls turning into men, and colors dissolving into sand. But this one took the metaphorical cake.

Lars thought about the e. e. cummings poem "White Horses" he had once read to Heather on a crystal meth-induced, all-night poetry marathon on their roof in Mexico:

> *after all are in bed*
> *will you walking beside me,*
> *if scarcely the*
> *wiggles in*
>
> *gesture lightly my eyes?*
> *And*
> *absolutely into me . . .*

"What does it mean?" Heather had asked, her pupils as small as a pen tip.

"Poems have different meanings for everybody," Lars had explained, confident in his junkie haze. "But I interpret it as Cummings asking his lover if she'll stay with him after all the madness dies, when it's just the two of them and nothing more." Lars had rested his hand along her neck. "Will you stay with me, Heather?"

Gossamer Hall, present-day, and Lars turned to

Heather once more while they ran down the hallway. "Will you stay with me?" he asked, and just like the night in Mexico, Heather did not reply.

"Nice idea, Lars!" Lily yelled in front of him. "Now this whole place is going to burn down!" She was holding Juan, but just barely.

"I wanted him dead!" Lars shouted back. He tightened his grip around Heather's hand while he struggled with keeping Hastings's weight on his shoulder.

"Well, thanks to you, we're all going to be dead!"

As the fire progressed, the air became toxic with smoke. Hacking coughs shook Lars's body. When he looked up and saw the red tubular contraption hanging on the wall, his free hand made a grab for it, but Lily, who saw what he was reaching for, beat him to it. She ripped the fire extinguisher off the wall and, finding its nozzle, opened the gauge and began spraying away into the hallway. The flaming monster raised his hands and succumbed to the bursts of cold liquid.

Lars let go of Heather's hand. "Lily," Lars began, "he's not dead yet."

"He's toast. What can he do?"

You'd be surprised. "Stop," he said, taking the extinguisher from her hands.

"Look at him now!" Lily cried.

Lars looked, flipping his Zippo open again. The monster was black, charcoaled meat lying on the grill of the hallway floor. The monster didn't even resemble the sort-of person he once was. Only a pile of black flakes remained.

"Lars?" a voice said next to him.

Lars looked up, expecting to see Heather, but instead it was Reagan, her wide, brown eyes reflecting more concern than fear.

Where was Heather?

Heather wasn't here. Heather was never here. It was just an illusion. Like seeing Mickey.

Lars placed his hands over his face. "What is going on here?" he asked brokenly.

"What do we do now?" Reagan asked. "What if there are more of those things?"

"My leg," a throaty whisper came from behind them. Lars and Reagan turned. Lily was crouching down, her left leg in front of her, Juan to her side like a discarded toy.

Lars flicked his Zippo and leaned over, taking her leg in his hand. He was no doctor, but he had seen his fair share of wounds, and the prognosis wasn't good. Blood was spurting, and a purple circle had formed around the wound.

She's going to die if we don't do something fast.

CHAPTER THIRTY-FIVE

MARK AWOKE WITH A PAINFUL, ALL-CONSUMING HEAD-ache that pounded his skull like a sledgehammer. The palette of black upon black painted the scenery around him. *I'd give my right arm to see light again,* he thought.

His wish came true when he sat up and his eyes made direct contact with the half moon above him. *Am I outside?* he wondered, and his question was answered when a cold gust of wind surged past him, chilling his cheeks with its autumn hands. Mark shivered, his mouth forming an O when he saw the destruction.

Something tells me we're not in Kansas anymore.

"Caleb?" Mark called, his head turning from side to side, looking for his newfound comrade. "You out here?"

Mark tried to stand, but a strong ripple of pain through his leg made him realize walking wasn't a good idea. *All I can do is sit here and wait,* he thought, and tried to work things out in his head, moving frame by frame through the night's events. When the list came to the present, he stopped and scratched his head, realizing he couldn't remember. It was like a black hole had engulfed this most recent event, and all Mark was left with was emptiness where a memory should be.

He breathed in the air. He did not mind the raindrops falling around him. There was a time earlier in the night when he didn't think he would ever see or feel raindrops again. *But here I am*, he thought, and opened his mouth, letting the drops fall onto his dry tongue.

So beautiful. But how did I get here?

Mark looked around again, lifting his BlackBerry to have a better view of his surroundings. Between his BlackBerry and the moon, Mark could make out that he was on the top level of Gossamer Hall, near the entrance to the stairwell.

And the roof? What happened to it?

It'd be nice to have workable limbs right now, he thought, glaring down at his broken leg as if it were the enemy. *It'd be nice to be able to walk.*

"Caleb!" Mark called once more. He refused to give up on the one person who had given him hope, the only other person who might be still alive in this nightmare.

Mark heard a rustling beside him, and then Caleb's voice. "Something knocked me upside the head," he said. "Shit, that's the second time today, man. The Lord's got something against me."

Well, if you weren't such a 'roid head, Mark thought to say, and decided against it. In the last hour or so, Caleb had proven he was far more than a common druggie. *He is actually not such a bad guy.*

"Do you know what happened?" Mark asked, craning his neck to see Caleb standing and dusting debris from his jeans.

"No, I have no idea what the hell happened," Caleb answered. "Are we outside?"

"Yes."

"Holy shit. How'd that happen?"

"Your guess is as good as mine."

Mark searched the roof again with his BlackBerry, hoping to find something that might help him remember. He gasped when he saw something unexpected. "Smoke's rising!" he exclaimed, pointing to the hole in Dr. Hastings's classroom where a light gray cloud was rising. "The building's on fire!" Mark paused. "Or, praise Jesus, do you think it's a signal?"

"A signal for who?"

"For whoever's looking for us!"

"Someone's looking for us?"

Mark shot Caleb an annoyed look. "I'm just being optimistic, okay? We can't be the only building in Austin affected by earthquakes." He added, "Please, please, don't let that be fire. Let's hope the rain kills it." He held out his hand, and the rain drizzled onto his palms. "Can you pick me up?" he asked Caleb.

Caleb nodded and leaned down, picking Mark up as easily as before. "Where are we going?" the jock asked.

"Let's see if that's fire," Mark said, pointing in the direction of the smoke.

"And if it is, what do we do?"

"Pray."

"I've never prayed a day in my life."

"Better learn quickly," Mark said as they came to the edge of the hole, where the smoke was barely floating out.

"There's no fire in there," Caleb said matter-of-factly.

"Or someone put it out," Mark suggested, and cried out, his eyes rolling back as another shot of pain torched through his leg.

Caleb noticed. "Hey, Mark, kid, you cool?"

Mark ground his teeth together. "Have you ever

had a broken leg before?"

Caleb grinned in the darkness. "Two of them. And one broken rib, four sprained ankles, one punctured lung . . ."

"Okay, I get it. I'm a wimp. You're a machine. Let's get out of the rain, shall we?" Mark suggested.

Caleb shifted him on his shoulder, inciting yet another round of toe-curling pain for Mark, and slowly walked to the stairwell again. "God, the smell!" Caleb cried, as he descended the stairs.

Mark sniffed the air. It was no longer simply the grotesque smell from an hour before. No. Also in the melting pot was the smell of burnt, charred flesh. Mark closed his eyes and shook his head, willing himself not to imagine what would bring about such a smell.

"Where is campus security?" Mark thought aloud.

"To hell with campus security. Where's that fucker who pulled a gun on us?"

Pulled a gun? A long pause followed as an image shot through Mark's brain like a bullet speeding through air—the image of a man (or *was* it a man?) threatening his life.

Of course, of course, I remember now.

The absolute fear. The shit-in-the-pants terror.

But the earthquake came, and . . .

"Oooh," Mark moaned, putting his hand to his face.

Caleb laughed. "What? You forgot about it?"

"I have a migraine; I can't think clearly," Mark answered. "But you've asked a good question. Where is he?" And an even better question: *What* was *he?*

"He's just some idiot still pissed about the steroid thing. The gun probably wasn't even loaded. He just wanted to scare me. You'd think they would be over it by now," Caleb said, sounding disgusted. "But in any case, I hope we don't run into him again; if we do, I'll beat the shit out of him, just like before."

A series of slurred words suddenly pierced the darkness.

"You."

Mark's heart picked up in pace.

"Can't."

Another added beat, another notch up the speed dial.

"Hurt."

Mark pressed his hand to his chest and squeezed his eyes shut.

"Me."

"Who said that?" Caleb asked. Mark could feel the jock's body shake underneath him, and realized he was just as afraid as he.

So much for the manly machine, he thought.

Think Han Solo.

Think Luke Skywalker.

You are a hero, and this building is your kryptonite.

"Is that Caleb-boy?" the stranger asked. "Is that

Mark with him? Well, ain't it a pleasure to meet you folks?" Mark could see the gun in the man's hand from the BlackBerry light, and his blood turned cold while sharp pains tore through his chest.

A heart attack, he thought. *I'm nineteen and having a darn heart attack.*

"What do you want?" Caleb asked.

"You ain't havin' no heart attack, Marky-Mark," the man said. "You're just a little pussy, that's all."

How did he know what I was thinking?

Mark felt Caleb's arms tighten around him. "You're one fucked-up dude," the jock said. "What's your problem, anyway? Did Ryan Gaskins send you?"

"Ain't nobody sent me but me."

"Caleb, I think we've got to get out of here," Mark whispered in what might have been the biggest understatement of his life.

"You two queers ain't goin' nowhere," the man said. "I got some business with you two. Yes, I do, yes, I do."

"This guy's one short of a six-pack," Caleb whispered to Mark.

"Get out of here," Mark whispered back. "Don't try to fight him. Just run. Don't you see he has a gun?"

"I told you, dude, it's not loaded—"

The gun went off just before Caleb could finish his sentence. Mark felt a sudden, sharp pain at the side of his face, and looked down in time to see a piece of his ear fall to the floor.

"Caleb . . ." Mark choked. Blood squirted from his ear as he reached his hands up to his head for no other reason than to assess the damage.

Caleb finally got it: the man was no prankster. The jock let out a demonic yell before his feet hit the stairwell. He moved faster and faster down the steps, never looking behind him.

We're going to make it, Mark thought. *A hero never loses.*

Think Indiana Jones.

Think—

The stranger's gooey hand reached up and grabbed at Mark's hands, ripping him off Caleb's shoulder just before the jock could reach the door. "Gotcha!" the man exulted. He left Mark screaming on the floor while he grabbed Caleb by the throat and pulled him backward.

"It's high time you answer for a few things, Caleb," the man hollered. Mark looked up to see the stranger's foaming, deranged mouth an inch away from Caleb's.

Between long, terrified pants, Caleb said, "Look, the steroid thing was just a joke . . ."

"Just a joke, just a joke. Everything's a joke to you, isn't it? ISN'T IT?" The stranger laughed. "I'm down for one, friend. One. The fun has just begun.

Ain't that the shit? Ol' Flat Shot here been sleeping for a long time. I'm a little rusty."

"Mister, whatever your damage, I'm telling you, it's cool, okay? How much do you want? I got parents in Florida. They've got a lot of money, just let me give them a call."

You can't buy your way out of this one, Mark thought. *He's not after money. Think Luke Skywalker fighting Darth Vader.*

The stranger laughed, and Mark held up his Black-Berry enough so he had a pretty good picture of what the stranger looked like.

He looks like a zombie comic-book character.

Correct that. He looks like a character from a zombie comic book specializing in the Old West.

Mark stared at the cowboy hat on the short man's repugnant head, and the muddy boots below his leather chaps.

Jesus, what are we dealing with?

Mark's blood froze. His limbs felt like popsicles breaking off.

But you can't be scared now. Luke Skywalker wouldn't give in.

Think like a Jedi knight.

The man howled when he pushed Caleb against the wall, the athlete flailing under his blow. Mark watched helplessly, yelling at the top of his lungs, while Caleb unsuccessfully tried to free himself by twisting one way, then the other, wiggling and squirming, contorting his large frame. But nothing could save him.

The athlete finally went limp against the wall, and the man snickered. "I ain't after your riches, bitches," he said, sticking the gun in the Adam's apple of Caleb's throat. "I already got enough riches to last me a thousand lifetimes. Yessiree. You ever hear of the Fredericksburg Massacre?"

Mark's ears perked up.

The Fredericksburg Massacre?

The man wiped his nose with the sleeve of his shirt and snickered again. "Now, who wants to go first?"

Not me, but just as Mark thought it, he saw the man raise his hand to Caleb's throat and pull the gun away in his direction. The barrel of the pistol was aimed directly at Mark's forehead.

"Reconsider. Please, reconsider," Mark begged, tears welling in his eyes. He tried to remember the speech Padmé had given Anakin just before he turned into Darth Vader. "You don't have to do this," he recited. "I'm sure you're a good person. Turn back."

The raw meat of the man's deformed lips turned upward in a dirty snarl. "Turn back? Reconsider? Naw. I've been considerin'. Considerin' and considerin.' I've been deciding between the two of you fools. Mark. Caleb. Mark. Now I know what you done," the man said, turning his gun so it pointed back at Caleb, "with snitchin' on your teammate and shit. Ain't no man with any balls larger than peanuts who snitches on his friends. But," the man pointed the gun back on Mark, "You're just a little know-it-all faggot. In fact, think I might take you out first," the man said. "Whatdaya say, Mark? Ready to meet your maker, the baker, the drink shaker?" He added, "What would Han Solo do? What would Luke Skywalker do, you little shit weasel?"

Mark covered his face with his hands while the fear freed his bladder. Piss exploded around his feet like an open well and pooled around the man's cowboy boots.

"Little turd," the man said. "Aren't you the weakest pig in the lot, Marky-boy? Couldn't even pin a tail on the donkey, honkey, could ya? What would Yoda do?" When Mark didn't answer immediately, the man screamed, "He'd blow your head off, Mark! That's what he'd do! Oh, yes, he would, oh, yes, he would, oh, yes!" And he laughed, and his laughter made Mark even sicker.

What would Han Solo do, what would—

Mark felt the sudden impact, and he was only conscious long enough to feel his brains blow out of his skull.

CHAPTER THIRTY-SIX

"HELLO, DR. KURCAN."

He was dressed in all black, from his cowboy hat to his leather belt to his boots. Gretchen had a strange feeling she should know who he was, but nothing immediately registered. She held her flashlight higher and gazed at his warped, melting face, and thought he looked more like a monster than a man.

Whatever his plans, Gretchen tried to stall him. "How do you know it is me," she asked, "when you have no eyes?"

The man had appeared after the fourth earthquake, when Gretchen had started banging on the windows and doors with a fire hydrant, trying to break the green mold on the windows and door. *Not that it worked*, she thought dumbly. Her mind was still trying to grasp the image of Josh Herzig in the hallway without a face.

She had turned from the windows, frustrated, sad, scared, tired, and there the stranger was, leaning against the elevator, and Gretchen didn't know exactly how to explain the dread that had overcome her, but let's just say, she knew he was no student.

"How can you know it is me if you have no eyes?" she repeated.

If the man had heard her, he did not answer. Instead he folded his arms over his chest, and Gretchen could see an outline of a smile graze his face.

"Dr. Kurcan," he said. "I wasn't expectin' to find you here."

"I wasn't expecting to find you, either," Dr. Kurcan admitted. "Whoever the hell you are."

He killed Josh Herzig, a voice inside her screamed. *Get out of here!*

Gretchen remembered Josh from the steroid investigations, what the staff and faculty of Brookhaven College had termed "Steroidgate." Josh had tested negative, but everyone who knew him said he was a close friend of Caleb Jacobs (who had also tested negative, but Gretchen didn't believe he was clean for one damn minute), and that he should be watched like a hawk until the end of the school year.

But not anymore, Gretchen thought sadly when she remembered the faceless body lying in the stairwell like an offering to a demonic god. The only reason she had known it was him was because she had looked through his pants and found his driver's license.

Lord, hear my prayer . . .

The stranger breathed in, and Gretchen could hear the mucus-filled sinuses. "I'm just interested in knowin'," he said, "if you know what my name is."

"No. Should I?" His immediate grunt gave Gretchen the impression she had given the wrong answer.

A series of thunderclaps followed, and Gretchen stepped back and leaned against the front door, working to regain her breath.

The man stunk. *So that's why this building smells like shit*, she thought. It wasn't the plumbing. It was him.

He pulled something from his side. Gretchen held her flashlight up and watched while the man adjusted the silver metal of a gun in his hand and pointed it at her. "My name is Mad Maron," he said.

"Bullshit. Mad Maron is dead," Gretchen said without hesitation.

"Mad Maron *was* dead," he corrected, and fired away.

CHAPTER
THIRTY-SEVEN

SCENE CUTOUTS AND PROPS, CLOTHES, AND BOXES filled the drama room from floor to ceiling. Under a plastic castle wall, Lars found a garbage bag of bundled togas. He immediately ripped them out and began pressing them against Lily's leg.

While he tried to stop Lily's bleeding, he assigned Reagan the job of finding "semi-decent" clothes for the three of them to wear. "Because another minute in my boxer shorts would be another minute too long," he said.

Reagan found a ragged shirt and pants for Lars from the Brookhaven production *Of Mice and Men* that he quickly donned.

(How handsome he looked in the 1920's poverty-wear was not lost on Reagan.)

Reagan picked Madge's soft blue dress from *Picnic* for Lily, and managed to slip it over the black-haired girl's head while Lars operated on her leg.

For herself, Reagan had thrown on the first out-fit she could find—the Blanche DuBois costume from last year's critically dissed production of *A Streetcar Named Desire*. It was a fifties-style dress, all chunky shoulder pads and flowers, hard silver buttons and straight lines. In a way, Reagan thought it made the perfect outfit. If anymore zombie cowboys crossed her path, all she'd have to do was hike up the dress and run like Stanley Kowalski was pursuing.

She took a seat on the floor beside Lars. He had positioned Lily on her back with her injured leg up on a patio chair. A mass of costumes surrounded her, and above her, Lars held the knife he had taken back from the monster's burning body minutes before. The Zippo burned beside him, the only light in an other-wise pitch-black room.

"I hope you know what you're doing," Lily said, and moaned when another surge of pain shot through her. "I hate you," she muttered pitifully, closing her eyes.

"I don't care that you hate me."

She sighed and opened her eyes again. "I don't

really hate you. I just hate the pain."

"I know. Keep still."

Reagan watched admiringly as Lars gently wielded his knife on Lily's leg, being as cautious as a surgeon with his patient.

(His rough, manly hands did not go unnoticed by her.)

"Those zombie things," Lily began, "do you think there's more of them?"

"I hope not," Reagan answered.

"I wonder what they are, where they came from," Lily said. "One minute I think they're just a couple of deranged lunatics, and the next, it's like they're not even human."

Lars snorted. "That seems to be the million-dollar question: *what the hell are they?*"

A long pause followed before Lily spoke. "I have something to tell you guys. You're going to think I'm crazy, but that one—the one we torched—I mean, Lars torched, excuse me . . . well, he knew . . . he knew . . . something about me. Ow!" Lily yelped, leaning forward. "Owwww! That fucking hurts." She raised her hand to slap Lars, and stopped, remembering he was trying to help her. "Sorry," she said, putting her hand back over her stomach and lying down again.

Lars ignored her near-hit. "Reagan, hold the Julius Caesar toga closer to her leg."

Reagan obliged, leaning over and pressing the white fabric against the wound.

"Lily," Lars said, "what do you mean, he knew something about you?"

"I mean, he knew about something in my life that not a whole lot of people know about. Are you almost done? God, where's Dr. Hastings's briefcase with the flask when you need it? Some whiskey would help."

"Dr. Hastings has a flask in his briefcase?" Lars asked. His lips stretched into a sideways grin. "I always thought that was a rumor."

"It is a rumor," a tired voice called from the corner of the room. Reagan, Lars, and Lily looked up to see Dr. Hastings had lifted his head off the floor, but as soon as Reagan opened her mouth to speak, to say something along the lines of, "Welcome back to the world of the living, Dr. Hastings," the old man's head fell back down and he became silent once more.

"I don't know what the hell is going on there," Lars said. "He was awake when he was in the hallway, too. I think he's just playing possum."

"He's a big enough asshole to do it, too," Lily said, and yelped again when Lars probed in her leg.

"I'm sorry," Lars said. "Do you think you can stop yelling, just in case another one of those fuckers is still roaming the hallway?"

"I'll try."

"Good. Tell me what the zombie said to you."

Reagan watched as the Zippo's flame revealed Lily's eyes glazing over in memory. A single teardrop slid down her cheek. "I was raped when I was seventeen," she said softly, and rubbed her hand below her eye. "And the zombie knew about it."

And so it is, Reagan thought. Even perfect people were never perfect. *We all have our demons.*

"How could he have known?" Lily asked.

"He might have heard about it from somewhere," Reagan suggested.

"Yeah, but . . . that's not all." Lily took a deep breath. "You're going to think I've lost my mind, but I'm telling you, for a moment, it was almost like the zombie had become him. Like, I looked at the thing, and there he was!"

"Him?" Reagan asked.

"My rapist."

"Oh."

Reagan looked over and saw Lars's eyebrows knitted into a frown, his teeth clenched in concentration. *He knows*, Reagan thought. He understood what Lily was saying. Reagan thought back to the hallway, when Lars had grabbed her hand while running from the monster. What had he called her?

Heather.

And the other zombie, back in the other room, had

known about Celeste, hadn't he?

Reagan shut her eyes. It didn't make sense.

But nothing about this night makes sense.

"It's like they know pieces of us," Lars said. "The worst, very worst pieces of us."

"Lars, please . . ." Lily begged, glancing down at her leg. "I don't know how much longer . . ." Her voice slipped away.

"I found the bullet. Are you ready? This is going to hurt." Lily nodded. Lars shrugged. "Okay," he said, and he reached in with his knife.

Lily's scream was married with the thunder; the noise took over the building, and Reagan had to shut her eyes to bear the weight of it. When she reopened them, Lily was breathing haggardly, and Lars was holding a bullet like a trophy up to her face.

"You see this?" Lars said. "It's gone."

"Good. Thanks. Oh, thanks so much!" Lily cried. "And what about my leg?"

"As long as it has pressure, it should be okay until we get to a hospital," Lars said. "If we ever get to the hospital," he added.

"But I can't move," Lily said. "How can I go anywhere?"

"That hasn't been a problem for Juan and Dr. Hastings," Reagan said.

"Yes, yes." Lars sighed and stood up, walked over

to the window, and leaned against it. He stuck his knuckle in his mouth and bit down thoughtfully, his one eye glaring into the darkness in deep concentration.

"Lars?" Reagan called.

Lars ignored her and slowly he turned around to the window. He reached up and began banging on the glass.

"What are you doing?" Lily asked.

"Trying to get someone's attention."

"The roof blew off the damn place, and no one noticed! Do you think knocking out a few windows is going to do much good?"

Lars turned around and glared at Lily, his one beautiful blue eye bulging out of his face with what looked like irritation. "I can't budge the window anyway. There's some sort of shit on it." Lars looked closer, prying at it with his knife. "It's green, like moss. But it's too hard to be moss. Christ, what is it?"

"Elephant moss is hard, but it only grows on the ground, like inside buried coffins after some years," Reagan said. Lars and Lily looked at her questioningly. She shrugged. "I took biology."

"Who cares what it is?" Lily asked. "Breaking windows isn't going to help us."

"Well, what do you want me to do?" Lars asked, sounding angrier. "Tell me, and I'll do it!"

"I can't tell you what I want you to do because I

don't know!" Lily shouted.

"Then shut up!" Lars yelled back.

"Both of you shut up!" Reagan interceded. "Let's stay focused here, please."

George wouldn't know me if he saw me now.

The three of them looked at each other for a long time before Lars said, between heavy breaths, "Reagan's right."

(The soft way he said her name was not lost on Reagan.)

He continued, "It's just that, I don't think you guys get what's really going on here. Hell, I don't get it, and trust me, I've lived in a world of shit for a long time. But this . . ." his voice faded, and began again, "is a whole different beast. It's like we are in the real-life version of *Night of the Living Dead.* Except, and correct me if I'm wrong here, in that movie, at least they had the luxury of lights."

"Yes, they had lights," Reagan remembered.

"Great bit of movie trivia there," Lily said, sitting up. "But may I make a suggestion? The best thing for both of you to do is leave me. Get out of here. Get help."

Lars shook his head. "What? So another zombie cowboy can find you alone and eat your brains for dinner? Don't be stupid. We're not leaving you, we're not leaving Juan, and we're not leaving Dr. Hastings's sorry, wrinkled ass!"

The room went silent, and no one else said anything for a long time. Reagan hugged her shoulders, her eyes gazing at the floor. She tried to do what she normally did in times of sadness or insanity, to conjure up a memory of Celeste, but nothing came. *And now what to do?*

There was nothing to hope for and there was everything to lose, she thought, and then shivered, feeling suddenly as if they were not the only people in the room.

Daggers of lightning filled the night, followed by thunder's loud boom, and Reagan looked up to see a man standing in the doorway.

Reagan managed to scream right before the man slammed the door and rushed over to her, folding his hand over her mouth.

CHAPTER THIRTY-EIGHT

IT WAS THE MOMENT JUAN HAD BEEN DREADING. HE stared out the window, side by side next to Lily, and watched while another rider drove his horse through the wind and dust.

"Who is it?" Juan whispered.

Lily did not answer. The rider rode up and stopped next to Josh. When Juan saw the rider's face, an unbelieving gasp shuddered in his chest, and he fell to the floor, pounding the wood panels with his fists.

"No! No! No!"

The rider looked differently than when Juan had last seen him. Juan was used to seeing him in black-rimmed glasses, wearing long-sleeved church shirts and beige pants, carrying a notebook with *Star Wars* illustrations.

The boy on the horse wore leather chaps and a tall, brown cowboy hat, and boots with spurs. His face was sans glasses, and a piece of hay dangled from a mouth that angled in a particularly menacing frown.

And yet Juan knew his good friend when he saw him.

Juan felt a pair of hands gently grip his shoulders. "Yes," Lily whispered.

"Did you know he was next?" Juan asked through gritted teeth and tears.

"No," she answered.

"You're lying."

"No, I'm not." Her voice was deadly calm.

Juan stood up and looked about again, brushing Lily's hand aside. *It isn't Mark out there*, he thought. *No. It couldn't be. Mark wasn't dead.*

"If I go out there . . ." Juan began.

"If you go out there, he'll kill you," Lily answered. "Don't even think about it, Juan. That's not Mark out there. Mark is dead."

Mark is not dead. He is not.

Juan suddenly felt the urge not to trust the woman he called Lily. Who was she, anyway? He knew she wasn't Lily, and it was impossible for him to call her by her real name, even though everything pointed to who she really was.

I can't call her by the name of a woman who's been dead for a century.

Juan didn't think about it another minute. *Mark won't hurt me. We're friends!*

Nothing will happen—

Juan bolted for the door.

"Juan! Don't!" Lily screamed, trying to grab onto his shirtsleeve, but it was too late. Juan was out the door and running toward the guy who had helped him score an A in his Organic Chemistry class, who had paid for the two of them to see *Star Wars: Revenge of the Sith*. A confidant to whom Juan had almost told his darkest secret that night at Amy's Ice Cream.

Almost, Juan reminded himself as each footstep brought him closer to his friend.

"Mark!" he yelled. "Mark!"

Mark was waiting for him, a shit-eating grin on his face. He spit out the piece of hay and tilted his brown cowboy hat, kicking his horse into a trot with Josh following.

He's smiling, Juan thought. *He's happy to see me. He's not going to kill me.*

"Juan!" Mark called out. "It's a pleasure to see you, my *amigo*!"

"Juan!" Lily yelled. He could hear her light footsteps following after him. "Juan! That's not Mark! Please come back!"

But it was too late. Juan watched, horrified, as Mark reached down to his side, and a glimmer of metal appeared in his hand. He lifted the gun and pointed it straight at Juan's head.

"Get down!" Lily screamed.

Juan ducked in time to dodge Mark's first bullet. His knees hit the ground, and the dirt blew up around him. His hands went defensively around his head, and he bent down begging tearfully for the nightmare to end.

"Stop!" he yelled at Mark. "Please, stop!"

Juan felt the grace of Lily's hands surrounding him, and somehow she managed to lift him enough to drag him across the dry earth. "Stand up!" she ordered. "To hell with you! Stand up now and run!"

Juan's took Lily's hand, and he rose as another bullet whizzed by his face. He frantically looked to the right and left, searching for the hotel's door. When he finally spotted it, he turned in its direction, still holding Lily's hand.

His legs pumped, and Lily went flying with him. He didn't stop to breathe until he reached the motel door. "What now?" he cried. "They're going to come in here."

"We're gonna fuck you up, buddy!" he heard Mark shout from outside. He could hear the horse's hooves beat against the ground.

"They're not going to come in here," Lily promised. She slammed the door behind them as another bullet pinged across the landscape. "Damn it!" she cursed.

Juan landed on the bed and hung his head into his hands. "Oh, God," he said, over and over. "Oh, God."

"Juan, look at me."

"No."

"Look at me."

Juan looked up. Lily stood with her hands on hips. "What have we learned today?" she asked, her eyes darkened with anger.

Juan's chest rose and fell with each hurried breath. "I'm sorry. I thought—"

"You thought," Lily chastened. "You thought." A silence filled the room. Lily sighed heavily and took a seat next to Juan by the bed. It was inconceivable for Juan to think that only a short while ago, he and Lily had made love on the same mattress where they now sat, one of them frightened beyond repair, the other one practically glowing with anger.

"Friends aren't friends when they're dead, Juan," Lily said in a voice that tried to be kind. She pointed out the window. "That rider out there—that wasn't Mark. Do you understand? That was whoever Mark was pretending to be in the séance your fucked-up history professor made you take part in. Zachary or Flat

Shot or Bezus, whoever. It doesn't matter, they're all murderers."

"I think I am starting to understand now. But . . ."

"But what?"

"Why isn't Mark—I mean, whoever it is out there—why didn't he follow us in here? Why did he stop at the door?"

"Ah. Now you're asking the right questions." Leaning over, she said in a voice just above a whisper, "He can't come in here because this is sacred ground. I was killed in this room."

CHAPTER THIRTY-NINE

STILL. VERY, VERY STILL. GRETCHEN KNEW NO OTHER way to be. The man stood in front of her, a gun in his hand, and all she could think of was the mess she had left her house in, the two cats that were hiding under the bed, the bag of pot sitting on the dining-room table.

She had cats because she couldn't have children, the same way she had a career because love wasn't meant for her, or at least, that's what her past said. She thought she had been happy once, with Bill, when they lived in Cleveland, when she kept his guests entertained and food on the table. If she hadn't seen the love note written by another man, she might still be with him, serving his every whim, from cooking his casseroles to burning the books for the tax man.

I took the road less traveled, she thought, reciting a Robert Frost poem, and closed her eyes. *And that has made all the difference.*

"Whatever you plan to do to me, do it," Gretchen ordered.

"You don't like to mess around, do you?" the man asked.

"Not if I can help it."

The flashlight. It was all she had. The big-ass flashlight she had taken from the firebox.

My only light, she thought. *But if I aim it just so . . .*

"What are you thinking, Dr. Kurcan?"

Gretchen narrowed her eyes. "What a fraud you are," she said. "Only pieces of shit have to make themselves out to be someone else to be important. Psychology 101."

"You think I'm not who I say I am?"

"I don't care," Gretchen admitted. "And if you weren't pointing a gun at me, we wouldn't even be talking right now."

The man smiled. "You're a tough filly, Dr. Kurcan."

"You have no idea," Gretchen whispered, raising the flashlight and throwing it at his face *(What a gamble. What if it backfires? Now I can't see anything!)*

and started running the opposite way.

It must have hit him. Gretchen didn't know for sure, but it must have hit and hit hard, because she had run at least a few yards before he started following her, his spurs hitting the floor.

"Dr. Kurcan," he said, "I ain't in the mood for no chasin'."

She passed into a room, what seemed like a chemistry lab. It hadn't been used in a while—the science department had been moved to a building in the center of campus, far more convenient for the biology and chemistry majors. Gretchen could smell the leftovers of methane and formaldehyde.

Gretchen crawled under one of the long counters, curled her legs, and tried to breathe. When the smell became worse and the spurs stopped clicking on the tiles, she knew he had entered the room.

It was true Gretchen had made a lot of enemies in her field (the path to the top was covered with many bones, as the saying went), but she couldn't think of one person out there who actually wanted to kill her.

A mental-asylum escapee, she thought. *A psychopath or someone who's just angry at the world.* She didn't even consider that he might be who he said he was. She didn't think for a moment he could really be Mad Maron.

His footsteps were quiet and drawn out, and

Gretchen could smell the disease of his scent growing stronger the closer he came. She closed her eyes, not wanting to see what would happen next. Another minute passed, and she opened them again, afraid of what she would miss.

A lonely Ph.D. with two cats, she imagined the obit would read. *The mediocre president of a mediocre school. Dead at the hands of a loony.*

"Dr. Kurcaaaan," the man sang. "Come out, come out, wherever you are."

The mere sound of his voice made her tremble like a leaf. She thought back to the green cement on the windows and door, the smell, the earthquakes, the dead kid in the hallway. Gretchen knew it all led back to this man.

She gritted her teeth and worked at staying calm. She was sure the man could hear her heart pumping at God knew how many beats a minute.

A light stretched out into the darkness, and Gretchen realized he was using the flashlight she had thrown at him to find her. *Not the smartest idea I've ever had,* she thought, and she watched, horrified, while he flashed the light back and forth along the tables.

The only way to escape him was to leave the room, she realized. The longer she stayed, the worse her chances became. There were only a certain number of places he could look before he would find her.

There is no way out on the first floor, but if I could reach the other levels and send a signal . . .

It was worth a shot, she surmised.

Tap, tap, she heard his boots on the floor, and she saw the light streaming closer, very close to where Gretchen hid, very close to finding her. *Don't make a sound,* she told herself while she gathered the courage to leave. *Don't make him think you ever left this room.* Gretchen looked out into the darkness, and realized she wasn't sure the exact location of the door.

Lord, be with me, she prayed.

The light passed by her legs.

Now! her mind screamed, and she took a deep breath and leapt forward.

CHAPTER
FORTY

"DON'T. DON'T SCREAM," A MAN'S VOICE WHISPERED into Reagan's ear.

Lily reached down and grabbed Lars's knife. "Get the hell away from her," she hissed. She might be one-legged for the time being, but she could still wield a knife. *If that's what it takes.*

"Please," the man said, "I just didn't want her to scream." To Lily, his voice didn't sound the least bit threatening. *In fact, he sounds as scared as we are.* She twisted her head and looked harder at him. A second later, the man took his hand away from Reagan's mouth, stepped away, and his face became clear under the light of the BlackBerry held in his hand.

"Oh, for the love of God," Lily moaned. "It's only you."

"Shut up," Caleb said in an undertone. "You're going to bring them in here."

"Bring who in here?" Lily asked, wanting to know if they were on the same page. *Maybe he doesn't know about the monsters.*

"Dick Cheney. Who the fuck do you think?" Caleb shivered, and looked at the three of them harder. "What's the deal with your costumes?" he asked, narrowing his eyes. "Did I enter a *Little House on the Prairie* convention?"

"Long story," Lars said, waving his hand. "Where are Josh and Mark?"

Lily watched a look of gloom cloud Caleb's usual cocky expression. "Josh left after the first earthquake. But Mark . . ." he began, and paused, seemingly unable to find the words.

He didn't have to say anything else. Lily looked at Reagan and Lars and knew they also understood what Caleb was unable to express in words. Mark was dead.

"Did you see it?" Reagan asked. Caleb nodded. "I'm sorry," she said. "How did you get away?"

"That's the strangest thing," Caleb replied. "I stood there, waiting for that fucking thing to shoot me, and my eyes must have been closed for five minutes, no lying, and I was talking to the thing, begging for my life, and then nothing happened. So I opened my eyes, and there was Mark." Caleb paused, tears welling in his eyes. "And . . . sorry, this is hard . . ." They waited, and Caleb finished, "But the monster was there, too, only he wasn't alive anymore, he was just this pile of bones and runny, snotty shit on the floor. It was fucking disgusting, and I'm glad he went out that way. I just don't know how it happened. I mean, it was like, right after he killed Mark, he killed himself, too, only I didn't hear another shot go off."

Thoughtful silence hung over the room for a time, until finally Reagan said, "One of them shot Lily in the leg," and motioned to the brunette lying on the floor, demonstrating someone else's misfortune as if to compensate for Caleb's horror.

Caleb looked over at Lily. "Crazy," he said when he saw the bloody clothes surrounding her.

"Yeah, quite an experience," Lily said with feigned nonchalance.

"The monster came out a lot worse," Lars said. "Did you check out the hallway on your way down here?"

Caleb cocked his head and rolled his shoulders back. "Yeah. I didn't see anything. Why, was something supposed to be there?"

Yeah, jackass, a burnt body! Lily wanted to scream *(jocks are so damn stupid)*, but instead replied, "He's out there, in the hallway. The monster."

Caleb shrugged. "I didn't see anybody."

"Bullshit," Lars said.

"I'm serious. Go out there, take a look."

"You didn't notice the burning smell?" Reagan asked.

"No, I smelt *that*—shit, how can you not? People in China are probably smelling that shit about now. I just didn't see a body."

"Okay, I'll take a look," Lars said, and shot Lily a disbelieving sideways glance before following Caleb out into the hallway.

The two girls sat in silence before Reagan asked, "What if . . .?"

"Don't even think it," Lily warned. "He's dead. He's got to be dead. We saw it. No one could have survived that fire."

But the face Lars gave her when he entered the room told Lily she was wrong. He shook his head and wiped his forehead with a tired hand. "We have a problem," he said. "There's no body out there."

CHAPTER FORTY-ONE

"IMPOSSIBLE," LILY SAID.

Lars shook his head. "I saw what I saw," he said. "You can take a look yourself."

"Oh yeah, let me just stand up and walk over there," Lily said sarcastically.

"That means he's in this building somewhere. Alive," Reagan said, and Lars could see her shivering.

Lars inhaled slowly. "I know this seems bad . . ."

"You better believe it's bad," Lily interrupted. "Very damn bad. Unbelievably bad."

"But," Lars continued, "there may be a ray of hope. I thought about a resource we haven't utilized yet."

"What's that?" Lily asked.

"Dr. Hastings's phone," Lars replied. "Remember? We were going there before all this other shit happened. The line may be up by now, and it's only a floor below."

"The cell line sure isn't up," Caleb said, pointing the BlackBerry at his face. "'No Service,'" he quoted.

"We may have a chance." Reagan looked up at Lars. A silent communication passed between them. "I'll go," she said, nodding.

"No. I'll go."

"We'll both go. Two is better than one."

"Then Caleb and I will go."

"Caleb should stay here and watch Lily."

"What? Do you think it takes a man to stand guard?" Lily asked.

Reagan shook her head. "Not just any man," she said, pointing at Caleb. "A muscled, football player type."

Lily chewed on her lip. "You have a point."

"I'll stay here," Caleb chimed in. He punched his fist in his hand. "I fought one of them once, I can fight them again." But his voice did not reflect the confidence of his words.

"Good," Lars said. "And watch over the other two, too. I think Dr. Hastings may be waking up."

"The other two? Dr. Hastings?" Caleb asked. Lars nodded at Dr. Hastings and Juan against the wall. Caleb did a double take. "Shit. What happened to them?"

"They've been out of it since the séance," Lily said.

"How did they get down here?"

"Well, that explanation kind of goes back to why we're wearing these costumes," Lily said, pointing to her country virgin dress.

They felt a trembling beneath them, and the four looked at each other as if to say, *Here we go again*.

"Another earthquake?" Lily asked.

"It can't be," Caleb said. "Five earthquakes in one night? In Texas?"

"God, I hope not. Another earthquake," Lars muttered. "That's all we need. Give me my knife," he ordered, and Lily handed it over to him. "Lock the doors behind us. It will stall them if they come again," he said, and grabbed Reagan.

"Good luck," Lily whispered as Lars pulled Reagan out of the room.

CHAPTER FORTY-TWO

THEY HELD HANDS AS THEY SLID AGAINST THE WALL, making their way to the stairwell. It seemed strange to Reagan, but somewhere within her fear and anxiety, there was a bizarre sense of security. *And it's because of Lars*, she thought, her fingers tightening around his. *Strange that earlier tonight I thought he would kill me.*

Lars carried his Zippo, and when they came to the door of the stairwell, he took his hand away to open the door and Reagan felt a loss of protection until his hand held hers again, and together they descended the staircase.

Reagan knew she had to be quiet, knew they were in a life-or-death situation, but she suddenly felt as if she wanted to tell him things she had not expressed to anyone in a long time. She wanted to ask him if he liked poetry, and if he was a morning person. Did he prefer baths to showers, and did he cry in movies? Did sunsets soothe him, as they did her? What did he want to do when he finished college, and did the future scare him?

If there is a future, she thought, and looked at Lars, wondering what he had looked like before he lost his eye, before the events of his life, traumatic as they must have been, forged him into the hard-ass person he was today.

The couple exited the stairwell, and Lars pulled Reagan with him against the wall. *I hope he knows where he's going*, she thought, because she didn't have a clue. They passed one door, then another. She could feel the jutting outline of wood trim under her fingertips.

"This is it," Lars whispered.

A noise came from the stairwell, a sound of footsteps ascending. Reagan gasped as a chilling fear began to bury her. Lars pulled her trembling frame against his body, and together they slid into the room. He put his finger to her lips, willing her to silence. Reagan nodded and the finger slipped away.

The footsteps continued, becoming louder as they

approached. Reagan held her breath and tightened her fingers around Lars's. *He's coming*, Reagan thought when the footsteps reached the door. *He's coming* . . .

The monster entered the room and shut the door behind it. Reagan could feel Lars lifting the knife out of his pocket, ready to do battle. Then he shoved her aside and launched himself.

The monster screamed.

CHAPTER FORTY-THREE

THE WOMAN JUAN HAD ONCE THOUGHT WAS LILY RAN her hand down her long hair. Juan shivered. He looked up at her solemn, tortured face. *It's as if she's reliving her death all over again,* he thought.

"I'm sorry," Juan said, and he meant it. "I kept insisting you were someone else."

"You had every right to believe I was someone else," she shot back. "Look at me. Am I not the spitting image of your Lily?"

"Everything but your eyes," Juan replied.

"What about my eyes?"

"Lily's eyes are hard. Yours are soft and, I don't

know, kind."

"Kind," she echoed.

Juan cleared his throat. "You said something a minute ago about the séance."

"Yes."

"Is that why all this is happening?"

"Yes. That séance," she said, contempt leaking from her voice. "They were all dead, Juan, all four of them. Texas's worst killers. And I . . . I was dead, too. Sleeping like a baby. Do you know what death feels like? Do you know what it's like to take a long journey somewhere, get home, and fall on your pillow?" She paused, her violet eyes moistening. "That was death."

"You're not dead," Juan said.

"Not anymore, I'm not." She paused. "Have you ever wondered how you can *make*, Juan? Did you ever know what it meant?"

"Yes. Well. Maybe."

"Maybe." She laughed. "You have the universe in your hands and you *may* have thought about how it got there. Just fabulous. A man blessed with no brains is like a night blessed without a sky. Don't ask me who said that. I might have made it up out of thin air. I *have* been dead for over a hundred years."

Juan stretched his hands in front of him and studied his fingers. He looked hard and found nothing. They were ordinary fingers, like anyone else's, and his palms were flat and lined, just like the average Joe's.

"There's no magic here," he said.

"You're only looking on the surface," she said. She pointed to her heart. "It's all in here." She reached up and touched her forehead. "And in here."

Juan remembered something his mother had said after they looked in the dictionary that day.

Your great-great-grandfather was a Monhu medicine man . . .

"The Monhu," Juan whispered.

"Monhu." Lily arched her back, massaging her face in deep thought. "Yes," she said finally. "That makes sense."

Juan looked over, his eyes wide with surprise. "You know about the Monhu?"

"Everyone in Texas knows about the Monhu."

"Not in the twenty-first century, they don't."

"Well, when I was alive, people knew of them. I remember meeting my first Monhu when I was seventeen. Daddy pointed them out in the square." Lily paused, remembering. "But let me ask you something," she went on, her voice sharper. "Do you really think it takes an ancient clan to *make* things, Juan?" She leaned over, her fingers brushing Juan's arm. "Any of us can *make*. It just takes knowing what you can *make*." Lily stood up, walked over to the bedside table, and opened a drawer, pulling out its unseen contents.

"What are you doing?" Juan asked.

"You want to know how all this trouble started, Juan? Do you?"

"My *make*."

She laughed again, a loud, hard-as-nails laugh. "Have you heard a word of what I've said? Anyone can *make*. But you carried a dangerous weapon into that séance your teacher talked you into. Heritage can be just as powerful as any *make*. Monhu or otherwise." Lily slowly leaned over and placed something on the bed. "Take a look," she ordered.

Juan leaned over and saw what was lying on the bed.

Strands of Lars's hair.

CHAPTER
FORTY-FOUR

"WHAT IS YOUR NAME?"

"Lars Case."

"Lars Case," Dr. Kurcan repeated. "Very different name. Is that Scandinavian?"

Lars thought the question was strange, considering the three of them were lying low in Dr. Hastings's office, waiting to be killed. *But we all handle stress in our own way.* So the psychology books say.

"I think," Lars said, "it might be Scandinavian. I don't really know my family history that well."

Lars watched as Dr. Kurcan reached up and traced her fingers along the minor cut around her neck. It was his hand, his knife that had left the mark.

"Sorry about that," he said.

"Under the circumstances, I understand. You thought I was a monster," she said, and then added, "I was the one who talked Dr. Hastings into teaching this class." She sunk her head into her hands, and her shoulders slumped.

Lars never thought, in a million years, he would see the dean of Brookhaven College express such vulnerability. *But there are a lot of things I've seen tonight I never thought I'd see. And I thought I'd seen it all.*

"Hiring Dr. Hastings doesn't really matter now," Lars heard himself saying.

"It does matter." Dr. Kurcan sniffed. "It does."

"The phone is not working," Reagan said, setting the phone receiver back in its cradle. "There went our last bit of hope." She shot Lars a defeated glance. "What now?" she asked.

"I don't know," Lars said. He looked around at the fourth-floor office of Dr. Hastings. The room was filled from floor to ceiling with books and papers. The desk did not have an empty space on it. The walls were covered with his diplomas and honorary certificates. Articles and reviews about Dr. Hastings's Mad Maron book were framed on the bookshelves, one leaning against the other.

"He wasn't proud, was he?" Reagan asked.

"Dr. Hastings has never been known for his modesty," Dr. Kurcan said. She cleared her throat. "I think we are dancing around the issue here. I suppose you have seen the man with the gun walking around?"

"Two of them," Lars said. "Murderous cowboy zombies seem to run in packs."

Dr. Kurcan shivered, closing her hands over her mouth. "The one I saw told me his name," she said between her fingers.

"'Crazy Murderer Freak'?" Lars asked.

Dr. Kurcan, unamused, shook her head. "Mad Maron," she answered.

The name echoed though the room, and its occupants went still. A cold chill ran over Lars. He looked up at Reagan. Her smile had fled, and a grimace was born in its place. "That doesn't surprise me," she said, her voice weak with fear. "The one who tried to kill me called himself Flat Shot."

"Flat Shot?" Dr. Kurcan looked up at Lily. "That was Maron's cousin."

"And fellow murderer," Reagan added. "He helped kill those people in the bank and on the street."

Lars walked over and reached out to touch the green lining along the window for the second time. His fingertip pressed against it, feeling its hard, yet mossy quality. *Elephant moss. The kind that grows in coffins.* He looked outside, into the night he could see but could not enter, and looked down to find that the floor of the earth was nearer than he would have thought.

We're sinking into the ground, he realized.

Gossamer Hall is no longer a building. It is a tomb.

The ground shook again as if to confirm Lars's suspicions, and he looked outside as the building settled once more. The mud oozed around the sinking stone, and the marble stairwell cracked from the top.

"What do you see?" Reagan asked from behind him.

Lars opened his mouth, hesitated, and finally said, "I see our death if we don't get out of here." He glanced over at the two women. "We are being buried. Those earthquakes we've been experiencing are not earthquakes. It's the ground shifting so we can enter it."

Reagan inhaled a sharp breath and walked over. "Where?" she asked. "Show me." Lars took her hand and pointed below. "Oh, my God," she whispered. She turned to Dr. Kurcan. "He's right. The building is going under."

Dr. Kurcan didn't look surprised. "There is no way out but the roof," she said. "Perhaps we could wait there, until day. Until the roof reaches the ground."

"Like sitting ducks?" Lars clicked his tongue against the roof of his mouth disapprovingly. "I don't think so," he said.

"What do you think we are now?" Dr. Kurcan

asked. "It is only a matter of time before they find us." She coughed, and her head fell into her hands again. "Damn him, damn him," she murmured.

"Damn who?" Reagan asked.

"Dr. Hastings."

"I told you," Lars said, "I don't think—"

"That Dr. Hastings is behind this?" Dr. Kurcan laughed hollowly. "Then you are a fool, Lars Case."

"Dr. Hastings?" Reagan asked. "But the man's a vegetable."

"He planned it beforehand," Dr. Kurcan answered.

"I don't understand."

Dr. Kurcan cleared her throat. "He sent me an e-mail tonight saying he was quitting Brookhaven College."

"To do what?" Lars asked. "Write another crappy Mad Maron biography?"

"It has to do with Mad Maron, but not in the way you think."

Dr. Kurcan walked to Hastings's desk. The drawer creaked when she opened it, and she began rummaging. "There's talk that in Mexico there were tribes that were able to *make* things. I think one of the students may have descended from these tribes, and Dr. Hastings knew about it."

"I'm sorry," Lars said. "*Make* things?"

"Yes, yes," Dr. Kurcan said. "First of all, lose the

tone in your voice that says I'm losing my marbles. Open your mind, because what I'm about to say is no more shocking than the men in this building who are trying to kill us." She paused before continuing, "I used to work with a man who was obsessed with studying the Monhu tribe. Last month Dr. Hastings called this man out of nowhere and got information about the ritual. I mean, Dr. Hastings really drilled him about it, like he was writing a paper. Only he wasn't."

"What do they do at these *make* rituals?" Reagan asked.

"The Monhu medicine men held a ceremony once a year where they *made* things."

"You mean just pull crap out of thin air?" Lars asked.

Dr. Kurcan shrugged. "That's what's said to happen."

"Sounds like a crock of shit to me. I mean, why aren't these people living it up? If they can make stuff, why don't they make cash and go to Vegas?"

"I think there are rules as to what they can make," Dr. Kurcan replied.

"Ha. Just like psychics. Forgive me if I'm skeptical but . . ."

"I was skeptical, too, Lars." Dr. Kurcan paused before adding, "Until tonight."

"What did the medicine men have to do for something to *make*?" Reagan asked.

Lars turned around and looked at her hard. "You're not buying this shit, are you?"

Reagan shifted her feet, looking uncomfortable. "I don't know. All I know is, in the last couple of hours, I've experienced four and a half earthquakes, a séance, and two murderous cowboys, so my mind is a little open at this point." She looked at Dr. Kurcan. "How do they *make* at this ritual?"

"I don't know how they do it," Kurcan said. "They either think about something really hard . . . or they hold a piece of what it is they're trying to create."

"So, what you're saying is, supposing Juan can *make*, he needed something of Mad Maron and those other three losers?"

Dr. Kurcan shrugged. "Hypothetically."

Reagan stiffened. "Well, I don't know where he would have gotten anything like that."

"I do," Lars said. He reached up and touched the back of his head, where he could still feel the tenderness of his ripped-out locks.

CHAPTER
FORTY-FIVE

UNCLE FRANK NEVER COULD KEEP A SECRET. ON THE night after their day of fishing on Lake Travis, Lars slept at Frank's house hoping he could stay up late and watch *Saturday Night Live*.

He had only been asleep an hour when he woke up to a bang followed by a string of curses.

"Damn it, fuckin' shit. Hey, fella? Help me out here, okay?" It was Uncle Frank.

Lars groggily crawled out of bed and went to where his uncle was sprawled out across the floor, his legs spread-eagled and his bloody hand gripping half of what remained of a Jim Beam bottle.

"Uncle Frank!" Lars cried, running over. "What happened?"

"Ol' Jimmy boy got to me." His uncle laughed as his hand waved back and forth in the air, blood forming crimson rivers down his wrist. "On a night like this, you can see everything," he said. "See everything," he repeated more softly.

Lars helped him up. The weight of his uncle was like lead as he tugged on the drunken man, willing him off the floor. Lars thought the mission was accomplished until his uncle stumbled, falling to his knees in the darkness of the hallway.

"Ah, shit," he said. "It's no use."

"It's just walking," Lars said. He was only eight and did not yet know the debilitating state of drunkenness.

(But I would learn. Learn tenfold.)

"One step after another," Lars said.

"I've got ten bucks in my bank account," Uncle Frank said suddenly. He placed the palms of his hands on the floor and looked up at Lars with bloodshot eyes. He reminded Lars of a dog begging for food. "Did you hear me? I've got ten bucks in the bank account. Your aunt's wiped me out." Drool trickled down his lips and onto the carpet.

Lars didn't know what to say. He didn't know what it was like for a woman to wipe a man out financially and emotionally.

(But I would learn. Learn tenfold.)

"Let's go to bed, Uncle Frank."

Uncle Frank murmured something under his breath. Lars wasn't entirely sure what he'd said, but it sounded like, *"If we knew where that gold was hidden."*

"What was that, Uncle Frank?"

"All that money. Somewhere." Uncle Frank pointed the finger at himself. "That money is ours, boy, ours! Somewhere in those hills. *In those hills,*" he sang.

Lars thought back to the discussion they'd had on the lake that afternoon. "You're not talking about Mad Maron, are you, Uncle Frank? You're not talking about his gold, are you?" he asked.

"Our gold!" Uncle Frank shouted with whiskey breath, his bloodshot eyes gleaming with newfound passion. He pointed at his chest again. "Our gold, boy! The man is our kin."

Lars finally managed to half drag, half pull Uncle Frank off the floor and walk him to the bedroom. The whole time Uncle Frank mumbled, "Kin, kin, kin, kin . . ." Lars did not even bother to help him out of his "I love animals . . . they're delicious," T-shirt before nearly throwing him into bed.

Lars went home the next night and watched his father drink on the couch with the usual TV tray of goodies beside him. His father wasn't a messy drunk like Uncle Frank. There was a near daintiness to the way he downed his whiskey sours while he watched CNN and graded his papers. There was something eloquently nineteenth century about the way his slender schoolteacher fingers gripped the glass and pulled it into the air and up to his mouth, and the way he lightly patted his mustache afterward with a lacy white napkin. Lars always thought there should be Bach playing in the background when his father drank.

When he saw his son staring up at him from the solitude of the hallway, he motioned him over with his drunken finger.

"Is there something you want to ask me?"

Lars walked closer into the room. "Mad Maron," he said, hoping his father would take the hint.

He did. "Ah. Mad Maron," his father answered, using a tone of reminiscence as if recalling an old high-school friend. He looked up with one arched brow. "Your Uncle Frank has been drinking again, hasn't he?"

Not unlike you, Lars thought, but simply answered, "Yes."

"Yes," his father repeated. "We shouldn't let you stay with him anymore. Your mother's right, he's a busybody." He reached over and clicked the remote control. Lars thought he was turning the TV off in order to talk to his son, but that wasn't the case. Instead his old man changed the channel from one news station to another.

"Is it true?" Lars asked.

His father looked at him. The haze of years of drinking too heavily and having to hide it seemed to cover him like a blanket, and Lars wondered if his father had ever loved him.

"He is an ancestor," his father confirmed. "A very distant one."

"Amazing," Lars said, his eyes brightening. The TV became a voice in the distance while he tried to register the wonder of being related to Texas's most famous gunslinger. "Does that make us special, Daddy?"

"Not really. When you consider what he did to all those people years ago."

"But what about the gold?"

"Old wives' tales," he said. When Dan Rather appeared on the TV, his father lifted his whiskey glass again to his lips, making clear the subject was closed.

Lars didn't want the subject to be over. He had been looking for a long time for something that made him special. Suddenly he was alive with images dancing in his head, Western cartoons and John Wayne movies and comic books illustrating gunslingers. Lars clapped his hands together in delight. He wanted to share his joy with his father.

"Dad!"

But his old man barely lifted a brow as the TV's screen reflected in his eyes. His son's joy came in second to national news.

"Leave me alone," he said with a wave of his hand. "Go bother someone else for a change."

CHAPTER
FORTY-SIX

ALL HE WANTED WAS A GLASS OF WATER. JUAN'S MOUTH
had gone dry over the past hours, and while he sat on
the bed with Brianna beside him, trying to wrap his
head around what she had just told him, all he could
think of was his thirst.

"You're thirsty?" Brianna asked, reading his mind.

"Yes."

"Would you like some whiskey?"

"No, thank you."

Juan sighed and wrapped his hands around his
head, willing himself to forget his thirst. "Let me get
this straight. You're telling me Dr. Hastings wanted

me to *make* the map?"

Brianna nodded, her face somber. "Yes. The map."

"But I *made* Mad Maron instead."

"Brilliant observation."

"And Lars . . .?"

"Of all coincidences, right?" Brianna chuckled to herself. "Some say there are no such things as coincidences, but I have to disagree with them. Or do you think the universe, God, whatever you want to call it, planned on Mad Maron returning back to life? If that's the case, I have to wonder about the intentions of the entity to which I pray." Her eyes narrowed, and her voice became softer. "You have to understand, Juan. I was not always in love with an evil man. Women were girls before they became lovers. Girls with dreams." She hugged her shoulders. "I had no intention for any of this to happen."

Juan moved back against the bedpost. He tucked his legs under him and wrapped his arms around his knees, his gaze never wavering from the beautiful woman who sat before him.

"Why aren't you over there? In my world?" Juan asked.

"Would you like me to be, Juan?" She cocked her head sideways, and a glint of humor touched her eyes.

"No," Juan said, feeling his face turn red. "I'm just asking."

"You didn't grab a lock of my descendant's hair, did you?" Brianna sighed. "That's the only way it can happen. And whoever thought it *would* happen? Congratulations for performing a miracle."

"And these are not the days of miracles." Juan looked away from Brianna to the window, where two horsemen resembling his former classmates waited to kill him. "There had to be another way," Juan mumbled, his words choking together from his dry tongue, "to get Mad Maron and the other two back here without killing more people."

A hoarse sound came from Brianna's throat. "If there is, I'd like you to tell me about it."

Juan's eyes moistened with sadness. *If I ever want to sleep again, I have to save them,* he thought. He looked outside at Mark on the horse. He might have been a scientist one day, a great doctor or biologist, maybe even a rocket scientist. But after tonight, the world would never know him.

An idea flashed before him. "Does this place," Juan motioned around him, "really exist?"

Brianna arched a brow. "Fredericksburg? Of course."

"No. I mean, yes, Fredericksburg, but I mean this Fredericksburg that we are in now?"

Brianna grinned. "In some contexts. Everything has its own time."

"I never took philosophy, so I'll take that for a yes.

Does that mean I can go anywhere?" Juan was feeling irritable. His body was trembling from dehydration.

Brianna tilted her head back, her face deepening into a pensive frown. "I suppose. As long as it existed in 1890," she said.

"In my day, the Monhu are spread throughout America, but in 1890, they're still clustered together, aren't they?" Brianna shrugged. *Let me try a different approach*, Juan thought, and said, "You said everyone knew the Monhu. Does that mean there are Monhu here, in Fredericksburg?"

"Not in Fredericksburg. But very nearby, yes."

"How nearby?"

Brianna cocked her head. "Nearby enough."

"A horse's ride?"

"Yes."

"I want to go there."

She shook her head. "I don't think that's possible."

"You told me anywhere is possible, as long as it existed now."

Brianna sighed. "Juan. Listen to me. The only way out of here is through them," she said, pointing outside.

"Yes. I know. What do you think I should do?"

Brianna tapped her fingers along Juan's hands. "I think you should *make*," she whispered.

"*Make* what?"

"What can you *make*?"

Juan recited everything he could ever remember *making* (except for the occasional porno video). When he was finished, Brianna looked unimpressed.

"That's quite boring," she said.

"Well, what is it you want?" Juan asked hoarsely. *My kingdom, my kingdom for a glass of water.*

"I don't know." Brianna craned her neck to look outside the window. "They can't be killed," she muttered. "It's a matter of outrunning them, or distracting them so they don't know we left."

Juan felt his fingers wriggle, and he looked down while a familiar tingle spread against his palm. *I'm about to* make, he realized. *But what?*

CHAPTER FORTY-SEVEN

CALEB LEANED AGAINST THE WALL BESIDE THE DOOR. Only Mark's BlackBerry cast a yellow light, and it was low and dying. Caleb looked at Lily lying on the floor. She was facing the ceiling, and her lips were pinched in an uncomfortable frown.

Partly to quench his nervousness and fear, partly because he actually cared, Caleb asked, rather hoarsely, "So . . . what do you like to do in your spare time?"

Lily turned her head to look at him, her expression pained. "My leg is killing me," she said. "I don't feel like small talk, if that's okay with you."

"Okay." Caleb looked away and began whistling

to himself. So, she was the uptight snob he had thought she was. *Sometimes*, he thought, *it's better when people prove to be exactly who you thought they were all along.*

A minute passed, and Lily said, "Fine. Do you really want to know? I play tennis on the weekends."

"That's cool. I never play tennis. I'm too clumsy. Is that all you do?"

"I watch television, too."

"Oh. What do you watch?"

"The news."

"The news? Why?"

Lily sighed. "Caleb . . . that's your name, isn't it?"

"Yeah."

"Do you know how stupid you sound when you ask me why I watch the news? Don't you care what's going on in the world?" She snorted. "It's people like you who elect the people who are in power now."

"For your information, I don't vote, but I'm glad that people like you use people like me to make yourselves feel better," Caleb said as the first flames of anger rose in him.

"You choose to be you," Lily said. "I didn't force you to be an idiot."

That's enough, Caleb thought, kicking his foot off the wall and walking toward Lily. "Snotty little bitch. Let me put this to you my way. *You* might be one of those who organize the game, promote the game, cheer at the game, but I'm the one who plays! Without me, you have a program with no act! You got that?"

"Shut up!" Lily spat. "You'll bring them in here, you fool!"

"People like you really piss me off," Caleb muttered, knowing Lily was right. He *had* been talking too loud.

The knock on the door came suddenly, without forewarning. It was so loud Caleb jumped.

Another, louder knock followed. Caleb waited for Lars or Reagan to say something, but no voice came.

Caleb looked at Lily as if to ask, *Should I open it?*

Lily shook her head. "What if it's the zombie?"

"What if it's Lars or Reagan?" Caleb whispered back.

The room darkened when the BlackBerry died out, and the two of them were left in complete darkness with a decision to make. *What should they do?*

CHAPTER FORTY-EIGHT

"UH, SO YOU'RE SAYING THERE ARE ZOMBIE MONSTERS crawling around Gossamer Hall because you're related to Mad Maron?" Reagan asked. Her face was frozen in stunned shock, like she had just survived falling off a cliff.

Reagan watched Lars look down at his shaking hands. "He's like my great-great-great-uncle, or something like that," he said. "My family never really shared the story with me."

Dr. Kurcan shook her head. "Un-fucking-believable."

Lars shrugged. "When I was a child, I told everyone I knew I was related to him, but when I got older, I don't know, it just didn't seem cool to be related to a serial-killing madman gunslinger."

"I just can't believe it," Dr. Kurcan said and stood up. "And I thought it was interesting to have a cousin who worked on the set of *Cheers*. You have me beat, Lars Case."

Lars flashed a vague smile. "Don't kick me out of school for it or anything." His smile slowly faded. "Do you hear that?" he asked. He glanced up at the door.

The room went silent. In the background, just a smidgen above silence, was a tap, followed by another.

"Footsteps," Reagan whispered, her eyes growing wide.

No, please, no . . .

Reagan glanced at Lars for confirmation. He nodded and stretched out his hand, and she took it, moving over to his side.

Lightning, followed by thunder, and the night continued to weep with blood from the sky. The shadows outside the window cast their secrets onto Dr. Kurcan's face while she crept to the other side of the door, her finger pressed up to her lips to silence the other two occupants.

As if we need quieting, Reagan thought. She had become old hat at being very still. She turned to look at Lars. He smiled at her one last time before flipping the lid of his Zippo, blanketing the room into total darkness.

If I die, I will not die alone, Reagan thought when she felt the rough lines of Lars's palms, followed by a voice from behind the door:

"*Gregory Maroon? Gregory Maroon? I've got your number, buddy.*"

The yell was followed by boots tapping against the marble as the cowboy walked closer. The all-too-familiar *click click* of spurs hitting the floor sent Reagan's heart beating out of her chest.

"*Gregory Maroooooon!*" the voice shouted again.

Reagan's eyes did not leave Lars's face. "Who is that?" she asked him.

But it was Dr. Kurcan who answered. "Who do you think?"

Reagan shook her head, her gaze turning to the dean. "No, I mean, who is Gregory Maroon?"

"Gregory Maroon!" the monster yelled. "I got my eyes out for you, boy! I sure am goin' to love chattin' with you. I wanna hear every detail about Mexico, about the girl, about Mickey, all the bits and pieces, buddy. You hear me, brother? I'm comin' for you!"

"Gregory Maroon," Reagan whispered. "He has to be somewhere in this school."

"What makes you think he's anybody?" Dr. Kurcan asked. "Maybe Maron's making him up."

324

"No," Reagan replied. "He's someone. Because those creatures, for whatever reason, know our names, and that means someone else in this building is here, and his name is Gregory Maroon."

"There's no one else in this building," Lars said quietly.

Reagan looked up at Lars again. "I beg to differ—"

Lars shook his head. "Please believe me," he whispered solemnly. His gaze told her there was much she needed to know, much he had to tell her, and little time to tell it.

"There's someone else," Reagan insisted, squeezing his hand.

"No. Really. There's no one else," Lars said. "Just trust me, okay?"

"Then why is he calling out for Gregory Maroon?"

Lars gulped. Reagan could feel his pulse quicken through the veins in his hands. Her eyes widened. "Tell me," she begged. "Tell me."

Lars's gaze did not waver when he said, "He calls for Gregory Maroon because that is my name. My real name is Gregory Maroon."

CHAPTER FORTY-NINE

DR. HASTINGS AWAKENED TO A SERIES OF VOICES IN THE darkness of a mind that was still half-dim with sleep.

Where am I?

He turned and looked beside him. The silver light of the moon revealed Juan Fuentes lying next to him, the kid's cheek pressed to the floor. His eyes were closed as if in deep sleep, and his chest fell with shallow breaths just loud enough for Dr. Hastings to hear.

Dr. Hastings tried to think back to what had happened, why he was on the floor next to his prize student. He twisted his head from side to side, searching for who or what else was in the room with them, but the darkness posed an impenetrable barrier.

Am I still in Gossamer Hall? he wondered.

"Don't open the door," a girl's voice whispered.

The voice was familiar to Dr. Hastings, but trying to put a name or a face to it was like reaching for air. His mind remained boggled that someone continued to knock loudly on the door.

Wednesday night. I had class. We studied Mad Maron.

The séance, Dr. Hastings remembered suddenly. His greed veiled by a seemingly honorable ode to the intellectual world, his homage to the great thinkers of the Enlightenment Period. Everything, Dr. Hastings thought, was going perfectly, better than he had hoped. The kids were really getting into it; even the creepy one-eyed guy seemed to enjoy playing Mad Maron. Dr. Hastings had felt victory was in hand.

Then something had gone wrong.

The earthquake! I fell through the floor!

Dr. Hastings felt the heavy weight of defeat on his chest. *The séance didn't work,* he realized. *I am still a poor man.*

(Too bad I sent that e-mail to Dr. Kurcan.)

Dr. Hastings sat up slowly, his jaw tightening when a surge of violent pain shot up his back. "What's the meaning of this?" he asked through clenched teeth. "Where am I?"

His words were met with a chorus of *shhhs* and the *pat pat* of feet rushing to his side, and a large hand pressing over his mouth. "Let me go," Dr. Hastings ordered under someone's sweaty flesh, and fought his attacker with a weak, tired fist.

But the man was strong and easily defended himself. "There is a murderer outside our door," he hissed in the professor's ear. "Try not to say a word." The man's voice was also vaguely familiar to Dr. Hastings.

The pounding on the door continued, followed by the sound of someone kicking through wood. "Oh, God!" a girl's voice squealed. "He's coming for us!"

The man uncovered Dr. Hastings's mouth. "Stop yelling," he whispered to the girl. "He knows we're in here."

"He's known we were in here!" Her muffled cry filled the room. "I have no chance . . . not with my leg . . ."

"You're in a world of shit," Dr. Hastings growled as he tried to stand, but his legs failed and he fell to his knees. The man tried to push him flat to the ground with two rough hands, but Dr. Hastings had found a will somewhere, and his would-be captor, it seemed, had a million other fires to put out.

"Who is kicking through the door?" Dr. Hastings asked. "I demand to know!"

Dr. Hastings felt a violent push on his chest and he tumbled over, face-first, to the floor. "Dr. Fuckings," he heard the man say, "you're right, we are in a world of shit, far more than you know." The voice was solemn and scared and angry at once, and Dr. Hastings finally recognized it.

"Well, well, well, if it isn't Caleb Jacobs," Dr. Hastings said, and laughed to himself. "I should have known a punk like you would be the one stirring up this trouble."

"Dr. Hastings, please shut up . . ."

The kicking grew louder, until the room came alive with the crash of a door hitting the floor and the rage of an unknown presence whose seething hatred chilled Dr. Hastings to the very bone. Caleb moved away from Dr. Hastings and, from what Dr. Hastings could see, jumped on the intruder.

"Die, you motherfucker, die!"

"Stop!" Dr. Hastings shouted, trying to breathe through the stench, but the two men continued fighting like drunks in a bar brawl. "The two of you must stop!" Dr. Hastings yelled. "I don't know what's going on here, but stop before I have you both suspended!"

I can't breathe, I can't breathe, I can't breathe.

The room erupted with more laughter from the invading stranger, followed by the sounds of desks breaking and screams from the girl.

I can't breathe . . .

Silence, oddly louder than the chaos, filled the

room, followed by soft moaning. Dr. Hastings knew that somewhere, very near, there was a winner and a loser. But who was who?

"Dr. Killian Hastings? Are you here to join us, partner?"

(I know what haunts you, buddy boy.)

Dr. Hastings didn't know who to respond to first, the intruder or the strange voice that had somehow echoed through his head. *It's not my voice*, he thought. *Not my inner thoughts.*

(Be careful, I can hear you.)

"Answer me, Dr. Hastings. I sure am darn tootin' dyin' to talk to you."

Dr. Hastings blinked and cleared his throat. "What is your name, young man?" he asked, though he was not sure that he was actually speaking to a young man.

"You should know my name, my pal. You should know my name real damn well. Hell, you spent half a year looking shit up about me. You probably know me better than I know me." And he laughed.

With each slow, threatening word the stranger spoke, a breath of smoke blew into the air and clouded Dr. Hastings's eyes with the threat of untold danger.

(Bezus Smith is my name . . . don't you know my name . . . don't you know?)

"I do not know your name," Dr. Hastings replied, blocking out the voice inside his head *(it can't be him,*

it just can't be). "But I do know you will be immediately expelled from school once I report you to the
disciplinary committee. As for you, Caleb Jacobs, you
should know better than to be getting into more trouble after the steroid episode you dragged yourself and
your fellow athletes into. You made a mockery out of
the marriage of education and sports."

There was no answer but

(How about a gift, Dr. Hastings?)

a pile of something that flew across the room, hitting Dr. Hastings in the eye, and knocking him onto
his back.

Dr. Hastings, one eye bleeding, reached over to
feel what had hit him. His hand landed on hair, followed by skin, and his blind fingers traveled down the
width of a muscular arm.

"Dr. Hastings," Caleb murmured. "Get out of here."

"Dr. Hastings, please stay," the other man urged.
"You are welcome company." The man's accent was
thick as sand in the Texas desert.

*(I'll eat you alive, you pansy piece of shit, come
closer.)*

"What are you doing in Gossamer Hall?" Dr.
Hastings demanded. "Who are you?"

"Hell's bells, Dr. Hastings, you know who I am."

(Bezus Bezus Bezus Bezus)

"Dr. Hastings," Dr. Hastings recognized as Lily

331

Blythe's voice. "Please, please leave. Go for help."

"I'll get to you, Lily-cat!" the man promised. "Don't you worry none. I'll get to you!"

Dr. Hastings felt a pudding hand reach out in the darkness and take hold of his arm. The next thing he knew, he was flying through the air and yelped with pain when he crashed into a cardboard cutout of drama-club scenery. He heard footsteps as the man rushed toward him again.

"Leave me alone," Dr. Hastings cried. "I am an old man."

The stranger's gooey hand grabbed Dr. Hastings's neck and squeezed. The professor gagged and kicked, his eyes bulging out of their sockets while the air left his lungs. "Stop . . . stop," he begged.

His answer was unyielding laughter. Then he was lifted off the ground and held in midair. The professor coughed; all he could inhale was the scent of death and the flames.

"Like what you brought back, Dr. Hastin's?" the stranger said.

(Don't pretend to not know.)

"What . . . I . . . brought . . . back?" Dr. Hastings asked.

"Take a good look!" the stranger ordered, and peeled open the black crust of his chest, revealing a fire burning where his intestines once lived. The flame flared out of his abdomen like a blowtorch.

Dr. Hastings looked up. The light from the monster's belly revealed his face. The black crust melted away, and the white, marshmallow substance formed in its place. *He is growing his face again*, Dr. Hastings thought.

The eyes rolled into their sockets, and the nose straightened. Lips formed above the chin, and the forehead heightened below a hairline slowly growing with brownish red hair.

I remember that face, Dr. Hastings thought.

(Of course, you do.)

Bezus Smith. *No, it couldn't be!* Bezus was a century-old corpse.

But there he was, there was no denying it. Flashbacks came to Dr. Hastings, all the times *(all that fucking time)* he had spent in the basement of Austin Public Library, looking at the photos, researching documents and books, stacks upon stacks of paper. And the photographs of those he had researched, staring up at him in the silence of the library.

"I've seen your face a thousand times, but never did I think I would see it in reality," Dr. Hastings whispered.

Bezus smiled at him. *It's all there*, Dr. Hastings thought. A thin, brown mustache. A tumor on his forehead the size of a grape. Eyes glowing blue with intense hatred.

Juan made Bezus, Dr. Hastings realized. *I wanted him to make a map, and he made a monster instead.*

(Bingo, partner.)

Bezus exposed his gray teeth in the semblance of a smile. "Greed is the seed which sustains all life, isn't it, Dr. Hastin's? Isn't that what you wrote in your book?" And he clipped the word "book" like it was a punch line to a joke. "Your desire for cousin Maron's gold," Bezus continued, "is your death sentence."

Dr. Hastings had forgotten the contents of his own book. He had forgotten that Bezus had gone to school in the East and received a fair education before returning to Texas and being corrupted by his cousin.

"It was not my intention to steal Maron's gold," Dr. Hastings whispered, as he tried to pull his face away from the burning fires of Bezus's stomach.

"But it is what it is, partner!" the cowboy said, and he threw Dr. Hastings back across the room again.

Pain shot through his entire body, and Dr. Hastings felt himself losing consciousness when Bezus picked him up again, holding him high in the air. "Please . . ." Dr. Hastings begged, legs pushing back and forth.

"You know as well as I do, partner," Bezus said, "there ain't a hell of a lot I can do. You're looking for Maron's gold. Well, then, that's your one-way ticket to the morgue, buddy. That's all there is to it."

(Ain't greed a bitch?)

Bezus bent Dr. Hastings's wrist back as easily as if he were snapping a twig. The professor's shriek echoed through the room, and the monster took the professor's arm and bent it back until it dangled like a broken leaf. Bezus lifted him once more and spun him around in circles before throwing him against the green-encrusted windows.

Pain, and more pain, and Dr. Hastings's mind traveled backward into a dim and dark time where he had no body, and his soul was but a spark burning out for eternity.

So, let it pass, he thought, closing his eyes for the last time.

CHAPTER FIFTY

"Juan? What's happening? Why is your hand shaking like that?"

Juan didn't answer. He couldn't pull his focus away from his hands, which were quivering badly, ready to rip from his wrists and fly. The *making* in him was strong, his power so large he felt it in every fiber of his being. Never before had he had this much magic.

But I do not know what I am making. *What can it be?*

"There's water coming out of the floor!" Brianna exclaimed suddenly. She kicked up a booted foot and showed Juan her damp heel. "Do you see that? How can it be?"

Juan turned his gaze away from his hands and looked. Her heel indeed was damp and dripping.

Water.

Juan's eyes opened wide. *I'm making water.*

"Juan, it's everywhere!" Brianna cried. She looked at him, astonished. Her cheeks were red with new rage. "Is that what you're *making*, Juan? Please tell me that's not what you're *making*."

Juan looked down, and sure enough, water spewed out of the ground like a geyser. Juan gasped and jumped up on the bed, grabbing Brianna's hand and taking her with him.

"I didn't know!"

"What do you mean, you didn't know?" Brianna raised her hand and slapped it across Juan's surprised face. "What do you mean, you don't know? I thought you said you had to envision the damn thing in detail!"

"All I thought was that I wanted a glass of water. I didn't mean to bring the Colorado River in here."

"Well, congratulations! Now you just need to *make* a glass!"

The water was rising. Juan saw it spreading upward through the room. The antique stool had already risen from the floor and floated on the water's surface.

"It's not going to stop," Juan said. "We have to leave here."

"You leave here, you're a dead man."

"If I stay, I'm a drowned man." Juan gave Brianna a defeated look.

Brianna shook her head. "Of all the things," she said.

"I'm sorry."

The water rose higher, up through the floor. It splashed against the corners and the walls, one wave after another, and when it crept onto the edge of the bed, Juan knew he and Brianna were in deep trouble.

I'll never think of a glass of water the same way again, Juan thought. He took Brianna's limp hand and squeezed it tightly.

"There's only one way out of this," he said, and he tilted his head toward the window.

Brianna nodded. "Wait until the water gets higher," she said. "Once the room is full, it will crash the glass and flood out, and maybe, just maybe, those boys out there will be too distracted by a flood coming out of a second-story window to notice us." She sighed heavily. "Just maybe," she whispered again.

CHAPTER FIFTY-ONE

Reagan had tossed and turned at night for five months during her daughter's short life, living over and over what she liked to call the "almosts." It was a mental list she kept of the times Celeste had been in danger throughout the day, examples being how Celeste had *almost* choked on Reagan's dropped earring, or how Reagan had *almost* dropped Celeste on their tile floor during a mad rush to catch the telephone. How Celeste had *almost* drowned when Reagan leaned over to pick up a fallen piece of soap and left Celeste there to balance in the baby tub alone, just for a split second.

But even so, the sleepless nights of "almosts," as

her OB/GYN had confirmed, were just post-pregnancy hormones running freely. No woman truly believed her child was going to die. The mother looked at her baby gurgling or sucking on a bottle, or feeling a soft blanket for the first time, and there was no place where death could penetrate.

All those hormonal "almosts" and "what ifs" disappeared like morning fog on the day of Celeste's funeral, and Reagan was left with the reality that her very worst nightmare had come true, and she knew nothing could ever happen again that would be as terrible as losing her child.

And there was no fear after that, she thought.

And so it was hard for her, when she smelled her daughter's scent again for the first time in two years, to return to the life where there was more than nothing.

Celeste's scent had entered the room; there was no denying it. *Lavender powder*, Reagan thought. The kind she had bought from a specialty shop a month before her daughter was born. She had spent ten bucks on it (more than George would ever have allowed, but Reagan was smart enough to keep some cash on the side for rare spontaneous buys). And it was worth it, every penny, because rubbing the sweet talcum on Celeste's skin after every bath had been a pleasure only mother and daughter shared.

Celeste.

The lavender scent overcame the putrid stench of the past hours, and Reagan, feeling giddy and stoned all at once, had to close her eyes to fend off the sweet impact of it.

She forgot to be afraid of the man looking for them in the hallway.

"I thought your name was Lars," Dr. Kurcan was saying. "Lars Case. Family from Scandinavia."

Lars sighed. "It is Lars Case. Now."

Dr. Kurcan narrowed her eyes. "Are you a convict?"

"No. In order to be a convict, you have to be convicted of something, right?"

"So you're a criminal on the run?"

Lars opened his mouth, only to be waylaid by the sound of Maron kicking through the door.

"Gregory Maroon!" he bellowed.

Reagan jumped back as panic took over her heart. She could feel the goose bumps growing on her arms, her blood running cold.

She did not expect the next idea that popped in her head.

Let me in if you want your child.

It was Reagan's thought, but it did not feel like her own. *Like someone is whispering in my ear,* she mused.

Don't you want to see Celeste?

Mommy, why did you leave me, Mommy?

It was a child's voice she heard on the other side

of the door, like the voice of a two-year-old. *The same age Celeste would have been if she was alive now.*

Come and get me, Mommy.

"Celeste?" Reagan said aloud. *Could it be? Could Celeste really be alive?*

A warm hand fell over her mouth. She looked up and saw Lars glaring at her. He shook his head. *Don't speak*, his eyes seemed to say.

Reagan watched Lars click his tongue on the roof of his mouth, getting Dr. Kurcan's attention. She raised one eyebrow. "What do we use for weapons? All I have is my knife," he whispered. Lars held his knife up, showing it to Dr. Kurcan. "It's all we have," he repeated.

"It's all we need," Dr. Kurcan replied softly.

"Bullshit. Have you fought one of these things yet?"

"You're right." Dr. Kurcan paused, mummified, listening to the kicking and banging on the other side of the door. She sighed and placed her hands on her face. "We have history books," she finally said.

"Great," Lars said. "So we can bore the bastard to death."

Lars squeezed Reagan's hand tighter, but she had no awareness of the reassuring gesture, only a man's voice speaking to her in her head.

Do you hear your daughter, Reagan? Can't you see she needs you? Why don't you open the door?

(Mommy, Mommy.)

"Celeste," Reagan whispered. She dropped Lars's hand. Why had they been holding hands to begin with? She could not remember.

Celeste is in this building, she thought. *My daughter is here.*

The intruding voice in her mind spoke again, *Come and get her. Ray-gon.*

And from the rooms in her heart, laughter emerged, sweeter and more beautiful than anything Reagan had ever known.

So real, Reagan thought. *Too real to be imaginary, too wonderful to be a fairy tale.*

"Gregory Maroon," Maron said, and the door vibrated with his kick. "Listen, buddy, I know we're related. You're from my father's side of the family, and as anyone knows, I don't shoot my kin, even if they are stupid like Zach, or mean like Bezus. Hey, man, you and me, we're on the same team. So don't be ugly, open this door or it's gonna be me who has to get ugly."

Open the door, Reagan. Your baby is out there.

Reagan reached out and touched her hand to the knob, only to be pushed away by a furious Lars. "What are you doing?" he mouthed.

"I want my daughter," Regan whispered.

"Your what?" Lars whispered back.

343

"My daughter is out there."

Lars looked like he was going to say something else when a loud *pop* filled the room, and the sizzle of a bullet slammed through the door, barely missing Lars.

"Hey there, cowboys and cowgirls, I told ya I didn't want to be ugly, but a man's gotta do what a man's gotta do," Reagan heard Maron say just before he shot again.

The knob fell to the floor with a crash. In a split second, Maron had created his passage.

"I'll handle him!" Lars yelled at Dr. Kurcan. "Take Reagan."

Dr. Kurcan nodded and reached across the empty space where the door once stood. She grabbed Reagan by the shirtsleeve, hurtling her up onto Dr. Hastings's desk.

Rubbing her sore shoulder where it had connected with the desk, the voice spoke to her again:

Don't you forget about Celeste, Ray-gon. I got what you're looking for.

"Please," Reagan cried, opening her arms wide when the grotesque stranger entered the room. "Please give me my daughter."

Maron gave her a cocky, black-gummed smile and spit tobacco on the floor. He took one step into the room and Lars was on him.

One hand plunged the knife into Maron's belly,

and with his other, he knocked the gun out of Maron's hand. It flew out into the hallway, and landed against a dark wall.

Maron hunched over and took Lars by the neck, lifting him in the air. Emitting a warrior's scream, Lars retrieved the knife, thrusting it into Maron's right eye. Maron screamed and let go of Lars, then fell backward and hit the ground, spurs clicking.

The only sound was now in Reagan's head.

You better get your little boyfriend off me if you want to see your daughter again.

But you'll kill him.

Do it.

Reagan didn't think about it another second. "Lars! Please, don't hurt him!"

Lars glanced at Reagan with an incredulous expression. Next to Reagan, Dr. Kurcan had removed a trophy from the wall and was climbing off the desk when Maron picked himself off the ground with an easy, sweeping move.

Dr. Kurcan bit her teeth into her lips and raised her arm, smashing the trophy against Maron's head. "Take that, you murdering, psychotic son of a bitch!" she screamed, and smashed his head again.

Reagan jumped off the desk and reached around Dr. Kurcan, trying to pull her away from Maron. "Dr. Kurcan. Don't! No! He has my daughter."

Dr. Kurcan ignored Reagan and threw a violent kick at Maron's side. Lars plunged the knife again and again into Maron's abdomen.

Mommy, please help me, it's dark. I'm scared.

You're killing your baby, Ray-gon.

"No!" Reagan cried. "Nooooo!"

But when Lars flicked his Zippo on again, Reagan saw it—Maron lying on the floor, motionless, blood oozing. Lars and Dr. Kurcan were on either side of him, gasping for breath, Lars's hands stained with crimson.

"You killed him," Reagan accused.

"No shit, Sherlock. What? Did you want us to give him a cookie?"

"He has my daughter!" she shrieked.

Dr. Kurcan stood up and rubbed Maron's brain matter off her forehead with the edge of her black coat sleeve. "What the hell's she talking about?"

Lars shook his head, his expression softening. "Reagan, I think . . ."

"I heard her! I heard her!" It sounded crazy, even to her, but she'd heard what she'd heard, and she knew what she knew.

"She's delusional," Lars said in a tone bordering on apologetic. "We have to get her out of here."

"Get *her* out of here?" Dr. Kurcan asked. "We *all* have to get the hell out of here! God knows how many of those things," she pointed down at Mad Maron, "are left."

"No, please!" Reagan cried.

I have to see her again. If only for a second. Just to tell her all that is in my heart. I never had a chance to say good-bye.

"Get her out of here!" Dr. Kurcan said impatiently. "Pick her up if you have to. God, you would think we had killed the pope!"

Hands reached around her and Reagan found herself being lifted over Lars's shoulder. "What are you doing? Put me down!"

"Lower your voice," Lars ordered. "You don't know what's still out there."

"My daughter . . ."

"Reagan, you're suffering trauma, okay? We're leaving."

"Please," Reagan pleaded, beating Lars's back with her fists. "He knows where to find my daughter."

Lars didn't respond. Reagan stared at the corpse of Mad Maron.

Celeste. My baby. I'm sorry I failed you.

The grief of her loss abruptly evaporated when she saw a flicker of movement out of the corner of her eye. Mad Maron rose and grabbed Dr. Kurcan by the ankle, pulling her to the floor.

Dr. Kurcan screamed, her fingernails clawing at the floor as Mad Maron reeled her in like a fish.

"You want to kill me, bitch!" Maron growled,

yanking her by the hair. "I'll eat you alive, you mess with me!"

"Help me!" Dr. Kurcan reached out to Lars and Reagan. "Help me!"

How long Reagan lay on the floor paralyzed with fear, listening to Dr. Kurcan's shrieks and cries, she did not know. It seemed an eternity before the screaming stopped, before Lars took her by the hand and lifted her to her feet. They ran down the hallway together.

"Lars, what happened?"

Lars's eyes burned with terror and shock. "She's dead. Maron bit through her neck."

CHAPTER FIFTY-TWO

WE ARE SWIMMING IN A VAST, OPEN SEA, JUAN CONVINCED himself, taking Brianna's hand. They exchanged glances, and there was a quiet agreement between them. "Don't worry about me," Brianna said. "I can't die again. I'm just going along for the ride." And she winked.

I love this woman, Juan thought, and with Brianna by his side, he took a deep breath and ducked into the water moments before it reached the ceiling.

We are in a sea . . .

Juan's eyes opened underwater, and he saw within its murky depths the windows to his right. A second later, the glass broke, and the water spilled through the openings, splashing and spraying the hard, brown land.

Here goes nothing, Juan thought when the water left the room and descended, spilling out the window. *Time to resurface.*

Juan squeezed Brianna's hand, and they swam to the surface, their heads bobbing up from the water as they gasped for air. Juan's relief did not last long, however, for as he approached the broken windows, he saw the cowboys were waiting, guns cocked and loaded.

Waiting to kill me.

With what seemed like the speed of light, Juan and Brianna were washed through the broken windows and cascaded on a wave to the sandy ground. The water delivered them to a spot near the motel's outhouse.

"Come on, get up!" Brianna ordered as four pairs of hooves galloped in their direction. "My horse is to the front!" Brianna said urgently, and bent over sharply as a shot plunged into her back.

"Brianna!"

"I'm fine! They can't kill me!"

Brianna's white and brown paint was tied to a post, and he watched dispassionately as the two approached.

"What's his name?" Juan asked offhandedly, as if another part of his mind had taken over to cope with his fear.

"Slowpoke," she answered.

"Oh. Well. That's reassuring."

Brianna quickly untied the reins and mounted, Juan jumping up behind her. She dug her heels into the animal's sides.

Juan looked back and saw Mark *(well, the boy who was once Mark)* a foot or so away, his gun aimed at Juan's head and a smirk twisting his face.

"Where you off to, Juan?" he called.

Juan had turned around and buried his head in Brianna's neck when a sudden pain stabbed into his back. Juan reached behind him and touched dampness. He brought his fingers to his eyes and stared at the red stain.

"Brianna," he said quietly. "I think they shot me." He sounded calmer than he felt. His eyes rolled back in his head as the slow, torturous hand of pain overcame him.

"Juan? Don't you die on me, Juan," he heard Brianna say.

"Brianna . . ."

"We're almost there!"

Through eyes that were mere slits, Juan saw Brianna was cutting around houses and through gardens. Suddenly she reached down, snatched a log from a woodpile as they passed, and hurled it at one of the cowboys. Juan heard a grunt, then a horse's whinny of pain as its wounded rider pulled sharply on the reins.

"One down," Brianna exulted, and laughed, hair blowing up wildly around her.

Juan tried to smile, but darkness was consuming him.

Fading, fading . . .

(This wouldn't be happening if I hadn't used the make.)

The "devil's gift," his grandmother had called it, but Juan had never believed it, not until this very moment. All this time he had convinced himself that what he did wasn't evil, but seeing the damage that had occurred in its wake made him doubt himself.

I am a demon, he thought.

"Don't think that way," Brianna said over her shoulder.

Juan smiled to himself as the colors of the world dimmed around him. He had forgotten Brianna could read his thoughts.

Juan felt them moving upward as if climbing a hill. He could still hear the single horse behind them. "Duck!" Brianna ordered, and Juan had only enough strength to lower his head to the side, but it was enough.

"Got him!"

Mark had not been able to avoid the tree branch Brianna so skillfully guided her horse beneath. On foot, Mark tried to follow but was quickly outdistanced.

"We're losing him," Brianna said, and she laughed

again. "This would almost be fun, if it wasn't for. . ." Her words trailed off, and she reached behind her and felt Juan's weakening pulse.

"Hold on, Juan," she pleaded. "Please hold on."

CHAPTER
FIFTY-THREE

CALEB FUMBLED AROUND ON THE FLOOR NEXT TO DR. Hastings's corpse. Mark's BlackBerry had long been AWOL, but the storm had passed, the night was failing, and outside the green-covered windows glowed the promise of morning.

Caleb glanced at his watch and saw the time was five thirty. Something fluttered in his gut. He searched for a word to describe it and discovered it was *hope*.

The feeling fled when he heard the dark laughter from above. Caleb put his hands to his face and willed the sound to stop, knowing it wouldn't, knowing he would once again have to stand and face the music.

"It's just you and me, Lily-cat," Bezus said. "I hope you don't mind me crashing your party."

"You go to hell," Caleb heard Lily spit.

Caleb's fingers scurried across the floor, searching for a weapon. *My fists aren't enough for this guy,* he thought, remembering the inferno of the monster's stomach. His fingers slid to the side, to the left and right, and moved through pieces of desk, costumes, and cardboard cutouts. Slowly, slowly he waded through the mess, knowing his only advantage was that Bezus thought he was dead.

There's nothing, Caleb thought before his hand hit something. He grabbed for it, molding his fingers around the item, searching to discover his treasure. He almost laughed when he saw what it was. *A hair dryer,* he realized, and remembered that last summer the drama club had performed *Steel Magnolias* to lukewarm reviews.

Not that I went to see the chick play. He death-gripped the blow-dryer.

If the guys from the team could see me now.

Caleb got to his knees in time to see Bezus standing over a frantic Lily.

The girl wasn't one to back off easily. She pushed off the floor and spat in the monster's face. "You lay one hand on me, buddy, and you'll hurt like nothing else," she warned.

"Oh, Lily, sweet Lily. *Shall I compare thee to a summer's day? Thou art more lovely and more temperate. Rough winds do shake the darling buds of May, and summer's lease hath all too short a date,*" Bezus recited Shakespeare's "Sonnett XVIII" in an accented voice that sounded more Princeton than prairie, and Caleb had to look at the monster again to remember it was Bezus Smith and not his English professor threatening Lily with rape and death.

Bezus touched Lily's face. "Nice, nice," he whispered. "Let's not bicker anymore, Lily-cat. There will be glorious times ahead of us if you do so wish it."

Caleb crawled along the floor with the steady, fluid motion of a cat. *Not so dumb after all, Lily,* Caleb thought.

Lily batted away Bezus's hand. "Don't touch me, you filthy fuck."

"Keep the poison coming, Lily-cat. You're only making my blood warmer," he said.

Everyone has a chance to be a hero at least once, Caleb remembered Dr. Kurcan once say, and struck the hair dryer on Bezus's head with all the raging, desperate force left in his battered and bleeding body.

CHAPTER
FIFTY-FOUR

A CLOUDED MOON ASCENDED OVER THE MOUNTAINS, bringing a first glimpse of night to the late afternoon. The threat of the horsemen had passed, but Juan was living with the horror of a wound that bled freely down his back. He passed in and out of consciousness while Brianna rode frantically toward their destination.

During a conscious moment, Juan studied Brianna as she scanned the landscape, looking from left to right, and realized she had changed in appearance. When she moved her head, he could tell her hair had lightened, and her skin had paled. Her eyes were no longer the shade of purple crystal but the color of warm summer skies. In his arms, he felt she had become more fragile and less sure of herself. When she talked to him, attempting to soothe his pain, her vocabulary was that of a well-bred lady and not a twenty-first-century teenager.

"We're almost there," she encouraged. "Stay awake, Juan."

He tried, but it was hard when it felt like the sky was falling on him, hard when every step the horse took felt like his brain was smashing to pieces, hard when the world drove around him in circles and he was suspended in a state of near-death.

Juan felt the horse slow. "Open your eyes, Juan," Brianna ordered.

Juan opened them and saw a clearing where the earth dipped into a narrow canyon. "Over there, where the smoke is blowing. You will find the Monhu. Your people." She looked over at him, her blue eyes burning in the dark day.

Juan freed his hands from around Brianna's waist. "I can't go alone. Come with me," he whimpered.

Brianna shook her head. "You know I cannot. This is your journey now. I have taken you as far as I can. Once you reach them, they can help. They were meant to help you."

Yes.

He did not understand the why of it, but somehow he knew that was the way it was supposed to be. He kissed Brianna for the last time. "Thank you," he said, feeling his sickness subside, if only for a moment. "For everything."

She accepted his kiss and returned it.

Juan dismounted, amazed to find his arms and legs still working.

"I will wait for you," Brianna said. "If you should decide to come back."

"Thank you." *I will miss you*, he wanted to add, but didn't. He reached around and touched his back. The bleeding, for whatever reason, had stopped.

I feel better, he thought. But how could that be?

He did not say good-bye to Brianna before he turned around and headed toward the canyon. He looked up into the evening sky, where the smoke blew from below the huge canyon rocks. Juan shivered. He felt as if he had waited to come here all his life.

His hands twitched.

Making.

The air was powerful. He had never experienced anything like it before. He could feel it dense around him, holding him prisoner with invisible chains. Juan fought to walk against it.

When he arrived at the cliff, he looked down.

The Monhu clan sat in a circle, with two medicine men in the middle. To any casual observer, it looked as if they were praying.

But Juan knew better.

Making, he thought as he descended the hill. Sand scattered around his feet and blew into his face.

A Monhu man waited for Juan at the end of the cliff. "Juan," he said. Wrinkles deepened around his eyes. "We've been waiting for you."

CHAPTER FIFTY-FIVE

CALEB HIT HIS MARK, AND BEZUS WENT DOWN LIKE A bowling pin. A scant second later the monster came up again.

"I thought you were dead," Bezus said, an open gash pouring blood over his eyes.

"You're dead," Caleb said, and took a swing at his jaw. The punch left the man's chin dented, and Caleb noted that what was once an almost fully formed face was sinking into a mural of blood and sagging flesh.

Caleb hit him again, and again. His hands found the cord to the hair dryer, and he took it firmly and swung it against Bezus's back, chest, to the side of the head, across his ear. Bezus howled and grabbed the cord, sticking it in his teeth, biting it in half. Caleb's grasp tightened around the handle, and he beat it over Bezus's head *(fuck, will this thing ever die?)* like a hammer on a nail.

Lily screamed in the background, "Caleb! Caleb! He has a gun . . ."

But her warning came too late, and Caleb felt something hit his butt, his back, his shoulder. He sank to the floor one knee at a time.

"Caleb, Caleb," Bezus berated, shaking his head, motioning with his gun. "You're gonna have to do better than that if you want to kill me."

Caleb was a raft losing air. Blood pulsed out of three holes in his body as easily as water out of a faucet.

Fight back. You're not done yet, an inner voice told him.

But how? I'm in pieces.

Thunder rolled outside, which Caleb thought was God's cheesy way of saying, "Just do it."

Caleb's last stand, he thought as he rose from the floor.

Go for it. Just do it.

"Back in action, are we, Caleb?" Bezus asked, lifting a moldy, deformed brow. "Have we not learned our lesson tonight, young man? You are a defeated clown."

Caleb's fist was his answer, and he aimed it at

Bezus's forehead, knocking the monster to the side. Caleb paused and clenched his teeth as he lost feeling in his leg. It was just long enough for Bezus to capture Caleb in an armlock.

"Too bad you ain't never taken steroids," Bezus said. "You might actually be worth a fight."

He grabbed one of Caleb's fingers. "Ever played 'Twist the Finger'? It's an old drinking game where I'm from. Allow me to teach you. Without the drinking," the monster said, and proceeded to twist the finger until it popped like a twig.

Caleb screamed as blood gushed. Bezus laughed harder. "That was fuuuun," he said. "Let's play again," and he took the left index finger and pulled it, too, until it snapped off .

"No!" Lily cried in hoarse, desperate protest.

Caleb felt nothing but pain, then nothing at all when the shock of losing two of his fingers became too much for his nerves to understand. Bezus, meanwhile, was having the time of his life—or death. He laughed, showing black, rotting teeth, and continued pulling at Caleb's fingers, twisting and popping each one like they were caps on a Coke bottle and throwing them at Lily.

A whole new meaning to giving someone the finger, Caleb thought idly just before he fell into unconsciousness. As the blackness took over, he heard a sound he had not expected.

A loud, angry bark. And not just any bark.

Gordy's bark.

The gunshot wounds and the missing fingers, the blows to the head and the death of people around him, had not yet sent Caleb to tears, but hearing his old best friend's bark was enough to water his eyes.

It can't be, he thought. He was delirious. He was imagining things.

But if it is a hallucination, it's a cool one.

The gray dog panted heavily in one corner.

The seventy-pound Catahoula-Aussie Shepherd badass that didn't get out of some car's way.

It's been a long time since I've had a dog like that.

He wasn't the only one to notice the ghost of a dog. Bezus paused from ripping Caleb's fingers off (he was down to the two pinkies and left thumb and enjoying every minute of his torture), when he turned to look at the big canine growling in the corner, illuminated by a mysterious, celestial light.

The monster grinned. His sockets, caked with just the smidgen of freshly baked eyes, gleamed with new merriment.

"Is that Gordy, Caleb? Is that your old friend? The one in your infamous e-mail?"

Caleb didn't answer. The dog moved to him slowly, his left hind leg limping as it had years ago.

Thick drool fell from his mouth, and his eyes were the shade of rotten lemons.

"A dog . . .?" Caleb heard Lily whisper from across the room.

"Gordy," Caleb said, and the name seemed to bring the room back to life again. The monster and the dog went to war, the man roaring, the dog howling, rolling over and over together on the chipped marble floor.

The jock watched as skin was ripped away and fell to the floor. "Get . . . off . . . me . . . boy," the cowboy panted.

"Not so fucking poetic anymore, are you?" Lily taunted.

"Get him, Gordy!" Caleb yelled.

Hope rose again, that motherless whore of an emotion. It was back again in the form of a mutt his mother had saved that morning so long ago.

Warmth overcame Caleb, and he forgot his injuries. He was about to join in the fight when he felt a sharp pain in his chest, and numbness blanketed him. Caleb cried out, and an unfamiliar voice answered.

If I kill him, you go, too.

He lives, he kills you anyway, but he takes the girl with him, and maybe the kids downstairs, if he lets you live a little longer. Until you die, he stays alive.

Caleb watched the fight and saw Gordy regarding him with his dead, yellow animal eyes.

Could it be—?

Yep. That's right.

Caleb shook his head. *So it is,* he thought.

Can you die, Caleb?

I don't want to die. I have a game this weekend. I'm taking Emily James to see Death Cab for Cutie tomorrow night. And I got plans for the later years. I wanted to coach, get married, start a family, check out Amsterdam.

(Behind door Number 1 is death, behind door Number 2 is death, your only choice is, will you die with glory or disgrace?)

I don't know, I don't know.

The dog could be lying to him. But why?

It's Gordy, for Christ's sake.

Caleb watched Gordy spit out Bezus's nose and go for his ears, his canine teeth pulling at the flesh. *He's always been a fighter,* Caleb thought proudly. Gordy ceased ripping off Bezus's lobes and looked up at Caleb with anticipation sparking through his eyes.

Take glory.

Caleb felt his chest. His heart beat slowly, like the drums in a funeral march. He inhaled with great difficulty, and realized his breath was preparing to leave his body, his lungs seemingly shutting down one cell at a time.

Caleb looked at Lily. She was hunched over, one

arm on her injured leg, the other bent against the floor, palm flat, watching the fight. Her eyes were wide, disbelieving.

I'll take glory.

"Tell them I never took steroids, okay?" Caleb said.

Lily's eyes widened. "What?"

"My friends, my family, the school. Tell them I never took drugs. Not once. The e-mail was only a joke. You'll do that for me, won't you?" He looked at Gordy, giving him a thumbs-up signal, and it almost seemed the dog nodded.

"Caleb," Lily cried, "What do you—?"

Before she could finish, Caleb sank to his knees, hands holding his heart, eyes glazed. He let out a long moan and fell into the ground face-first.

Behind him, Gordy *(the best dog in the fucking world)* had Bezus Smith's sick black heart crushed between his sharp teeth.

Lily screamed, and the ground shook again, more terribly than any time before.

CHAPTER FIFTY-SIX

THE GROUND RIPPLED.

"Lars, the floor!" Reagan warned when she saw a widening crack that began at the far wall and headed their way, slicing through marble with deadly precision.

The loud hammering sound of the ground shifting rang out through the building. "Jump!" Lars ordered when the crack reached their feet. He tightened his grip on Reagan's hand, and together they jumped to the other side of the hallway as marble split from under them.

Lars pushed Reagan against the wall before he felt his own foot slip through a crack. He grabbed the ledge as he fell.

The next thing he knew, Reagan's outline was kneeling above him, offering him a hand. "Take it," she said.

"You're not strong enough."

"I'm stronger than I look."

"Reagan, you can't hold me. This isn't a snub. It's simple physics."

"Okay," she said, surrendering. "Tell me what to do and I'll do it."

Lars strained to hang on. "Just give me a moment," he said. His grip strengthened on the ledge, and he swung his dangling legs back and forth, wider each time. "Step back," he warned, and he raised his leg, flinging it over onto the floor. He felt Reagan's hands holding on to his arm, and with her help, raised his other leg.

"That's better," he said.

"Lars," Reagan whispered. Her hand was still on his arm. He could hear the fear in her voice.

Lars took her by the shoulders and leaned down to whisper in her ear. "Reagan, listen to me," he began, "My Zippo is gone. We don't have another source of light, the floors are cracked in a gazillion places, and I'm sure Maron isn't done with us yet. We're going to have to go slowly and not say another word. No more hallucinations about your daughter, no more hallucinations about my dead girlfriend. Deal?"

He could sense Reagan nodding beside him. "Okay, then," Lars said, releasing her shoulders.

He thought the little powwow was over when Reagan grabbed him by the shirtsleeve. "Lars?"

"I told you not to say anything," Lars half whispered, half hissed.

"I know. But I just wanted to ask you, if we get out of this, if you wanted to go out for coffee sometime. To a place that isn't Starbucks. There's a café downtown—"

Her words were lost when Lars's mouth crushed down on her own. Everything stopped, the building fell away, the lightning cleared, the thunder silenced, and it was only the two of them in a place that stood still inside time.

Lars combed his fingers through Reagan's long, red hair. *So this is what redemption feels like.* It had been a long time since he had experienced such sweetness.

Their lips parted. Lars's fingers traced her mouth.

"Was that a yes?" Reagan asked.

"Let's get out of here."

Slowly, very slowly, Lars told himself, and began crawling.

Lars wasn't sure how long it was before the diseased rotting smell of Maron entered the hallway. As the stench worsened, he could make out the faint clickety-click of Maron's spurs hitting the ground.

"Gregory . . . oh, Gregory . . ."

Lars didn't move a muscle. Reagan was completely still behind him.

Maron's footsteps were closer, and his voice sounded near when he said, "You know, Gregory, you ain't much better than me, partner! Why don't you tell your girlfriend what happened in Mexico?"

Yeah, let's relive the worst year of my life.

"Tell her about Heather, Gregory. Tell her about the bag."

He was close, so close. Every minute, the smell grew worse, Maron's breathing became louder, and the room grew smaller.

Lars curled up in a ball, pulling his legs into his chest, his back into his feet, his head into his arms.

Let him pass. Don't let him see us.

A split second later, something remarkable happened. The lights came on.

CHAPTER FIFTY-SEVEN

JUAN WAS BARELY OUTSIDE FREDERICKSBURG, BUT THE world he had entered looked light-years away from the desert land he had crossed only moments earlier. The surreal images before him spread out like a dark dream, a canvas of odd fortitude—the old, decrepit men, their haunting chants, the smell of rain and fire blanketing the surrounding wall of purple sky. In the distance, a coyote called.

The four men looked at least a century old, each one more ancient than the other. They sat Indian-style around the campfire, their hands folded as if in prayer. Their long, silver braids ran down their naked chests, and they wore nothing save for leather loincloths and beads around their necks. Attached to the beads, each man wore a different-colored symbol based on the element he represented. The blue medallion was water; the red, fire; the green, earth; and the yellow, air.

The man who wore fire, the one who had first spoken to Juan, motioned for him to sit beside him. He opened his mouth and uttered an unfamiliar word Juan could only assume was *here*.

"Have you really been expecting me?" Juan asked, taking his place beside the man.

The man's lips pursed. "Gossamer Hall," he began, "is submerging in the mud. You have stirred something in the ground that was not meant to be awakened."

"Mad Maron," Juan whispered.

"And the others," said a different voice.

Juan looked over to see another medicine man staring at him, his wrinkled, leathery face pinched with something close to anger. He wore the water medallion.

"The bones were never meant to be awakened," the man said.

"The bones?" Juan repeated.

"The bones were waiting for you," still another voice said, and Juan looked at the man sitting across from him. He wore the earth medallion. His expression was particularly accusing.

"Maron's bones," said the man of fire.

Juan swallowed. "Tell me what I can do."

"There is nothing you can do," said the man of earth, and threw something resembling salt into the fire. The flames heightened and crackled, their red luster glowing hot against the cool night.

Juan touched his back when he felt a spot of moisture along his spine. *The wound,* he thought, bringing his fingers forward to see the crimson staining his skin. He glanced up and saw the men staring at him.

"Your back?" asked the man who wore the air medallion. He tilted his head to the side, and Juan could see the long beak of his nose.

"Yes," Juan answered. "How did you know?"

"You stink of blood."

"You will die if you stay here," the man of fire said. "The only way to stay alive is to descend again to the living place."

His words were followed by sparks cracking from the fire. They shot into Juan's face, burning his eyes, and he bent over with a cry. A cloud slowly rose above the flames, filling his lungs with smoke. He hacked long, hard coughs that tore through his throat.

"Are you trying to kill me?" he asked, wiping the tears from his eyes.

All four men grunted at once. "The ground has spoken," said the man of earth. "You must go back."

Juan shook his head. "Go back and do what? Go back to a building of corpses?" He looked up to the twinkling, dismissive stars. *A building of corpses. Yes, there is no use in denying it,* he thought. *This is all my fault.*

"Gossamer Hall will not exist when you return," said the man of earth.

"You will be alive, but buried underground," said the man of fire. "You will have to dig your way out."

The flames flickered like little demons across Juan's face, the heat adding to the nervous sweat already building on his brow. "And Maron?" he asked. "What about him?"

"He will be dead."

"And Lily? And Lars?"

"Dead. You will be the only survivor. This is the way of things."

CHAPTER
FIFTY-EIGHT

SHEER TERROR. IT WAS LARS'S FIRST REACTION WHEN
the light suddenly flickered on and cleaved the darkness. A lump built in his throat. It was neither the time
nor the place to be seen, not when Maron was on the
same floor with him and Reagan, hunting them down
like dogs. *But there you have it,* Lars thought, and
jumped up with Reagan still holding his hand. *Better
to find Maron before he finds us.*

"Where is he?" Reagan asked. Lars could feel her
fingers trembling under his own.

He isn't here. A moment before, it had seemed
Maron was right beside them, but now he was nowhere

to be seen.

"Stay close," Lars ordered.

They tiptoed over the piles of marble lined up along the shredded floor. Fully lit square fixtures dangled like chandeliers from the ceiling, blinking on and off. A water fountain hummed nearby, and a clock ticked from one of the classrooms.

Strange, Lars thought, looking at the debris around him. It was unbelievable. Had Gossamer Hall ever been a normal building, a place of learning? Had it always been a hunting ground?

Lars glanced at Reagan. Her brown eyes were roaming the room in awed shock, her mouth drawn open in an O.

"I had forgotten what the color of light looked like," she said.

"Remember," Lars warned, "we are not safe. He's here. Somewhere."

"I wish you had your knife right now," she admitted.

"I wish Juan was awake to *make* one for us."

His words were followed by a beep and then the rattling of something at the end of the hallway. Lars and Reagan looked in the direction of the sound and saw the elevator was climbing up—a red light on the ground floor, red on second, and moving upward.

"Lars," Reagan said, trying to stay calm, "you don't suppose they're coming to our floor, do you?"

Lars didn't answer and instead listened while the elevator shaft rattled to the fourth floor and stopped.

"I suppose they are," Reagan concluded leadenly.

Lars nodded. "It looks like we have company."

CHAPTER
FIFTY-NINE

Lars pushed Reagan into a nearby room as the elevator door chimed open. The next minutes dragged with silent terror while they waited for the click of spurs that would no doubt follow.

When they heard only silence, Lars craned his neck around the corner and sighed with momentary relief.

"Who is it?" Reagan asked, shivering.

Under the flickering lights Lars saw the dark-haired girl lying flat in the elevator, her leg bound by the white sheets he himself had applied. A desperate expression darkened a face pale with looming death.

"It's Lily."

"Lily," Reagan repeated, and Lars nodded. Her face brightened with hope. "She's still alive then."

But who knows for how long? Lars saw the blood streaming from her leg, soaking through the makeshift bandage.

"Reagan? Lars? Are you there? Help me," Lily begged, her voice quavering in the air like a damaged butterfly. Her hands moved forward along the floor as she crawled out of the elevator. The smacking of her palms hitting the marble echoed through the hallway.

No, don't come in here! Lars wanted to scream. A shout would only alert Maron. *Wherever the hell he is.*

Lars moved into the hall. When he caught Lily's fearful eye, he placed a finger to his lips.

Lily stopped. *Lars*, she mouthed. *Thank God.* Her eyes darted. She made her fingers into a gun and pointed to the ground, her face forming a question mark. *Are the monsters here?* she asked with her eyes.

Lars nodded affirmatively. *Where is Caleb?* he mouthed.

Dead, was Lily's reply.

Dr. Hastings?

Dead.

Juan?

Lily pointed up to the ceiling.

Lars frowned. *Why did you leave him?*

Lily shrugged. *What else could I do?*

Why did you come down with the elevator?

Lily pointed upward again and shook her head. *Because I couldn't go up.*

Lars looked over at Reagan. "What is it?" she asked between chattering teeth.

Lars paused before answering, "Caleb and Dr. Hastings are dead."

"Oh, God. And Juan?"

"Upstairs." Lars looked back at Lily. *Go back to the elevator,* his lips told her.

Lily understood and slowly crawled backward. Lars motioned to Reagan to follow him. His hand tightened around hers. The determination of life and death was upon them; Lars could feel it.

Lars turned the corner, Reagan trailing behind him. The elevator was mere feet away, but for Lars the trip seemed endless.

He and Reagan were halfway there when he felt the scenery shift around him, like an invisible band had imprisoned the landscape. He looked at the crippled girl scooting backward into the elevator. Her eyes betrayed the horror that was invisible to him. Her mouth opened wide, she trembled with sudden fright. "He's behind you!"

The sword of a voice penetrated the hallway. "Gregory, boy, don't you go anywhere!"

Lars didn't stop to look behind him. They fled into the elevator as Lars felt fingers grab at his neck.

He turned and landed a swift kick in Maron's groin, knocking the gangster back, buying them enough time for Lars's thumb to press the sixth-floor button. "Why isn't this thing working?" he growled when the doors refused to close.

"No sixth floor," Reagan reminded him. She was bent over, her hands on her knees, trying to regain her breath.

"I told you I couldn't go up!" Lily cried.

"Down it is," Lars said, pressing a trembling finger to the first-floor button.

"But—" Lily stopped short, her words turning into shrieks when Maron's bloody, rotten fingers pried open the doors and reached in, grabbing her arm. She batted his hands away before the doors slid closed again, and the elevator descended.

Silence filled the elevator as the threesome waited in their boxed hell. The mocking, cheerful background music of Barbra Streisand played from invisible speakers.

"You have to be fucking kidding me," Lily said. "As if this night wasn't bad enough."

"I don't mind her," Reagan said. "She reminds me of my grandmother."

Lily rolled her eyes. "What if Maron is waiting for

us?" she asked, turning to Lars.

"He can't get down there fast enough," Lars said. "Remember, he's a hundred-year-old corpse."

"Well, he's been doing fine so far."

Lars jolted forward when the elevator halted to a stop. Then the elevator started moving in the other direction.

"We're going up," Reagan said, her voice frantic. "Did you hear me? *He's coming on.*"

"Not if I can help it." He examined the ceiling of the elevator; around the walls were antique rails. *If I can get high enough, I can break through the top.*

"What are you doing?" Reagan asked.

"Hey, I was kidding about Barbra Streisand," Lily said with a hollow laugh.

"Fuck Barbra Streisand. I'm looking for a way to get us the hell out of here," Lars grumbled. His legs extended far enough to pop open the ceiling panel with a heavy blow. He glanced down at Reagan. "Get the elevator going back down," he ordered before chinning up into the small opening.

"I'm trying," Reagan said while madly pressing buttons. When her thumb hit the emergency button, the elevator stopped abruptly.

"What did you do?" Lily exclaimed. "We're between floors!"

"We stopped, didn't we?" Reagan shot back.

Lars peered into the elevator shaft. Small cracks of light illuminated the darkness, revealing wires and pulleys. Best of all, Lars realized, at the top of the shaft, he could see the sky. *It should be at ground level by now*, Lars thought, and another minor tremor shook the earth as if in answer.

The sound of someone beating a door filled the shaft, and on the level above Lars, he saw a door being pried open.

"Gregory!" Maron sneered. "I know you're right under me. I can smell you, cuz! Your Marlboro Reds, that faggy gel you put in your hair, your caffeine guts. I can *smell* you, bitch!"

"No," Lars said and climbed back into the elevator as the door opened, revealing the light from the fourth floor and the hideous madman.

"I see you!" Maron laughed, his voice echoing. "I see you, partner!"

Lars's feet hit the bottom of the elevator.

"I heard him," Lily said, her voice sounding numb.

"Yes," Lars said, nodding. He inhaled before adding, "He's pried open the door. But there is hope."

Lily cocked her head. "Yeah. That an Al-Qaeda suicide squad bombs the place before Maron gets to us?"

"Escape is right above us," Lars said. The earth trembled again, and the elevator lights flickered. "The sixth floor is almost to ground level. I could smell the pine trees outside." Lars laughed nervously, feeling suddenly light-headed. "I could see the stars, and the moon, and light from the east."

"This elevator won't go up to the sixth floor, re-member?" Lily said.

Lars opened his mouth to answer and looked up just in time to see Maron falling into the elevator, spurred boots slamming into his shoulders. Instinctively, he grabbed the boots, trying to hurl Maron off him. The rotting madman lurched, and Lars was left holding a single boot, wrenched from the withering foot.

Pain coursed through Lars's spine, and he fell back-ward against the wall. Reagan instinctively reached for him.

"That's it," Maron said with a laugh. "Help your boyfriend, Red. It don't make a damn bit of difference. You're all gonna die."

Lars looked up through blurry eyes. He was half-blinded with pain, but he could make out Maron's face of death. Layers of loose skin hung around his putrid green neck, his face was red and oozing dark blood, and a lipless jaw gaped wide, revealing black, rotten teeth. The tongue, covered with open lesions, was coated with pus that crept over the broken teeth like moss on a grave. Mucus ran thickly from his nostrils. Sullen eyes were sunken deep in hollowed sockets.

"Welcome to hell," Maron said and laughed,

holding something up.

Lars saw what it was—Dr. Hastings's lighter. It had been missing since early in the night. Now Lars knew why.

This is gonna hurt, Lars thought with resigned defeat just as Maron set himself on fire.

CHAPTER
SIXTY

"NO ONE GETS MY GOLD!" MARON BELLOWED, HIS FACE melting away in flames. "No one!"

Reagan felt the heat of flames against her skin, and she choked on the smoke. Hunched over, an insanely rational thought occurred to her: *Maron has nothing to lose. This is why he kills. He is already dead.*

Reagan understood the feeling, though her similar thoughts were beginning to flee. *I am not a lost cause*, she thought with renewed vigor and turned toward the elevator buttons, shielding her eyes with one hand while the other searched for the fourth-floor button once more. Her palm finally slammed into it, and the elevator moved upward.

The inferno turned in her direction. "What do you got planned, missy?"

This is it, Reagan thought as Maron reached a flame-engulfed hand toward her rapidly beating heart. Reagan closed her eyes.

The elevator stopped at the third floor, and the doors opened. Reagan stumbled out. Eyes still closed, she ran blindly down the corridor, knowing Maron was following her, hearing his spurs beat against the floor.

With a roar, Lars tried to stand but fell over, his back giving way to waves of pain. He watched Maron's fiery body chase Reagan down the hallway. He tried to stand again, and this time pain did not outweigh his determination.

"What does she think she's doing?"

"Buying us time," Lily said. "She's the only one still standing."

"Lars, the elevator!" Lily screamed, pointing upward, but it was too late. The fire had softened the wires, and the elevator was breaking free of its cable, one snap after another—loud, explosive pops.

"Hold on!" Lars jumped through the hole from the rails, grabbing a wire just before the elevator gave way under his feet. He reached out and grabbed Lily's clothing, his breath catching in his chest, his mind spinning in circles as his muscles took possession of

Lily's weight. The elevator plunged into the abyss.

Lily moaned as she dangled from Lars's weakening hand. "Oh, God, oh, God!" she cried.

"Lily, don't panic."

"Don't panic? Don't fucking panic? I'm hanging from your hand, you're hanging from a wire, and there's a fire below me burning my ass, but you don't want me to panic? Screw you."

"I can get us out of this."

"Well, like Dr. Phil says, it's a short leap from words to action."

"Do me a favor and save the daytime talk-show mumbo jumbo for someone who gives a damn." *What to do, what to do?* He could only imagine Reagan's fate if Maron caught up with her. Lars had to get them out of the shaft and quick. His hand tightened around the wire. Just above, the door of the fourth floor waited.

"Lily, use my body like a ladder."

"What?"

"Climb me. It's the only way."

"Lars—"

"Remember Dr. Phil. It's a short leap from words to action."

"Don't use my words against me!"

"Lily. Please."

CHAPTER SIXTY-ONE

EVERYTHING HAD CHANGED.

Juan felt like he was hanging, suspended in some netherworld that had no relationship to the Monhu tribesmen or the place below the cliff where they sat.

The darkness had consumed his sight. Even the bright fire beside him seemed to only reflect from within itself, selfishly shedding no heat upon the men sitting around it.

Juan felt his hearing soften, as if it were going dead from a very loud sound. Yet, there was no noise at all, no feeling of vibration in his head, no harsh music or screams.

His hands could no longer feel, and his sense of place and time had dissolved like sand upon the fire, stupefying him. He could no longer be certain whether he was moving or standing still.

One clear thought rang through his senselessness.

I cannot go back to the living world.

I know what I have to do.

If I can make, *then I can* unmake. *For every yin, there's a yang. East and west, hot and cold, summer and winter.*

"I will die," Juan decided aloud.

"Your wound will not exist once you return to your time," said the man of fire. "It will be like nothing happened. But if you stay . . ." Juan cleared his throat. "Did you hear me? I do not want to live. Let me die."

The men looked at each other. The man of water said, "That is not the way it should be."

"It is the way if I wish it," Juan answered. "And I wish it."

He took a deep breath. What would he do for the rest of his life, knowing he was responsible for the massacre at Gossamer Hall? How would he ever live with himself?

Juan studied the men's faces. Each of them seemed reconciled in the gift that both tormented them and fascinated mankind, the secret that could do so little good and create so much destruction.

The gift of *make*.

Juan stared into the fire and imagined Brianna's voice.

A yin, a yang. A make, an unmake.

"No more," Juan whispered. A memory of his mother danced in his head, and he slumped his shoulders as he spoke to her pale image. "I am not evil, *Madre*. But I no longer wish for this gift. You will have it your way and you will not. Your son will no longer have this gift, but your son will no longer be your son."

His mother's image did not answer, but turned away from him and dissolved into the depths of a mind growing cold with resolution.

Juan lifted himself from the ground, still staring into the flames.

"Don't do it," the man of water said. "There is no going back. Death is death, in this life or the other."

"Yes, that is my intent," Juan murmured and closed his eyes.

Now, now, now . . .

It is time.

Another second could be another second too late.

No more monsters, no more *make*, no more earthquakes, no more deaths.

Good-bye!

The universe, the Lord above, the Greek gods, whatever entity held the heavens in its grasp, was a kind stranger to Juan. Before his body hit the fire, his soul had already departed. Brianna was the first to welcome him into the world of spiritual light and everlasting darkness, and it was in her embrace he discovered the peace he had hoped to find for so long.

CHAPTER SIXTY-TWO

REAGAN TURNED THE CORNER WITH MARON FOLLOWING in a blaze of fire. "Bitch!" he screamed. "I'm coming for you, Ray-gon! You and your dead daughter will be together real soon."

Reagan hesitated when she came to the end of the hallway. Her hands beat against the walls and her knuckles bled against the hard stone. There was no going back, no escape. Maron was behind her. She could hear him. She could feel the heat from his burning form. She turned around.

He was glowing like a demented Christmas tree under the bright lights of a hallway torn apart from wall to ceiling. When he came closer, he laughed, and his laughter was poison to her senses. Putting hands to her ears, she ran past him and into a classroom.

"You're just too damn hardheaded, ain't ya?" Spurred steps closed in on her. "No one gets their hands on my gold, girl."

"I don't want your gold!" *There is only one thing I want, and you can never give it to me.*

"Don't be too sure of that, Ray-gon," Maron answered, as if reading her thoughts. "You never thought you would see that little booger eater of yours again? Hell's bells, girl, the dead live where I'm from. That's right. The dead live." Maron turned over one desk after another like dominoes, engulfing the room in a sea of flames. "The dead live. THE DEAD LIVE! You're coming with me, Ray-gon. I could use a girl like you where I'm from."

Three desks, then two desks away. So close. Reagan could make out the malicious face that still existed inside the flames. He was smiling, his melted lips wide like a clown's. He had her, but he was taking his time.

Then, finally, he lunged. Reagan closed her eyes and waited for the impact, but it never came. A minute passed, then another. Scared, perplexed, weary, Reagan opened her eyes, only to see Maron on his knees, face tucked into his arms. Around him and upon him, not a trace of fire burned, nor was there any evidence a fire had once raged over his face and torso.

Almost as if there had been no fire at all.

Lars came around the corner, staggering. "Reagan! Come on. Let's get out of here!"

"Lars! What happened?" Reagan pointed at Maron.

Brows furrowed, Lars violently kicked Maron's body over. There was no malice left in the vacant face, only an expression of withered defeat.

"He's dead," Lars said with disbelief in his voice.

Reagan shook her head, her hand covering her mouth. "He can't be dead. I didn't kill him."

"It must have been the fire, then . . . It doesn't matter, Reagan. What's dead is dead. We have to go."

"Where is Lily?"

"She's waiting by the stairs."

"I don't get it," Reagan said, looking back at Maron. "What just happened—?"

"Good God, Reagan, who cares? This place is burning like Michael Jackson in a Pepsi commercial. Come on."

Lars half dragged, half carried Reagan to the emergency stairs where Lily waited. "Can you make it?" He pointed at her bleeding leg.

Lily nodded. "If you can make it, I can make it. Let's get the hell out of here," she said and opened the stairwell door.

Maron really is dead, Reagan thought, but there

was no relief in this conclusion, only mystery.

He is. Really. Dead.

And she wondered if it was true what Maron had said, if there really was a place where the dead lived.

I can only hope.

They wrestled their way through the next level before Lily stopped and turned to look at her fellow survivors. "We have to get Juan," she said, chin tilted at a determined angle. "I'm not leaving without him."

"Is he where you left him?" Lars asked, out of breath.

"Yes."

"I'll get him. You and Reagan keep climbing."

Lars punched through the door of the fifth floor without looking behind him. Reagan waited, stunned he was once again going inside the haunted, fiery corridors of Gossamer Hall.

"You heard him," Lily said, taking her hand. "Let's keep moving."

"What if something happens?" Reagan asked, and immediately felt a crumbling under her feet, and the ground began to shift. Reagan cried out, lost her balance, and fell backward against Lily; the women went flying down the staircase.

The following moments were filled with tumbling light and shadow, screams and cries, fire and earth, as Reagan felt the world spin around her, her head swimming into unconsciousness.

She felt her mind slipping away into a permanent midnight, and then a voice penetrated the darkness. "Reagan!" she heard Lily exclaim, and a hand grabbed her by the arm, stopping her free fall.

The spinning stopped. Everything went still. Reagan dared open her eyes. "Lily?" she inquired weakly. She flattened her palms against the marble steps and tried to rise. "Lily?"

Lily sat beside her, her hand still on Reagan's arm, her head pitifully folded in her arms. "Good God, I can't go any farther. My legs . . ."

Reagan stood up, trying to ignore the pain coursing through her limbs. "Let me carry you," she begged. "We can still get out of here."

"No. I'm beyond repair. Please. Save yourself."

"Shut up. Put your arms around me. I'm not as weak as I look." Reagan thought momentarily of all the times she'd had to walk around the grocery store with Celeste's car seat in her arms because Celeste hated lying in the grocery cart. She thought about carrying the stroller before unfolding it, or picking up a diaper bag full of baby gear because, God forbid, George help her in any way. She thought about the portable crib, the swing, the high chair, any number of things baby-related she'd had to haul around for the few months Celeste was alive.

Yes, I am stronger than I look, Reagan thought. *In*

more ways than one.

Reagan bent down and wrapped Lily in her arms, lifting her from the floor with every ounce of strength left in her body.

I can do it, I can do it . . .

She began her ascent, braving the gauntlet of fire. It was everywhere. *And the moss*, Reagan thought, looking at walls covered with gooey green vines that refused to budge or melt from the heat. The smell of smoke, the smell of earth permeated the air, and the deathly stench of the corpses tucked eternally inside the building, never again to leave.

And Lars, Reagan thought. *Where is he?*

The voyage up the stairs seemed endless. Reagan felt herself dragging, slower and slower. Even with the threat of fire below her, nearly nipping at her feet, it seemed the night of sleeplessness and terror was finally shutting her down, one function at a time, and not even the encouraging murmur of Lily's voice could move her faster through the stairwell.

And then . . .

The sky.

Reagan saw it finally, when she took her last step on the stairs. She saw the sky, the sky of stars and a slit moon, the sky of evaporating darkness turning discretely into hues of light and blue.

"Yes," Reagan whispered, and the building sank

under her feet with a lost, long roar. Then Reagan felt Lily slipping from her shoulders. The dark abyss of Gossamer Hall had not freed them yet.

Reagan found herself fighting for ground while the floor disintegrated under her feet.

"Reagan!" she heard Lars shout. He appeared as if out of nowhere, his hand encircling her arm. "Hold on!" He pulled her and Lily onto the grass just in time to see the building crumble and collapse into its grave, acre by acre, stone by wall by ceiling by stair. The three looked on in muted shock.

A different kind of thunder filled the morning, blasted with dust of stone and dirt of earth. Lars took Lily from Reagan and step by step they moved farther away from the swallowing hole.

"Where is Juan?" Lily asked.

Lars shook his head, eyes wild and sad. "I couldn't find him."

"What do you mean, you couldn't find him?" Lily's fists pounded his chest. "I told you he was right where I left him!"

"And I'm telling you, he wasn't there! Lily. . ." he said, grabbing her fists with his free hand. He sighed when her weak fight ceased.

"Lars," Lily sobbed. "I just left him there."

"He wasn't there. Lily, I tried, okay? I did try. I don't know what else to say."

Lily slid from Lars's shoulder. She bent down over the earth, weeping. Reagan watched and felt her own sad thoughts cling like fog on an autumn morning. She glanced over at the place which had once been Gossamer Hall and saw only a grave where a mighty building had stood, and shivered with an emptiness that had changed her heart forever.

CHAPTER SIXTY-THREE

SKIP JONES AWAKENED TO AN ACOUSTIC VERSION OF Pearl Jam's "Jeremy," followed by the loud, mind-altering voice of DJ Steve.

"Alrighty, it is seven a.m., time to get your lazy butts out of bed. This is DJ Steve with you on this gray Thursday morning. Hey, how about that storm last night, kids? Call in for your best bad-weather stories. I got Jennifer here from UT. Jen, what's your story?"

"My electricity was off all night, and I missed the *Nip/Tuck* marathon on FX!"

"Okay, thanks for your call. Next caller, we've got a Ken on the phone with us. Ken's calling from Lake

Travis. Ken, what's your story, buddy?"

"Dude, last night, I, like, saw a building across the lake from my house fall down."

"Fall down?"

"Yeah, dude, like totally collapse. It was so cool."

"Alrighty there, Ken, let's put the pipe away. We're going to take a break now and pay some bills. Remember, this is Hot 95.5 FM, you're listening to the morning show, I'm DJ Steve." While his voice went off the air, a car dealership jingle followed:

"Ford has got the best deals, Ford has got your trucks, ain't no need to steal, yeah, Ford has got your trucks . . ."

The jingle was immediately interrupted when Skip's fist landed on the "stop" button of his alarm clock. His eyes opened slowly, and he saw he was inside Brookhaven College's security booth. He reached around and massaged his neck. It was painful to sleep sitting in a stool, but it wasn't like he had a choice. He had been deathly tired. He hadn't meant to stay awake all day sailing around Lake Austin with Shelley, but when she had asked, he couldn't say no. When she asked him to stay longer, he went mute. And when she gave him Bill Clinton sex in a secluded part of the lake, he decided sleep was overrated. Besides, if he got tired, he could always sleep at work. It wasn't like anything bad ever happened at Brookhaven College.

The storm had helped him sleep better. Something about thunder and lightning and the pitter-patter of rain always sent the nineteen-year-old high-school dropout to the Sandman quicker.

Time to do the rounds, Skip thought, and rolled off the stool. He popped his knuckles as he stepped out of the booth, avoiding the mud on his way to the security golf cart. Excitement built in his blood when he realized that in just one short hour he'd be free to go home and take a shower, call Shelley, and grab a bite to eat at Z-Tajus before going back to work again.

Skip cranked up the golf cart and rode through the campus, mentally checking the buildings as he went. Rice Hall. Check. Banner Hall. Check. Graves Hall. Check.

What next?

Skip rolled his eyes. *Gossamer Hall.* He hated the building and its whole Dracula-meets-Bates-Motel look, but at least he would have a chance to see the lake. There was a beautiful picnic area on the other side where he could sit down and smoke a blunt before Marcus came to free him from his shift.

Assuming I didn't lose my pot again, he thought, his hand hitting his side pocket to assure the presence of his grass. He remembered two weeks back when he left his weed *(like an idiot)* on the sidewalk only to have the head of campus security find it that afternoon. It became part of Dr. Kurcan's "Hugs, Not Drugs" campaign at chapel that week.

At least no one knew it was mine.

Thoughts of weed and Shelley continued to dance in his head while Skip rode up to Gossamer Hall.

Or where Gossamer Hall should have been.

Skip blinked hard.

Could it possibly . . .?

No. He was just in the wrong place. The weather, the weed from the day before, all those hours of rough sleeping were playing with his mind.

Skip jumped out of the cart and turned to the left, to the right, and behind him on the other side of the trail.

Feeling something close to nausea, Skip succumbed to his first inclination and slowly walked to the place he had first thought Gossamer Hall was located.

His breath caught in his chest when he saw what the tall grass hid.

It was a hole, a hole the size of . . . well, the size of Gossamer Hall.

What the hell . . .?

Skip inched closer, his heart skipping a beat. He peered into the hole, and his eyes glazed over with shock when he saw the inside of a classroom. Desks were in disarray, a chalkboard dangled off the wall, ashes blanketed the floor.

And there was more, Skip realized, stepping closer. His hands flew to his mouth when it became clear it was a mutilated body that stared up at him with hollow sockets where the eyes should have been.

A dead body.

A damn dead body.

Adrenaline stirred in Skip, and he found himself running backward, his screams bouncing off the hills and vibrating through the morning solitude.

CHAPTER
SIXTY-FOUR

MODERN BIOGRAPHY *MAGAZINE*, *REVIEW OF SAM Deniz's* Gossamer Hall *by Oliver Wood*

Athletes don't fare well in biographer Sam Deniz's account of the buried-like-a-grave mystery known as Gossamer Hall, entitled (oddly enough), Gossamer Hall. Deniz, a Brown graduate, launches the opening chapter with a full description of the condition in which one of the athletes was found (with his face ripped off). By Chapter 8, we learn of the death of another football player, also faceless, with all but two of his fingers removed.

If we ignore the needless, grotesque details of the students' deaths, then we can enjoy Gossamer Hall *for what it is—an amazingly well-researched documentation of one of the greatest mysteries of our time. But don't expect an immediate rush into the fateful October night that killed eight people, including the dean of Brookhaven College, Dr. Gretchen Kurcan, and the honored Mad Maron expert, Dr. Killian Hastings. Deniz has produced a book with an inspiring wealth of information, as impressive in scope as the state of Texas itself, creating a portrait not only of the building and its mysterious demise, but also the history surrounding it.*

Did anyone really know, for example, that Gossamer Hall was meant to the be the center of the campus, but after four men died in a freak scaling accident on its walls, the school chose to move the campus elsewhere? Such jewels of trivia are what raise Deniz's book above the standard bio.

Once the past is made clear, meet the characters of Gossamer Hall: Mark Green, a talented biology student who was set to be, as one of his teachers described him, "the next Einstein and Bill Gates, all in one"; Dr. Killian Hastings and Kurcan (both, coincidentally enough, friends of Deniz). Was it chance that Hastings sent Kurcan a resignation notice on the night of the tragedy? Was it the reason the reclusive dean came out of hiding for the night? Maybe, maybe not.

Perhaps the most intriguing mystery of all is Lars Case. In the book, Deniz finds that the person who went by that name actually lives in Michigan with his family and had lost his passport in Mexico the year before. So who was the real person behind the fake name? "We may never know," Deniz writes, also noting Case's was one of two bodies never recovered (Lakeway native Reagan Tanner is the other. Her car also disappeared that night.)

Deniz ends the book with a rare and heartfelt interview with the only survivor, Lily Blythe, who was in class on the night Gossamer Hall sank in the ground. "Everything happened like we were inside the eye of a tornado," the book quotes. "One minute you're at your desk, the next you're not, and everyone is dead."

But what really happened in Gossamer Hall? Deniz gives us many clues and too few theories, which is where the book falls short. How, for instance, did elephant moss end up on the windows, and for the love of Jesse James, whose bodies were found in the building? Deniz never truly explains what needs explaining, and instead stoops to storytelling about "the mysterious men whose faces were caved in and gnawed to the bone, who wore cowboy boots and clothes similar to those worn in Maron's era."

Mad Maron came back from the dead and started killing again? Now, there's a theory worth exploring.

CHAPTER SIXTY-FIVE

AT HALF PAST SEVEN, WHEN THE OAK TREES WERE losing their shadows, disappearing like ghosts, giving way to the first shades of darkness descending on the Houston streets, the black-haired girl walked onto her balcony and watched her two visitors climb up the steps to her apartment.

The three of them had known each other for less than a year, barely talked in the last six months, and yet were bound together by an invisible cord no one could sever.

The couple greeted the girl with warm hugs. "We came when we got your letter," the redhead said. Not too long ago, she had gone by a different name, but these days, she called herself Sara.

"We were surprised, to say the least," the man said. His name, his third, was Dan.

The black-haired girl, whose name was, and had always been, Lily, nodded and motioned toward the apartment. "Follow me," she said, and walked through the door, leaving it open enough so her friends could follow. She did not apologize for her modest home, or the emptiness of its rooms, nor did she thoughtfully offer them food or beverage or a place to sit. She was preoccupied with a single thought.

Lily walked down the hallway toward the two bedrooms and opened the door to the first. She turned to her friends and placed a finger to her lips.

"Her name is Clarissa, after my mother," Lily whispered.

The brown-haired baby slept in a portable crib in a corner by the window. A crocheted pink blanket was wrapped around her, and hanging above the crib was a silent Care Bears mobile.

The redhead gasped. "She's so beautiful. Lily, you must be so proud."

"She's a handful," Lily replied, a smile lighting her tired face.

"But you love her." Dan grinned.

"Of course."

"Her hair is lighter than yours," Sara noted.

"But she has my eyes," Lily said. "I wish she was awake so you could see them."

Dan touched her tiny arm. The baby, without opening her eyes, took his finger and squeezed it in her little fist. Dan smiled, and Lily noticed the man was not as frightening, not as thuggish as she had once thought he was. He was actually quite handsome. *But being in love might have something to do with that*, Lily thought, and looked at the beaming redhead standing at his side.

"And the father?" Dan asked.

Here we go. Lily combed a hand through her un-brushed hair. "That's why I sent you the letter," she said quietly, and sat in the room's only other piece of furniture, a small rocking chair by the closet. "I don't know who the father is. And it's not because I went on a free-for-all, multiple-man-screwing spree, either. Just the opposite." Her violet eyes widened, and she glanced over at her sleeping daughter before whispering, "I didn't sleep with anyone the night she should have been conceived."

Sara and Dan remained silent as they absorbed the information. Lily continued, "I know I did not sleep with anyone the night she was supposedly conceived, because the night would have been the night of . . ." She let the sentence hang, and both Dan and Sara understood.

Dan shook his head. "I don't mean to pry," he said, "but is there any chance the doctors could be wrong?"

"It doesn't matter if they were wrong about the night. I haven't slept with anyone in a year."

"That can't be," Dan said, shaking his head.

"After that night, is there anything you do not believe?" Lily didn't let Dan answer before saying, "I didn't know I was pregnant until the seventh month. All the sickness I felt, all the weakness, I thought it was just the aftereffects of . . . you know. When I first found out, I didn't know how to feel, what to think. I was living with my mother in Houston. Have the two of you thought about finishing school somewhere else? I have, but I don't think I will for now, not until she's older."

"We thought about going back to school, but something else has come up," Dan said, and he glanced at Sara. She nodded.

Lily caught their exchange. "What is it?"

"Do you remember when I ripped Maron's boot off him that night?"

"I remember you carrying it, yes."

"Well," Dan continued, "I think something might have fallen out, and attached to my shoe. A map. *The* map. We think we know where the gold is buried." He grinned. "How would you like to furnish your apartment and buy Clarissa a real crib?"

CHAPTER SIXTY-SIX

THE RED SUN WAS THE PUPIL IN THE EYE OF A SWELTER-ing Austin day. The three travelers opened and reopened their Dasani bottles, pouring soothing water down their dry throats as they stared out into an open field by a serene and expansive lake. The vacant land was a place none of them had ever thought they'd see again.

"So, this is it," Lily said, wiping her sweaty forehead with her forearm. "Looks different empty."

"Looks different during the day," Sara said.

"Without Gossamer Hall," Dan added. He took the crumpled map out of his pocket and perused it one last time. His fingers traced the spot where Maron had signed his initial, a place, judging by the crudely drawn hills and water, not ten miles from Mansfield Dam, near the edge of Brookhaven College. "This has to be it," Dan said, refolding the map. He narrowed his eye at the area mere yards from where Gossamer Hall once stood. "It has to be."

"We're going by a crude map that was drawn over a hundred years ago," Lily said.

"And this," Dan said, pointing to his head, then his heart.

"You mean intuition?"

"Always trust it," he said, and smiled.

"It won't be that far down," Sara commented hopefully. "According to Dr. Hastings's book, he wouldn't have had that much time to bury it."

"It's far enough down no one's found it for a century," Dan replied. "Come on, let's get moving and shaking."

They took their shovels and started digging. A time or two Lily stopped to call her mother and check on the baby, and once Sara paused so she could rest the arm that had never fully healed. Her discomfort did not go unnoticed by Dan, who brought her water and wrapped his warm hands around the offending limb, massaging it with tender fingers.

The couple had been together constantly since that fateful night in October, although Dan had tried to give her the spiel.

You don't want anything to do with me. I'm a loner. A rebel.

Sara hadn't bought it. "A loner is just what I need. You and Lily are the only ones who know what happened."

"You would have to change your name. You'd have to live in hiding."

"I can change my name. I can hide," she said as she had held him in the Exxon parking lot miles out of Austin.

Dan and Sara had taken her car in their escape, which was good, because Dan had doubted that his piece of shit Datsun would have done the trick. *Probably would have broken down before leaving the campus,* he thought. One of Maron's men, whichever one was left, if there was one left, would have easily caught up with them.

Is Maron really dead? Dan often wondered at night while Sara tossed and turned beside him. He had seen his body lying lifeless in the classroom, but still . . .

Dan was never 100 percent sure about anything anymore.

Lily had taken her car, insisting she would be okay, that she had to get to the hospital, and they had to get away. Neither Dan nor Sara thought they would see her again—but just days later, before Sara changed her name, she received a phone call from her mother, the only person Sara had talked to, saying a girl by the name of Lily was looking for her. Dan followed Sara to Pflugerville, just south of Austin. The three of them sat in silence, which Lily finally broke.

"I was a bitch to Caleb before he killed the monster for me. And Juan. How could I have just left him like that?"

"I felt like I didn't do enough," Sara admitted.

"Dr. Kurcan's face . . ." Dan began, then drifted into silence.

They didn't see each other again, not until Lily wrote a letter announcing the birth of her daughter.

"When we're in Costa Rica, we'll try for our own," Dan told Sara one night as they lay in bed after making love.

Sara sighed, lifted her arm over her head, and touched his lips. "I don't know if I can do it again," she said.

"You're still young. So am I," Dan whispered, kissing her fingertips.

"It's not about being young."

"A child could seal our fate."

"A child is not redemption." But after a time, Sara said, "Perhaps a boy. I would like to see him play in the surf." And she turned over and buried her head in Dan's chest.

Dan closed his hands around his shovel and

worked faster, harder. The dream of a life away from the Texas that haunted him, the dream of living in a house on a foreign beach away from his sins, his horrors, was the force that made him push through the dirt harder and quicker.

For hours the three of them dug in the stifling heat. "Not that far down, my ass," Lily mumbled to herself, but as soon as she said it, her shovel hit something hard.

"Tell me that's not what I think it is," Lily said, her dark eyes melting to the color of twilight purple.

Sara put her arms around Dan's waist.

Dan returned the embrace, his boot kicking the dirt where a hint of gold glimmered under the noonday sun. He pressed his lips briefly to Sara's forehead and whispered a single word:

"*Jackpot.*"

erin samiloglu

DISCONNECTION

There is a serial killer on the loose in New Orleans. Someone is branding, stabbing and strangling young girls. Their mutilated bodies are being found in the depths of the Mississippi River.

Beleaguered Detective Lewis Kline and his colleagues believe the occult may be involved, but they have no leads. And the killer shows no sign of slowing down.

Then Sela, a troubled young woman, finds a stranger's cell phone in a dark Bourbon Street bar. When it rings, she answers it. On the other end is Chloe Applegate. The serial killer's most recent victim.

So begins Sela's journey into a nightmare from which she cannot awaken, a descent into madness out of which she cannot climb . . . as she finds herself the target of an almost incomprehensible evil.

ISBN#1932815244
ISBN#9781932815245
Mass Market Paperback
US $6.99 / CDN $9.99
Available Now
www.erinsamiloglu.com

mary ann mitchell
street
of
death

It is 15th Century Spain and the Inquisition is raging. Countless hapless souls find a torturous death bound to the fiery hell of burning stakes.

Though her father is burned as a Jewish heretic, Susanna Diego escapes and gives birth to her daughter, Teresa, at a convent. Her prayer is that the child will never know of her Jewish background and suffer persecution from the Inquisition. And then, as Susanna lays dying, she asks that her skull be fixed above the lintel of the Diego family home.

Twenty years later, the nuns send Teresa to care for wealthy Roberto Velez, a former Jew, who has converted to Roman Catholocism. Teresa quickly learns, however, the conversion is false . . . and it is not the only danger the family, and now she herself is in.

Roberto's son Louis is bewitched by the lovely Teresa. To keep her at his side after his father's death, he informs her he knows who her birth mother was—and where her skull resides—and offers a burial in a Christian cemetery. But, caught with the skull, Louis is arrested by the Inquisition, and Teresa is accused of being a witch. Has Teresa finally found her fate, the fate of those who lived on The Street of Death?

ISBN#9781932815847
US $7.95 / CDN $9.95
Mass Market Paperback / Horror
Now Available
www.maryann-mitchell.com

The Vampire Shrink

LYNDA HILBURN

Denver psychologist Kismet Knight, Ph.D., doesn't believe in the paranormal. She especially doesn't believe in vampires. That is, until a new client introduces Kismet to the vampire underworld and a drop dead gorgeous, 800-year-old vampire named Devereux. Kismet isn't buying the vampire story, but can't explain why she has such odd reactions and feelings whenever Devereux is near. Kismet is soon forced to open her mind to other possibilities, however, when she is visited by two angry bloodsuckers who would like nothing better than to challenge Devereux by hurting Kismet.

To make life just a bit more complicated, one of Kismet's clients shows up in her office almost completely drained of blood, and Kismet finds herself immersed in an ongoing murder investigation. Enter handsome FBI profiler Alan Stevens who warns her that vampires are very real. And one is a murderer. A murderer who is after her.

In the midst of it all, Kismet realizes she has feelings for both the vampire and the profiler. But though she cares for each of the men, facing the reality that vampires exist is enough of a challenge . . . for now.

ISBN#9781933836232
US $15.95 / CDN $19.95
Trade Paperback / Paranormal
Now Available
www.LyndaHilburn.com

S O M E T H I N G
B A D

RICHARD SATTERLIE

Gabe Petersen can't cross the borders of his rural Tri-county area—even the thought triggers the erratic cardiac rhythm and breathing difficulty of a panic attack. And he doesn't know why. His memories stop at twelve years of age, his early years nonexistent.

But when a strange little man arrives in town, Gabe feels an unsettling sense of familiarity. Then families begin to die, all because of bizarre natural disasters, and the events trigger glimmers of memory for Gabe. Memories pointing to Thibideaux, the strange little man.

Returning memories open a door on rusty hinges in Gabe's mind. Behind the door is a catatonic Catholic priest who fled the area years ago after he was found sitting on the church altar surrounded by the slaughtered remains of several animals. And Gabe now remembers . . . he was there. Along with Thibideaux.

The past explodes, revealing Gabe's deepest fears. This time, his family is Thibideaux's prize. And Gabe's only weapon to defend them is his mind . . .

ISBN#9781933836133
US $6.99 / CDN $8.99
Mass Market Paperback / Horror
Now Available

THE DREAM THIEF

HELEN A. ROSBURG

Someone is murdering young, beautiful women in mid-sixteenth century Venice. Even the most formidable walls of the grandest villas cannot keep him out, for he steals into his victims' dreams. Holding his chosen prey captive in the night, he seduces them . . . to death.

Now Pina's cousin, Valeria, is found dead, her lovely body ravished. It is the final straw for Pina's overbearing fiance', Antonio, and he orders her confined within the walls of her mother's opulent villa on Venice's Grand Canal. It is a blow not only to Pina, but to the poor and downtrodden in the city's ghettos, to whom Pina has been an angel of charity and mercy. But Pina does not chafe long in her lavish prison, for soon she too begins to show symptoms of the midnight visitations; a waxen pallor and overwhelming lethargy.

Fearing for her daughter's life, Pina's mother removes her from the city to their estate in the country. Still, Pina is not safe. For Antonio's wealth and his family's power enable him to hide a deadly secret. And the murderer manages to find his intended victim. Not to steal into her dreams and steal away her life, however, but to save her. And to find his own salvation in the arms of the only woman who has ever shown him love.

ISBN#9781932815207
US $6.99 / CDN $9.99
Mass Market Paperback / Paranormal
Available Now
www.helenrosburg.com

JOSEPH LAUDATI

IN DARKNESS IT DWELLS

Teen-aged filmmaker Tom DeFrank, through his hobby of stop-motion photography, conceives a monster: he builds and animates a demon puppet. Unbeknownst to Tom, however, the "toy" creates a subliminal bond with a dark entity. As he labors with the miniature beast, making his movie, the boy unwittingly summons a force that wreaks the terrible vengeance of Tom's repressed rage.

Only reclusive psychic Stephen Parrish and his daughter Julie know of the ancient evil awakened in their little town. As romance blooms between the teens, Parrish senses the strange presence within the troubled young filmmaker and seeks to unravel the mystery of the demon.

But people are dying as bitter grudges come to the fore. Rumors abound of a strange creature loose in the countryside, and a fearful public turns suspicious on Parrish. Will he be able to leash the monster and the will of its creator — a boy little conscious of his power to create . . . or destroy?

ISBN#9781932815702
US $6.99 / CDN $9.99
Mass Market Paperback / Horror
Available Now

g . a . r . y   f . r . a . n . k

FOREVER
will you SUFFER

Unsuspecting Rick Summers had simply gone to the cemetery to visit the graves of his mother and sister, killed in a car accident years earlier. He had the cabbie wait for him. But when he got back into the taxi, he didn't have the same driver. His new chauffeur was a re-animated corpse. And he was about to take a drive into hell.

The doors to hell open in the house of his ex-lover, Katarina, where he is delivered by his not-so-sweet smelling driver. Rick learns that Katarina is missing and has been recently plagued by a stalker. That's just the beginning of the bad news. When the house changes right before their unbelieving eyes, taking them somewhen and somewhere else, a horrifying mystery begins to unfold. At its heart is unrequited love. And Rick Summers.

It seems that several lifetimes ago, Rick, then Thomas, spurned a woman named Abigail. Not a good idea. Because Abigail's great at holding a grudge, some of her best friends are demons, and she's dedicated to keeping a promise she made to Rick long, long ago. "Forever will I remember; forever will you suffer . . ."

ISBN#9781932815696
US $6.99 / CDN $9.99
Mass Market Paperback / Horror
Available Now
www.authorgaryfrank.com

For more information
about other great titles from
Medallion Press, visit

www.medallionpress.com